KING'S REIGN

NINA LEVINE

Editing by Becky Johnson, Hot Tree Editing

Cover Design ©2018 by Romantic Book Affair Designs

Cover photography Wander Aguiar

Cover model Jacob Rodney Hogue

DEDICATION

This one's for all my amazing readers.

1

King

Some say the art of war is to subdue the enemy without fighting. I didn't buy that shit for a second. I've always said show the fuck up with the biggest army you can amass and crush the motherfuckers with brute fucking force.

I was here to crush Tony Romano's empire with the kind of force that would tell the world never to fuck with Storm again.

We'd arrived in Melbourne just after 8:00 p.m. and had staked out both his home and his business headquarters for the past two hours. Biding our time. Something I wasn't good at, but Axe had convinced me this was the best course of action to ensure we were running on good information that left little room for surprises when we did attack. I'd left a skeleton crew back in Sydney and brought just over forty men with me. Zane and Griff were in charge of surveillance, pulling intel on how many men we were dealing with inside.

Last week, they'd found the floor plans for each building and had mapped out different scenarios for how to infiltrate and attack. The thing I wanted to make sure of before we went in, guns fucking blazing, was that there were no women or children who'd be caught in the crossfire. The intel so far led us to believe there weren't, but Zane was making sure that information was accurate.

Hyde approached me as I watched the entrance to Romano's headquarters. A van had just arrived and five more men were about to enter the building. "You sure you don't wanna just burn the joint down and be done with it, brother?"

I turned to him. We'd been going back and forth over this question for about an hour, and disagreed on it. As far as we knew, there were about thirty guys in the building. Hyde held concerns that was too many for us to deal with. "I want to look these motherfuckers in the eye and see them bleed. And I want to make sure every last fucking one of them dies. There will be no survivors here today."

"Okay, we do this your way, but if shit gets out of hand, I'm torching the place and getting us the fuck out of there."

I clenched my jaw, pissed that he kept arguing over this. "No." No fucking way was I not getting my hands dirty with these cunts. If they wanted to come at me the way they had, they would feel the full extent of my wrath.

He returned my scowl. "King, you're running on emotion, and we both know that's a dangerous headspace to be in with this kind of shit. I don't wanna see our club wiped out because you couldn't fucking think straight."

"I fucking said no, so drop it. And if you can't, you can stay the fuck out of this entire operation," I barked before turning back to continue watching the building.

"Fuck," he fired back before stalking away from me,

muttering some other shit under his breath I couldn't work out, nor had any fucking interest in trying to.

As he left, Zane made his way to me. "Best we can figure, there won't be any collateral damage if we go in now."

"You're sure?"

He gave a quick nod. "Yes."

I glanced at Axe who'd also joined us. "You agree we're good to go?" My brother was the only person whose opinion I ever gave this much weight to. He'd proven his skill in this kind of situation a long time ago, and while it sometimes killed me to take his suggestions on board, I almost always did.

"I do. There may not be a better time than right now. Most of the guys inside are concentrated in the back corner of the building. That neutralises a lot of the risk associated with this. And there's no one at Romano's home, so it's good timing there, too."

I texted Nitro who was at Romano's home and told him to proceed. I then spoke into my handheld radio that connected me to Kick and Devil who were at various points around this building. "Go!"

We moved fast and silently towards the perimeter, entering the building as Zane and Griff had planned. That was after Axe and I slit the throats of the two guys guarding this side of the building. Griff had shut down the video surveillance, allowing us to enter with ease. That I finally had some of Romano's men's blood on my hands lit my fucking mind up.

I needed more.

I fucking hungered for it.

This shit had been going on for too long; I was like a jittery fucking addict waiting for his next hit.

My finger twitched at the trigger of my gun.

If only Romano were here.

Fuck, I wouldn't kill him on sight; I'd take him with me so I could keep him like a fucking toy that needed to be played with daily. Pull that fucker out every hour and give him some King love. *The kind of love my father taught me.*

Once inside, I led the way to the back corner room, meeting the two other teams of men who'd entered at different access points. Darkness blanketed the building, the only light spilling from the back like Zane had predicted.

Devil, Kick, and Hyde locked eyes on me. Without pausing for even one fucking second, I stormed through the door and opened fire the minute my gaze landed on the first of Romano's motherfuckers.

Surprise rolled across his face before terror as he took in my gun. I zeroed in on that terror, feeding the craving that lived deep in my soul. Satisfaction filled my veins exactly like the addict I was, and every instinct I had for death and torture roared to life in a way it never had before.

There will be a bloodbath here today.

I'd been shutting my shit down for far too fucking long.

Keeping a tight fucking rein on my crazy.

No more.

I would allow every impulse I had to take over and run its course. And when the chips fell wherever they did, I would pick those fuckers up and do it all over again with the next enemy on my motherfucking list.

The sound of gunfire filled the room, mine leading the way. There had to be twenty guys in here, some cutting coke, some counting cash, some watching over the operation. That they only had four guards on the building—the two where we'd entered, and two more at other points—told me whoever Romano had left in charge didn't know his ass from his elbow. With this kind of shit going on in here, I would have blanketed the building with protection.

We were thirty to their twenty, and we had the element of

surprise. But while I didn't think much of whoever was running this show, I had to give it to them—they were ready enough for an invasion like this. Guns swiftly appeared, and we had to react fast to avoid bullets. That only sparked my mania.

My mind disconnected from everything but the task at hand.

Kill.

Annihilate.

Ruin.

The carnage surrounding me stoked the fire of hate burning deep inside me.

Romano had kept me down for long enough; I was back on my fucking feet now.

Give me all you've got, motherfuckers.

"King!"

My gaze sliced to where Kick pointed, and I roared with rage as I eyed one of our men going down. A moment later, I had my arm hooked around the neck of Romano's guy who was about to bring his blade down on my man.

Squeezing tight, I snarled, "You ever felt the cut of a knife, cunt?"

He thrashed against my body trying to break free of my hold. "Fuck you, asshole!"

I jerked him against me again, making sure I choked some of the life from him. "It hurts for sure, but I'm not here just to deliver some fucking hurt. I'm going to sink that blade into your body and twist and dig the fuck out of your insides until your screams are burned into my brain. And until you're eyeballs roll back and you're dreaming of hell because even it'd be better than meeting me."

"Do your fucking best," he managed to get out as I shoved him to the ground.

Dropping my gun, I ripped the knife from his hand as our

eyes locked. I bent over him and sliced his shirt down the middle. I needed to see the blood drain from his body. Needed *that* seared into my brain. Romano wasn't here, but I would take what I required from this motherfucker. And what I fucking required was to channel every ounce of my fury and pain into making someone else hurt like I did.

I plunged the blade into his chest. The kind of rush a junkie would do anything for surged through me. But it wasn't enough.

The second thrust of the blade sparked a disconnect between my mind and my humanity.

I detached myself from everything with the third.

Almost there.

I floated outside of myself as I stabbed him the fourth time.

Now I was chasing pure darkness.

Succumbing to the needs I'd forced to the far edges of my soul.

Running like a madman towards the evil that infected the parts of me I could never eradicate.

His blood was my blood.

I fucking bled the same pain he did.

His cries were my cries.

And finally, when he took his last breath, he was as dead as I was.

My frenzy finished when blood and guts lay sprawled out before me, a feast for my black heart.

I stood and dropped the knife on his dead body. Blood covered every inch of my skin. I barely noticed it, though. The high buzzing my veins stole my attention. Every single last speck of it.

I was just getting started.

Tonight we would blaze chaos through this city.

Anarchy was the only answer to Romano's deeds.

Hyde stepped in front of me and snatched up the knife. "It's done, brother."

My eyes cut to his briefly before glancing around at the slaughter. Death surrounded us. It filled my senses in exactly the way I needed it to. But my wrath still raged, and I knew it wouldn't be sated until I had Romano's blood on my hands.

I looked at Hyde. "Everyone?"

He nodded.

I picked up my gun. "Light the fucking match."

Sweeping my gaze over the room one last time, I stalked out, my mind already shifting to the next stop on tonight's death train. My men followed, Hyde and Devil torching the joint, leaving Romano's empire in a state of destruction. Next stop, his allies. If they didn't agree to our terms for how we would conduct business going forward, they would suffer my wrath, too.

2

King

The headache I'd had for days sank its claws deeper into me. Nothing I took came close to easing it. Not even the shit Lily had given me.

Fuck.

I exited the clubhouse bar and headed to my office. Shutting myself in, door closed, I dumped my phone on the desk, switched the lamp on, and reached for the bottle of whisky that had become my saviour. I guzzled a mouthful, hardly noticing the burn as it slid down my throat.

Sitting, I rested my head back against the top of the chair and took another swig of whisky. I couldn't get this shit into me fast enough. My only goal tonight was to knock myself the fuck out and silence the thoughts and feelings slowly killing me.

Last night we'd cut a path through Melbourne, making it very fucking clear Romano no longer held any power in that

8

city. Blood had been spilt. Fuck, for some, it had flowed. But in the end, I'd made every last motherfucker understand that Storm now ran Melbourne. And they'd spread that news around today. I'd taken a lot of fucking calls when we'd arrived back late this afternoon. We'd stepped on a lot of toes, pissed a lot of people off. I couldn't have cared less. I'd already told Winter to pack his bags and prepare to move to Melbourne. He'd be heading up our operation down there. I'd never been interested in that city; now I'd take it over.

A knock sounded at the door, and Axe stepped inside. His gaze landed on the whisky in front of me, and he frowned. "You okay, brother?"

"Yeah. What's up?"

He moved further into the office, a look of concern on his face. "Just got word from my guy. He's been able to confirm that Romano is working with the feds. They turned him."

I threw some more whisky down my throat. "And his location?"

Axe shook his head. "Still nothing on that."

I motioned my hand at him. "Get him on the phone."

"No."

I worked my jaw, unable to calm my rising irritation. "Axe, get him on the fucking phone."

His eyes turned hard. "What, so you can fuck this up? I let you talk to him, we won't have a contact in the feds anymore."

"Fuck," I roared, slamming the bottle down. Standing, I met him where he stood, my body tense with determination. "You've got skills I don't, brother, but right now, we don't have time to fuck around waiting for you to work this guy. It's time for me to have a word with him."

Deadlocked, we wasted a minute while Axe got to the realisation I wouldn't let this go. He could be a stubborn motherfucker sometimes.

"Jesus, Zac," he muttered, smacking his phone into my hand. "Try not to screw this up for me. I've used this guy for a few years now, and he knows his shit. I don't want to lose him."

His use of my name lightened my mood. I lifted a brow. "You only use that name when you want something."

"I want you to tread carefully. You think you've got that in you? 'Cause I sure as fuck don't."

"No." He was right—I didn't have that in me. Scrolling through his phone, I said, "What's his name?"

He rattled off the name and I dialled the guy. While I waited for him to answer, I looked at Axe. "The time for restraint has passed, brother. We're not taking any fucking prisoners anymore."

He scrubbed a hand over his face and turned away from me. He hadn't been this pissed off with me for a long time, but I couldn't bring myself to give a fuck. This wasn't anything new for us. He'd come around.

His guy answered my call, "Axe, man, it's late."

"Johnny, it's Zachary King, Axe's brother. We need to have a talk about Tony Romano."

Silence for a beat. "No, we don't. I only talk to Axe."

I gripped the phone harder, willing my impatience to take a back seat. "Not tonight you don't. Tonight you tell me everything you know about what the fuck Romano's doing with your friends."

The stillness on the other end of the phone was deafening and maddening, causing my agitation to flare. "Okay, let me put this another way, Johnny. You give me what I want or I'll come at you in ways you won't like."

Axe swore under his breath, pacing the office. His angry eyes met mine, but I ignored what I saw there.

I just fucking need to know where Romano is.

"Your brother there with you?" Johnny asked, his own anger bleeding through the phone.

"Yeah, but for the record, he's not down with this request." I could be a good brother sometimes.

"Put him on."

"How about you listen to me, Johnny? You give me the information I want, and then you can talk to Axe for hours if that's what you want."

"I've heard a lot of shit about you, and now I've had the pleasure of this conversation, I'm guessing all of it was right," he gritted out. "I've told Axe everything I know. They've got this investigation locked down tight like I've never seen before. Whatever shit Romano knows, it's big."

"I'm giving you twenty-four hours to find his location. That's all I need at this point."

"Fuck. It's gonna take me longer than that. They don't muck around when they've got someone in witness protection."

I decided to take a new tack. "Here's what we're gonna do. You speed this up, get me that information by this time tomorrow, I'll leave you alone *and* throw in ten grand in cash."

He blew out a long breath. "Forty-eight hours."

I balled my fist. I did not want to wait another day, but I knew the truth in what he said. It could well take him that long. "The cash offer is only good until tomorrow. Hurry this the hell up."

I ended the call and shoved Axe's phone back at him. "Where's Zane?"

"In the bar as far as I know."

I stalked out there and found both him and Griff. They were going over something on Zane's laptop. I pulled up a seat at their table. "I've got a job for you two. Romano's in protection. You think you can track him down within the next twenty-four hours?"

We'd suspected they had him in witness protection, but it hadn't been confirmed until now. It slanted this differently than if he was being held in prison. It meant that if we could locate him, we could deal with him ourselves rather than finding someone inside to do it.

Zane nodded. "Yeah. It's possible."

"That's what I thought," I said. Johnny might have been a fed, but he didn't have the equipment and skills Zane did. There was a reason Zane was in high demand since he'd left the military.

I stood as I saw Devil enter the bar. "Keep me updated." Leaving them, I met Devil as he found somewhere to sit. "How'd you go?"

Exhaustion lined his face. Fuck, it lined all our faces. "Her sister is still in a coma."

"And Lily?" My gut knotted. She'd invaded my head since I'd walked away from her. I couldn't escape her.

"She's at the hospital. The kids are at her mother's with their father. The boys have reported there's been no suspicious behaviour at the house. They're safe, King."

"Talk to her neighbours tomorrow. Get me a description of anyone they saw at the house that day." I wasn't leaving it to the police to bring justice for Lily's sister. I would deliver that myself. By my own fucking hand.

I headed back to my office, ready to finish that bottle of whisky. I hadn't made it to the office when a text came through that made me sit the fuck up and pay attention.

Unknown Number: Sara needs to see you.

Jesus, what the fuck was Bronze doing?

Me: You're in Sydney?

Bronze: Yes

Me: When?

Bronze: Now

Me: Give me 30

I stalked out of the clubhouse. Bronze was about to incur some of my wrath. I hadn't set him up just so he could come back and fuck himself in the ass.

"You should be a million fucking miles from here, Bronze." I'd arrived at the café before him and had sat for the past five minutes growing increasingly pissed off. "This was not the fucking plan."

He returned my scowl as he sat across from me. "You know me better than that, King. I did exactly what you would have done in the same situation."

I ground my teeth together as I ran my gaze over his face. "You look like shit." He looked a hell of a lot worse than shit. It had been ten days since I'd seen him, but it looked like he hadn't slept in a month.

"Yeah, you too, asshole."

I leaned back in my seat, trying to shake the wild energy coursing through me. I was fucking hyped up from everything going on and everything I still had to get done. It was a high I would crash and burn from eventually. Usually I'd screw my way through it, but the only warmth I craved was the one I wouldn't seek.

Huffing out a breath, I demanded, "So, what gives?"

"I've been doing some digging on Romano and his crew.

One of his guys seems to be his main choice for getting shit done, so I dug deeper on him than the others. Turns out he changed his name years ago, and when I followed that, I found his history of violent crime including multiple counts of murder. I figure he's probably the guy Tony sent to take care of Jen—"

"Romano's crew has been taken care of, Bronze. This information isn't useful anymore."

He narrowed his eyes at me. "When? Because I had a buddy track this guy's credit cards, and he used one a few hours ago."

I frowned. "Where?"

"Here. Sydney." When I didn't respond, he asked, "You found Romano yet?"

I shook my head.

He slid a piece of paper across the table. "We find this guy, he might lead us to him."

I glanced down at the paper.

Fuck.

Brant.

"He's in Sydney?"

"Yeah."

"Fucking hell."

We'd taken him off our radar after Romano was arrested.

And we'd bought into the story he'd fed us about why he'd shown up on our doorstep.

For Ivy.

I yanked my phone out as a thought slammed into my head. To Bronze, I said, "What else do you know about this guy?"

"Not much, but it seems he's a loner with a taste for stalking women. He fixates on them until they become an obsession. Two of them took restraining orders out on him. One of them ended up dead three months later. I talked to the first one, and she gave me a rundown of his history with this. Turns out he's done it a few times. Somehow he escaped a murder charge and later, changed his name."

When Axe picked up, I said, "Pull Zane off tracking Romano. I need him to find Brant."

"Why?"

I gripped the phone harder. "I think he has Ivy." I paused. "And I think he's a sick fuck who will do God knows what to her."

With everything going on, we'd been distracted and taken our eyes off the motherfucking ball.

Ending the call, I said to Bronze, "You hear that Ryland's off the case now?"

"Yeah."

"Fuck, Bronze, you trust whoever's giving you information? That their goal isn't to draw you in so they can arrest you?"

"I'm taking precautions."

I leant forward. "Why? Why would you risk everything to help us? Your debt to me was repaid a long fucking time ago."

He stared at me for a long time. Silent. Like he was trying to figure that shit out, too. "For Hailee. You guys go down, she goes down, and I refuse to let that happen."

I didn't buy that for one moment.

Not fully.

Bronze had crossed a line somewhere along the way. A line in his soul. I'd watched it happen. He'd let stuff slide, had turned away when he'd seen me get my hands dirty. He may have given the impression he wasn't on board with a lot of my shit, but not once had he truly challenged me.

Bronze was caught between worlds, and his actions told me he had more than one foot in mine.

I stood. "You got somewhere safe to stay?"

His mouth curled at the ends. "Why? You gonna put me up at your place?"

My brows lifted, waiting for an answer.

He jerked his chin at the door. "I'm good, King. Go take care of business."

3

Lily

"I can pick the kids up from school this afternoon," Linc said, distracting me from staring out the kitchen window. From thinking about Brynn.

"Huh?" I'd heard him, but for the life of me, I couldn't connect dots in my head. *Why's he offering to pick the kids up?*

He moved close to me, concern in his eyes. "Did you get any sleep last night, baby?" He stroked my hair, and I let him. I knew I shouldn't. God, I was letting him do a lot of things I knew I shouldn't, but my sister had been shot three days ago and I had no idea if she'd ever wake up from the coma she was in, so all the right things had flown out the window.

And the one man I wanted to do the right things for me? He'd walked out of my life without a backwards glance.

I shivered as I remembered the way he'd looked at me before he left. *Cold*. Colder than I'd ever had anyone look at me.

He'd told me we didn't belong in the same worlds.

Told me we were done.

We'd made no promises to each other, but I hadn't expected him to cut and run in my hour of need.

That was cruel.

Heartless.

"Lil," Linc said, his hands curling around my biceps. "Did you hear me?"

I blinked and pushed my thoughts of King away. They weren't productive. I was best to forget him as fast as he had me. "I got a couple of hours of sleep." A slight exaggeration. Either way, it didn't make much difference whether it was one hour or two. It didn't change the fact my sister was in a coma.

He placed a kiss on my forehead and let me go. "Sit. I'll make coffee."

He shouldn't kiss you.

You should tell him not to kiss you.

Before I could respond, Holly and Mum wandered into the kitchen. Exhaustion and sadness hugged them, too. *How long would this nightmare haunt us?*

I reached for Holly as she walked past, my hand sliding down her arm as she continued towards the fridge. "You okay, Hols?"

She wasn't okay. None of us were. But what else did you ask in a situation like this?

She nodded but didn't say anything. Her nod was all I needed.

Mum moved past me, barely registering my presence, and joined Linc near the kettle. We didn't need words to know how the other was. *Because neither of us will ever be okay again if Brynn dies.*

Linc told Mum to sit down, he'd make her a tea. She told

him she could make her own. I tuned out as they argued over it, and left the kitchen.

I needed to be alone.

I had nothing to give any of them.

Not even my kids.

Not today.

Today Linc could step up again, like he had the last few days.

I shut myself in the bathroom, stripped, and stood under the shower. Closing my eyes, I let the water cascade down my face. It soothed me a little. A momentary reprieve. No thoughts. Just me and the water and silence.

I don't know how long I stood there. It wasn't until Linc came in, held out my towel, and said, "Lil, you've been in here long enough. The kids need the bathroom," that I joined the world again.

He should not be in here.

I turned off the shower and stepped out, ignoring the way his gaze dropped to my naked body.

I allowed him to dry me off and wrap the towel around me.

I let him comb my hair.

All the wrong things.

I didn't have the energy to argue over any of it.

My mind drifted to King again.

I'd known the man just shy of three weeks. He should not have been a thought I so easily chased. Memories of his face, his eyes, his hands... they should not have crashed into me so effortlessly.

And yet, they did.

They pummelled me.

I wanted *him* to make me coffee. Argue with my mother over her tea. Tell me I'd been in the shower too long. I wanted *his* hands drying me off. Wrapping the towel around me.

I wanted King to be the one who was here for me.

But he wasn't.

And I didn't have Brynny to help me through this.

All I had was Linc.

So I let him do all those wrong things.

And avoided thinking about the way he looked at me. Because when the only energy I had was barely enough to get me through moment to moment, I had none to think about the fact my ex was likely misreading everything and making plans to move back into my life.

Linc dropped Mum and me off at the hospital after he took the kids to school, on his way to work. If I wasn't so wrapped up in myself, I would have cheered over the fact he'd found a steady job. As it was, I only just noticed a car that pulled out of a parking spot abruptly, almost knocking me over. Everything happened in a blur. Mum pulled me towards the footpath, away from the car before I was hurt. After, we stood in shock staring at each other until she wrapped her arms around me and cried.

We stayed like that for a long few minutes, shedding tears we didn't know we still had in us. It seemed tears lived deep inside, in limitless quantities.

By the time we stepped off the lift near the intensive care unit, Mum's face showed how close she was to shattering. I wasn't convinced she'd be able to sit here for another day, watching tubes and machines and doctors and nurses helping my sister fight for her life. Two days of this had revealed the desperation that long days filled with nothing but silence and beeps from those machines caused. I'd sat by Brynn's side, teeth chattering from the frigid air, heart aching with pain from sadness and uncertainty, and I'd prayed like I'd never prayed even though I didn't believe in praying anymore. I'd made God promises I wasn't sure I could keep. And even when there were no tears streaming down my face, they drowned my soul.

I can't lose her.

A new wave of agony washed over me as we approached the unit. It knocked the breath from me, and I grabbed at the railing on the wall to hold myself up. The world spun, and black dots stole my vision.

I can't do this.

I can't do life without her.

Oh God.

I can't breathe.

I hunched over and tried like hell to suck air deep into my lungs. I felt like wire had wrapped itself tightly around my chest, suffocating the life from me.

Just as my knees buckled and I started to go down, strong arms circled me, and a deep voice sounded at my ear, "I've got you."

Devil.

He stopped my fall and held me until I breathed, "Thank you." I turned and frowned. "Why are you here?"

A look crossed his face that I couldn't quite place. Regret, maybe. "I wanted to check in on your sister. And on you."

"Why?" Devil seemed like a good guy, but it wasn't like we were friends. I was missing something here.

His forehead crinkled as he hesitated to answer my question. Finally, he said, "Just making sure you guys are okay."

The puzzle fell together. "Did King send you?"

More hesitation. "We want to—"

I cut him off. "No. King made it clear what he wants, and it's not making sure I'm okay. Tell him I don't need you guys

21

checking on me. And tell him to take his men off watch duty, too. The police have a lead they're following up, and they think it was a random robbery gone wrong. Whoever did it isn't coming back, so we're safe."

"He's not going to listen to anything I have to say, Lily."

I wrapped my arms around myself. Was he trying to insinuate this would have to come from me? There was no way I'd be calling King to say any of this to him. I didn't have that in me today. "You need to make him listen, Devil. Please."

He exhaled sharply before jerking his chin towards the intensive care unit. "How's your sister doing? And that's not for King. I want to know."

Tears filled my eyes. I didn't even try to stop them falling. Before Brynn was shot, I tried to never cry in front of people. Now I wore my tears like a second skin.

Swallowing my fear, I said, "The doctors don't know. She's still attached to the machines."

The regret I thought I'd seen on his face before was now clear as day. "Fuck, I'm sorry, Lily."

I nodded. There wasn't anything else to say so I left him and walked towards the unit where my sister lay battling for her life.

Will our lives ever go back to normal or will there be a new normal now?

"I'm just saying, I have to hand this assignment in by Thursday, so we need to either buy a printer for here or go home and use ours," Holly said that night, her voice a harsh tone I'd never heard her take.

Linc took one look at me and stepped in between us. Holly and I had been going back and forth over this damn assignment for the last fifteen minutes and weren't getting anywhere. She'd pounced on me after dinner and wasn't letting it go. I wasn't up for this discussion; I had a headache from hell and craved a bath and some silence.

Brynn's still in a coma and I'm standing here arguing over a damn printer.

Surreal.

"Hols, I'll call your teacher and organise an extension. The school won't expect you to get this in on time. Not with what's going on," Linc said.

"No!" Holly exploded, her anger crashing into me, startling me from my thoughts. "I'm handing it in on time."

I stared at her, confused by her behaviour. She'd visited the hospital twice since Brynn was shot and avoided talking about her aunt. Anyone who didn't know us, wouldn't realise she was going through something as devastating as she was. I knew everyone experienced hard situations and worry differently, but this seemed extreme.

I touched her arm. "Baby, don't do this," I said softly.

She frowned, pulling her arm away. "What?"

The hole in my heart grew a little bigger as I watched my daughter struggling. "Don't shut down on what's happening."

Her face pulled into a scowl. "I'm not shutting down, Mum. Some of us just have stuff we still have to do. If I fall behind on school, it'll only be harder to catch up after this is all over."

I didn't understand what she meant by that. "You mean after Brynn comes home?"

Her eyes stayed locked to mine while she remained silent. I knew by her refusal to answer my question that she didn't have faith she'd ever see her aunt again.

Oh God.

Pain sliced me.

I have to keep the faith.

She looked at Linc. "Can we just go buy a printer?" Harsh again. Bleak. *My poor baby.* But I couldn't reach her. God, I could hardly reach myself.

Linc nodded and they left me alone with my thoughts. Mum had refused dinner and had locked herself in her bedroom. Zara and Robbie were also in their rooms. Thank goodness my mother had a big house. Beds for all of us, even Linc who had taken it upon himself to move in and help us through this.

The police had given us the go-ahead this afternoon to move back home, so Linc had spent a few hours there cleaning up after he collected the kids from school. He'd had to get the key off me, and that had brought King front and centre in my mind again. The man was such a strong presence even when I tried to push him to the side.

And now I was thinking about him again.

Ugh.

I stalked to the kitchen to grab a smoke. My attempt at quitting had flown out the window completely. Everything had flown out the damn window.

Once I'd located a cigarette, I headed out the front door to check the mailbox. Linc may have already checked it, but I wasn't sure. As I bent over to check the box, a car pulled up down the street. Straightening, I narrowed my eyes to watch it. A guy got out and walked to another car that was parked in front of him. *King's men.* I watched them have a conversation, anger rising in me. It struck suddenly, seemingly out of nowhere, but I knew it had to be a reaction to everything I was dealing with. And yet, even though I realised that, I channelled every ounce of that anger towards King as I stomped down the street towards his men.

It was irrational.

It was ungrateful.

But I was pissed at the world, and I couldn't stop myself.

"Why are you guys still here?" I yelled as I approached them.

They both glanced at me, their faces not revealing any surprise at my behaviour.

The one I recognised as the guy King had called Mace once when I was at the clubhouse, said, "King wants your family watched."

"I don't care what King wants. *I* want you to leave. I don't need his protection."

He pulled a face. "Sorry, babe, no can do."

I looked at the other guy who watched me with care. "Let me guess—you only take your orders from King, too?"

"Yeah. And I agree with him. There's no harm to you if you just go about your shit while we go about ours. Keeps everyone happy."

He was right.

I knew that.

But I had this overwhelming need to remove King from my life after he'd removed himself from mine. If he didn't want anything to do with me anymore, I would slam that door closed and hammer bolts in it. The hurt he'd inflicted wasn't something I wanted to experience again. After years of keeping my heart to myself, only sharing little pieces of it here and there, I'd been ready to crack it wide open again. Not anymore.

"Give me your phone," I said to Mace, holding my hand out.

He shook his head. "No."

"I'm not going anywhere until I speak with King, so one of you needs to get him on the phone."

Mace's gaze hardened. He appeared to wrestle with his thoughts, until finally he muttered, "Fuck, Lily, you don't make shit easy for a man."

I lifted my brows, waiting for the phone.

Stand your ground.

Do not let these guys steamroll you.

He pulled out his phone and made the call, passing it to me before King answered.

Nervous energy engulfed me as I held the phone to my ear waiting for King. My tummy went crazy with nerves, annoying me. I didn't want to feel anything. Didn't want to be this affected by King.

But I was.

Damn.

"Mace," King barked, "is everything okay?"

My hand shook as it gripped the phone hard. "It's not Mace, King. It's me."

Silence.

"Lily."

Oh God.

No.

The gravel in his voice hit me first.

Then, the hint of softness.

Totally unexpected.

And confusing.

King didn't do soft, so it made no sense.

But it couldn't be denied—King had just toned himself down a level for me.

4

―――――

King

Christ, I'd needed to hear her voice. Three days without it, and I was questioning my own fucking sanity. What kind of man thinks about a woman non-fucking-stop when he's only known her for three weeks? I'd made a mistake telling her we were done. We were a long fucking way from done.

I didn't give a fuck that she was about to let loose on me.

I'd take Lily however she came right now.

"You need to tell your men to leave. I don't need them here anymore."

I leaned back in my seat and stretched out my legs, ignoring the noise in the clubhouse bar around me. "You do need them. I'm not removing them."

"Don't you take that tone with me."

"What tone?"

"The arrogant one you like to use when you're being over-bearingly assuming about something. Don't assume to know what I need or what's happening with the investigation. The police have told me—"

"The police know jack, Lily. And I'm not assuming. I know this shit for a fact."

"God," she huffed out before turning silent.

"How are you?" I asked, needing that information more than anything else.

She was quick to give me a tongue lashing over that. "No, King... just no. You don't get to ask me that anymore."

Before I got a word in, she continued, "Look, you made your choice the other day, and you didn't choose me. So please tell Mace and his friend to go home. Every time I see them, it makes me think of you, and I have other things I need to concentrate on at the moment." She paused before adding a little less harshly, "Please."

I stood. "Put Mace back on."

"You'll tell him to go?"

"Lily," I growled, "put him on."

She grumbled something I couldn't make out, and then after some rustling, Mace came back on the line, "Yeah?"

"Stay put, brother. We're not pulling out yet." No fucking way were we pulling out. I'd go over there and make that clear to her myself.

"Done."

I ended the call and headed into my office to grab my shit.

Zane met me in the hallway. "I have some good news for you for once."

"You found Brant?"

"No, still nothing there. This is about Don and Kree. She's safe now. We got Don to drop the parenting order."

I scrubbed my hand over my face, still not happy with the outcome he'd worked. We were moving closer to me putting that bullet in Don's head. "That's a temporary fix."

"No, it's permanent."

"How do you know that?"

His nostrils flared. "Fuck, King, you're not gonna be happy until he's dead, are you?"

"You've got that right. She's your cousin for fuck's sake. Do you really wanna leave her out there vulnerable as fuck while that cunt is still breathing?"

"No, but we've always known that you and I handle shit differently. Murder isn't an option in my toolbox."

"It should be. When it's family, it fucking should be." If it wasn't Zane I was dealing with here, I'd go around him and take care of this myself, but I had history with him and respected him enough not to.

"Don's gotten himself in some shit, owes money he can't afford to repay, so my guys have taken care of that in return for him staying away from Kree."

"You're fucking kidding me, right? A man like Don doesn't just walk away from his woman and kids. He's the kind to show up with a fucking 9mm and end all their lives so no one else can have her."

His phone sounded with a text. Glancing down at it, he said, "I'm keeping an eye on him, King. I'll keep you updated." Meeting my gaze again, he said with some force, "Restrain yourself from doing whatever the fuck it is you're thinking of doing. There's other shit at play here that I don't have time to go into. But it's the kind of shit that, if you put a bullet in Don's head, you'll cause worse problems for Kree."

As he walked away from me, I made a mental note to get Griff to do some of our own digging on this. I wasn't happy with Zane's plan. Far fucking from it. And there was no way I'd put Kree back out there with the way things stood.

———

Half an hour later, I pulled up outside Lily's mother's house. Mace sat down the street right where I'd told him to stay. I hadn't heard from him since our last conversation, and there was no sign of Lily, so I figured he'd managed to handle her. However, as I exited my ute, she came barrelling out of the house, rushing at me like a bull to a red flag. He may have dealt with her, but I'd be the one handling her.

I traced my gaze over her body, because hell, she wore a fucking skimpy black robe that barely covered her ass. I had to fight like fuck not to reach out and undo it. My imagination went wild thinking about what it hid.

"I thought you were going to call Mace home!"

I found her eyes. They screamed the wild storm raging through her. She was a beautiful hurricane I couldn't walk away from. Lily was passion and calm all rolled into one. I needed the calm to centre me, but it was the fire I craved in a woman. Beauty never spoke to me long enough to keep my attention. Fire did, though, and she blazed with it.

I was here to re-claim her.

She could fight me all she liked; I would win in the end.

And I fucking loved a good battle.

"I never said that."

Her eyes bulged with fury. "Why are you being so difficult about this? I don't freaking understand you!"

"You don't need to. You just need to turn that ass of yours around and go back inside and let me do my thing."

Eyes still wide, she threw out, "Your *thing*? What does that even mean?"

"It means that it's shit I'm not worrying you with. Go inside. This isn't getting us anywhere."

"Just so you know, when you tell a woman you've got stuff on your mind that you don't want to worry her with, it makes her worry. I'm not going anywhere until you spit it out."

"Lily," I growled, "this isn't shit I'm sharing with you. We can stand here and argue all night, but I won't change my mind."

She crossed her arms over her chest and shifted her weight to one leg like she was settling in for the long haul. "Fine by me. I've got all night."

My gaze dropped as I caught a flash of skin when her robe fell to the side, revealing the inside of her thigh. At the same time, a red Falcon pulled into the driveway and Linc jumped out and stalked our way.

"What the fuck are you doing here?" he roared.

Lily dropped her arms and grabbed hold of him trying to stop him coming close to me. "Linc," she warned, "don't get into this. Holly's watching."

He ignored her, his eyes firmly locked to mine. Shrugging out of her hold, he moved into my personal space and spat, "You need to fuck off and leave us alone to get through this. We don't fucking need your help."

My jaw clenched as I worked hard to keep myself in check. Lily's daughter stood next to her father's car watching us, and her other kids and mother were in the house. As much as I wanted to knock the motherfucker out, I didn't want to do that while her family were close. Squaring my shoulders, I said, "I'm not here to help *you*. I'm here for Lily."

"Yeah well, she's good. I'm back now."

It fucking pissed me off that he'd worked the shooting of her sister to his advantage, but I couldn't fault her for allowing him to help her through it. "Step the fuck away from me, asshole. I'm not here to get into a fucking fight with you."

He didn't. Instead, he shoved his face closer to mine and said, "Did you hear what I said? That I'm back with Lily now. Because if you didn't, you need to pay attention to that."

At the same time Lily reached for him again and said,

"Linc, don't," I swung my head to face her and demanded, "That true?"

Motherfucker.

I'd missed his point the first time.

Now he had me fucking worked up.

Anger burned in my veins at the thought of him forcing his way back into her life.

Her eyes met mine, challenging me. "That has nothing to do with you."

Linc finally took that step back from me. Sliding his arm over Lily's shoulder, he pulled her close and hit me with a satisfied smile. "It's true. Now get off my property."

Every inch of my body tensed as my patience stretched to breaking point. It wasn't his fucking property, but Lily hadn't corrected him. She also allowed his hands on her. And she didn't challenge anything he said. The only fucking challenge she threw down was to me.

Seeing another man's hands on her drove me fucking wild. I wanted to rip those hands off her. Wanted to crush the motherfucker and ensure he never had the chance to put them anywhere near her again. Fuck, I wanted to claim her then and fucking there, and lay the fucking law down. That her body would know only my hands in the future.

I'd been mistaken when I thought I could shut my feelings down. Lily had worked her way into my black heart, clawing at it piece by fucking piece. Hell would fucking freeze over before I'd give up on her. I'd also been mistaken worrying that her connection to me would put her in danger. My thinking had been fucked up for too fucking long with the shit the club had going on. After taking care of Romano's men, my mind blazed bright with clarity, and I was thinking straight again. And what all that thinking told me was that motherfuckers could come at us, but they would never defeat us. And they sure as fuck wouldn't get their hands on my woman.

I turned my gaze to Linc. "I'd like a word with Lily. Alone."

"Not fucking likely," he said, squeezing her tighter against his body.

She wiggled out of his hold. "Give us a minute, Linc. I'll be inside soon."

He stared at her long and hard before muttering, "Fucking hell," and doing as she'd asked.

I tracked his movements until he was inside. Then, pinning my gaze to Lily's, I said, "We're not done."

She frowned. "Yes, we are. That was your choice the other day, King."

"I don't give a flying fuck what I said the other day. I'm telling you now—this thing between us is far from over."

Her frown disappeared, leaving an expression that told me how annoyed with me she was. "You don't get that right anymore. You don't get to tell me anything. And fuck you. My sister is lying in a coma that I'm not sure she'll wake up from, and I've got a lot on my mind, and you wanna come around and discuss *this*? No. I'm not okay with that. Not when you made it perfectly clear where you stood the other day. Go home. I'm done with this conversation."

Not giving me a chance to respond, she walked inside, leaving me staring after her.

I was a selfish bastard. I'd pushed her away to protect her, and here I fucking was demanding her back. It completely went against my reasons for removing her from my life. Dragging her back into it would only put her at risk again. But I couldn't do it. I couldn't *not* have her. I had no idea where this need came from. I sure as fuck didn't want to feel this way. And yet I did. Hell, I wanted Lily in ways I'd never wanted a woman.

Once she was safely back in the house, I walked to where Mace was parked. Tapping my hand on the top of his car, I leant down to talk to him through the window. "Go home, brother."

"We're done here?"

I shook my head. "No. But I'll do tonight's shift."

"I'm good, King. And besides, haven't we removed the threat to her now?"

"Go. Get some sleep and be back here at six tomorrow morning. We're keeping eyes on her until Romano is dealt with." Fuck knew who else he had on his payroll.

"Okay, so long as you're sure."

I nodded and pulled out a smoke. "I'm sure."

I lit the cigarette as he pulled away from the kerb. Dragging nicotine deep into my lungs, I thought about what I was doing. Not much of it made sense to me, but that was the fucking story of my life. The last thing I wanted was a woman by my side. And fuck knew where we'd end up. But even though I was in the middle of a fucking war that needed my full attention, and although I had a million reasons not to pursue her, Lily had become my new addiction.

5

Lily

I pulled the curtain to the side to glance down the street. He was gone. The fact that disappointed me also annoyed me. I wanted King just as much as I didn't want him now. His arrival last night and his announcement that we weren't done had thrown me. Completely freaking screwed me up. I'd hardly slept, especially since I knew he was outside. I'd watched from my window after I left him standing on the footpath, waiting for him to leave. But he hadn't. He'd stayed all night. I knew this because I'd bloody checked almost every half hour until I finally fell asleep around three.

God.

I was going to lose my mind over this man.

I was sure of it.

That was the reason why I'd let him think Linc and I were getting back together. I'd hated letting him believe that, especially when I'd seen his reaction. His response had surprised me. When Linc had thrown it out, I'd thought King wouldn't even blink. I mean, the man told me in no uncertain terms we were over. A small part of me had been happy to see how affected he was by the thought of me back with my ex. But I didn't like playing games with men, so mostly I'd felt like a bitch for misleading him.

I had to guard my heart, though, so I'd chosen not to correct his thinking.

He'd move on soon. He'd find another woman to sleep with, and I'd be long forgotten.

"Mum," Zara said, knocking softly on my door. "Breakfast is ready." She peaked her head in. "Are you okay to come out and eat or do you want me to bring it in here for you?"

I smiled at my beautiful girl and moved to her. Wrapping my arms around her, I pressed a kiss to her head. She was coping with Brynn being in a coma differently to her sister. Zara was me, through and through. Right down to her boy-crazy bones. It was why I worried so much about her having sex with her boyfriend. I knew her next move before she did most days.

"I'm okay, baby. How are you?" It was a lie; I wasn't okay. I was exhausted from too little sleep over the last few days. I was anxious over Brynn. I was worried about how my kids were doing. I was concerned about this situation with Linc. And I was twisted up over my feelings for King. Somehow, I'd managed to go from being hardly aware of living this time yesterday to hyper-aware of everything today.

She looked at me sadly. "Do you think it means something bad that Auntie Brynn still hasn't woken up?"

My heart crawled into my throat. Getting my kids through this was the hardest thing I'd ever had to do as a mother. Because as much as I wanted to reassure her, I wrestled with the same thoughts and fears. Lying had never been part of my parenting style, but I was going to have to consider it now.

And I was going to have to reach deep inside myself to give her an answer that didn't alarm her further.

I ran my hand gently down her long hair, smoothing it. "Auntie Brynn is in a critical condition, sweetheart. I'm not sure the doctors are ready for her to wake up yet. Yesterday, they told us she needs to rest in order to grow strong enough to breathe on her own. The machines are helping her do that." I actually couldn't quite recall what the doctor had said, but I was sure it was something close to this.

Zara nodded. "Okay. That's good then I guess." Her voice betrayed her inability to fully buy into that, but at least she didn't appear further distressed.

"Yes," I agreed.

Her features shifted into a frown. "What's happening with you and Dad? Like, is he moving back in with us?"

I really need to deal with this.

Like, really really.

"No, he's not. He's just helping me look after you guys while Brynn's in the hospital. And he's getting our house ready for us to move back into. That's all."

"Oh, okay." She paused before adding, "I think he thinks you guys are getting back together."

I sighed. "I'll talk to him." I lifted my chin towards the door. "Go start your breaky. I'll be out in a minute."

After she left, I pulled my phone out and sent a text to Adelaide.

Me: Sorry I didn't reply to your text last night. I was dealing with King and then I completely forgot. Sorry, babe.

Adelaide: Girl! Don't you dare apologise to me. Can I call you?

I rang her.

"How are you today, hon?" she asked as soon as she answered.

I took a deep breath. "Not good, babe."

"Okay, so I've organised the day off so I can spend it with you. You want me to swing by your place and pick you up and take you to the hospital?"

I sat on the edge of my bed and smiled through my sadness. "Has anyone told you you're the best bestie a girl can have? I would love you to do that. God knows I need to stop relying on Linc to drive me."

"Yes. How is he? Are you guys getting along okay with him being there? And wait, let's back this up a beat. What were you dealing with King for? I thought he'd fucked off?"

"Yeah, he had, but he turned up here last night after I rang him and told him to send his men home."

"Oh, they were still there?"

"Yeah. Anyway, we argued over it a little and then Linc turned up and told King we were back together. King then told me we weren't over."

"So let me get this straight. King doesn't want you except when he thinks you're no longer available? Bloody asshole."

That was a thought I hadn't been able to shift all night. The more I thought about it, the more annoyed at the whole situation I grew. "Seems so."

"Oh, babe," she said softly, "I'm sorry he's a dick. I know you thought there was something there between the two of you, but I think he did you a favour when he walked away the other day. You don't need a man who pulls that shit."

"Yeah," I whispered as tears fell down my cheeks. I felt dumb crying over him, and told myself I was only doing it because of everything else going on, but even I didn't buy that. I'd been ready to give King more than I'd been ready to give any man for years, and he'd hurt me. I'd pushed this hurt to the side for the last few days so I could just get through the days, but it had forced its way to the surface now.

"Right, we're not going to talk about him again today, okay? Let's go back to Linc. How are things there?"

I leaned forward and rested my elbows on my knees. "I'm fairly sure he truly does believe we're getting back together. I don't think he was just saying that for King's benefit. So I have to have that conversation with him today." The more I thought about what I had to do today, the more I wanted to crawl back into bed, hide under the covers and shut the world out.

"This morning?"

"Yes, I'm about to go and have it with him now."

"Good. I'll be over in about an hour or so."

"Thanks, Addy."

"Always."

We ended the call and I gathered all the strength I could find to go and talk to Linc. I found him alone in the garage, cleaning rubbish out of his car.

"We need to talk," I said when he glanced up at me.

He came my way. "You okay, baby?"

"Linc, you can't call me that anymore. I've told you that before."

He hit me with a confused look. "I thought we were working on something here."

I wasn't convinced I was up for this conversation. Not while anxiety and worry had me in their grips. My emotions were all over the place, and that wasn't a good starting point when dealing with my ex. Linc had a way of twisting my words to suit himself, and a way of muddling my thinking. I'd known him for sixteen years. We'd been together for most of those years. He knew my triggers, and he wasn't afraid to push them to get what he wanted. I'd had to learn how to manage my boundaries with him, and that usually required me being completely on my game. Today was not that kind of day.

"I appreciate everything you've done to help me through this, but I never once said we were working on something. I'm sorry if I gave you that impression." I really didn't think I had, though. But people often took what they wanted from an interaction, and miscommunications had always been a big part of our relationship.

He stayed silent for a good few moments and then his face twisted into an ugly expression. "Is this because that asshole showed up last night?"

Before I knew what was happening, a strong desire to defend King rushed up from deep inside. It was immediate and it was fierce. And I had no idea why the heck it forced itself on me, because defending him was the last thing I wanted to do after he'd hurt me. But hearing Linc say nasty things about him drew out my protective side.

"Don't call him that. And no, this has nothing to do with King."

His brows lifted. "If you're standing up for him, that says something, don't you think? Fuck, Lil, doesn't our marriage count for something? All those years we worked towards building—"

"You really wanna go down that path? Because if you do, I've got a whole heap of stuff to get off my chest concerning the work *we* were doing on our marriage. And none of it has anything to do with King, so let's just leave him out of this, okay?"

"No, let's fucking not. He hasn't been here for you the last few days. Not like I have been. So I have no clue why you'd even look at him, let alone wanna be with him. And what about the fact you just stood by while I told him we were together? Are you playing both of us?"

He had my blood boiling now. It was as if all the sadness and worry I felt collided with my frustration and irritation, causing the perfect storm of anger. "Have I ever played you, Linc?" I yelled. "Have I ever been anything but supportive of you? God, you make me so freaking mad some days I could scream at you for hours. I'm sorry you got the wrong end of the stick about us, but I honestly didn't say anything to make you assume I wanted you back. For the record, I will never take you back. You broke my heart when you cheated on me, and I could never trust you enough again to be with you. And as for King, what I do with him is none of your business."

His lip pulled up in a snarl. "It is if it affects *my* kids."

My eyes widened and I went at him with a ferocity I didn't know I had in me. "Do not threaten me. You will not like the outcome if you do. I've worked hard to keep our relationship civil. You wanna threaten me? I won't give a fuck about civil."

He leaned closer to me and yelled, "Fuck you, Lily. You think you're above me, but you aren't. Just because you went and got yourself an education while I stayed home with the kids doesn't mean you're any fucking better than me."

This was an old argument of ours. Linc had never moved past the insecurities he had over me earning more than him. And while I'd studied for my degree, he'd spent most of the time bitching about me being away from the family. If it had been any other day, I would have walked away at this point, but it wasn't. It was today, and he'd pushed me too far. "I've never thought I was better than you. That's your hang-up, not mine. I don't care what people do for a living or whether they've got an education. All I'm interested in is whether they care about those they love, and you proved that you don't. You can stand there and tell me you love me and that you wanna be together again, but your actions speak a lot louder than your words. I don't care about words or promises anymore, Linc. I don't even hear them. I hear actions."

Steam practically billowed from him he was that angry. Huffing out a shitty breath, he backed away and snapped, "Fine, you wanna be like that, I'm done here. I'm out. You can fucking sort your own shit out." He stared at me for a few beats, like he was waiting for me to change my mind. When I said nothing, he shook his head angrily at me and stalked inside.

I took a minute. He had me all worked up that I shook with the adrenaline coursing through me. Sagging against the wall, I got my breathing under control while I thought about our argument. It struck me how easily he turned on me. He turned mean. That definitely wasn't a characteristic I wanted in a man I gave my heart to.

Following him back inside, I found him telling Holly he would drive them to school this morning but he wouldn't be here when they got home this afternoon.

Robbie and Zara were in their bedrooms so I went back to mine. The less time around Linc, the better. My phone sounded with a text as I walked through the bedroom door.

Skylar: Hey Lily. Just checking in on you to see how you are. I'm thinking of you.

My heart sped up as I read the message. I couldn't think of Skylar without thinking of King.

Me: Thanks babe. I'm okay.

She'd been texting me every day since Brynn was shot. In a short amount of time, I'd grown to adore her. Kinda like how I'd fallen for her brother in a crazy short time.

She didn't send another text. She rang instead.

"I really doubt you're okay," she said when I answered the phone. "Give it to me straight. We're friends now, and friends don't bullshit each other."

I smiled, and for the first time in days, it was a genuinely happy smile. Funny how those who truly cared about us could do that for us even when we were going through something that had no joy in it. "I'm not okay, but I kinda am if that makes sense. I've got some really good people around me, including you, and that makes things so much better."

"Good. Now, I've organised some home-cooked meals for you with the girls here. They've all pitched in and cooked a heap of casseroles and stuff for you guys. I'm going to ask King to drop them over late this afternoon. Will you be home?"

A new wave of emotion overwhelmed me and tears streamed down my face. How was I so lucky to have people like Skylar looking out for me? I squeezed my hand tighter around the phone as I tried to talk through my tears. "You're amazing," I choked out. "Thank you."

"Oh shit, I'm sorry I made you cry."

I dashed the tears away. "They're good tears, I promise. And besides, I cry far more at the moment than I don't, so this isn't anything unusual."

She was quiet for a moment. When she spoke again, her voice softened. "How's your sister?"

I swallowed hard, the unrelenting pain slicing through me at the thought of Brynn lying unconscious on her hospital bed. It knocked the wind out of me, and I had to sit on the bed to stop myself collapsing to the floor. "I don't know," I whispered through more tears. "She's still on the ventilator. The doctors don't know when she'll wake up."

"I'm so sorry." Her voice held tears now, too. "I'm going to come and see you today. Will you be at the hospital?"

"Oh no, don't do that. You're still on crutches and in pain. I'll be okay. And besides, they won't let you into the intensive care unit. It's just family."

"I'm fine. Don't you worry about me. I'm still doing all the exercises you gave me, and getting better every day. And I don't care if I can't come in. I just wanna be there for you in case you need someone to talk to or cry with. I'll sit outside. What time will you be at the hospital? I'll ask King to drop me off for a few hours."

She'd mentioned King twice now. I'd ignored the first mention, but my body wouldn't allow me to do that twice. Because although my head stayed firmly committed to not starting up with him again, my body had completely different ideas. Kind of like my heart did.

Skylar King had the same level of determination as her brother, so I knew there was no point arguing with her. "I'll be there in the next couple of hours until around school pick-up time."

"Okay, I'll see you later. Do you need me to bring anything for you?"

"No, you're already doing so much."

After the call ended, I took a deep breath. Today would get tricky if she managed to convince King to do those things for her. Hopefully he'd be far too busy to say yes.

6

King

I stretched my neck before shoving two Advil down my throat. I avoided washing them down with whisky. There was a hell of a lot of shit to get through today; whisky wouldn't help with any of it.

It had been a long night sitting outside Lily's place. I'd headed home for a few hours of sleep after Mace covered me early this morning, but it had been broken. Sleep was the last fucking thing on my mind, though. I could run on sheer fucking determination if I had to.

"Where'd you get to last night?" Axe asked, joining me in the office.

I settled my ass against the office desk. "Had shit to do."

He gave me the look that told me he would wait for further information.

Scrubbing my hand over my face, I muttered, "I gave Mace the night off."

His eyes narrowed at me. "He was watching the physio-therapist, right?"

"Yeah."

"Since when do you take on that kind of job?"

"Fuck, brother, do we really need to play twenty-fucking-questions? I'd rather go over the shit we've gotta take care of today."

"Jesus, King, how long since you've had some good sleep? You're being extra fucking whiny today."

I glared at him. "Tell me you've heard from Johnny."

"I have. He thinks he has the location. He's confirming it now and said he'll be back in touch within the next hour with any luck."

I wouldn't ease off this guy until I had that address in my hands. "Keep on him."

"Will do."

A knock sounded at the door and Skylar called out, "King, you in there?"

I pushed off the desk and opened the door. "What's up?"

She made her way in, using her crutches like a pro. Lily had worked her magic on Skye's recovery. She went from strength to strength daily. "Can you drop me off at the hospital this morning?"

I frowned. "You don't have an appointment today, do you?" It wouldn't surprise me if she did and I'd forgotten. My head felt like it could explode with all the shit in there.

"No. I want to go and see Lily. I feel so useless and unable to help her, but I figure I can sit and just be there in case she needs someone to talk to or be with her, you know?"

My gut tightened at the mention of Lily. I knew exactly what Skylar meant. I felt useless, too. And fuck, what I wouldn't give to make shit right in her world again.

I checked the time. We'd be cutting it fine because I had a

meet scheduled with Eric Bones in just over an hour, but I'd make this happen. Nodding, I said, "We'll leave in ten."

She smiled. "Thank you."

As she exited the room, Hyde came in. "You good to leave in about twenty for this meet?"

Bones had called yesterday after word had travelled about the visits I'd been making around Sydney. Visits letting everyone know Storm wouldn't take shit lying down. I'd had Eric on my list, but he'd called me first.

"Change of plans," I said to Hyde. "I have to swing by the hospital on my way, so I'll meet you there. If I'm running late, start without me. We've got too much to get through today to slow shit down."

"Agreed. See you there," he said and left us.

Axe met my gaze. "I'll call you as soon as I hear from Johnny. You gonna have time to get this done this afternoon if he comes through with an address?"

"I'll fucking make time for that." I would move heaven and earth for that. The fact Romano still breathed infuriated me. The kind of anger that made a man willing to go places he'd never considered before lived inside me over Romano. The only other time in my life I'd felt rage like this was when Margreet had been killed. A bloodbath had been my response to that. I wouldn't hesitate to do the same this time if that was needed to ensure the safety of my family and my club. *And of Lily and her family.*

"You haven't visited her yet?" Skylar asked, surprised when she realised I didn't know where the intensive care unit was. We'd arrived at the hospital five minutes ago and the need to see Lily compelled me to park the ute and go inside with

Skye. I'd known it would. It was why I'd told Hyde to begin without me when he met Bones.

"I've been busy, Skye," I muttered.

We found our way to the lifts and headed up to where Lily's sister was. Skylar sent a text to Lily letting her know she was here. When we arrived outside the unit, Lily was nowhere to be seen and I wondered how long I'd have to wait for her.

I didn't have a lot of time to spare.

And yet, the tension punching through me told me I'd wait.

I needed to see her for myself. Had to see she was okay.

Skylar took a seat in the tiny waiting room. I didn't. Instead, I paced the area, my thoughts completely on Lily.

"God, King, sit down," Skylar grumbled.

I checked the clock on the wall. Fuck, the silence in here was deafening. We were the only ones waiting, and the corridor was quiet, too. I disliked noise, but I would have done anything for something to take my mind off shit.

"Send her another text."

"No. I told her I wouldn't get in her way today."

Fuck.

"I'll be back in a minute," I said, exiting the room to make a call. As I stepped out into the corridor, Lily pushed through the door from the intensive care unit, her eyes coming straight to mine.

Stopping dead in her tracks, she said, "King."

I'd caught her off guard, which wasn't my intention, but it seemed to slow down any inclination she may have had to tell me to leave the minute she saw me. Either that or she'd decided to stop fighting me. The way she looked at me was a hell of a lot different to the way she'd looked at me last night. She appeared to have thawed a little.

48

I ran my eyes over her. It wasn't because I wanted to fuck her, although that desire was stronger than ever. This was based on my need to know she was okay. It was a habit I'd picked up somewhere along the way in life. When I spent time away from those I cared about, I found it necessary to check for any harm that may have come to them while I was absent. It was a habit I couldn't shake.

Lily was okay. Physically, at least.

"What are you doing here?" she asked as I checked her over.

Meeting her gaze again, I said, "I dropped Skylar off."

Her brain appeared to catch up to my presence when the thawing of her ice shifted back to freezing temperatures again. "Thank you for dropping her off. You can go now."

Her words were automated. Cold. Emotionless. Like she was talking from a fucking script. It was as if she didn't even fucking know me; like I'd never been inside her. That shit pissed me off. Where the hell had her fire gone? I could handle her hate and her disappointment and her regret. Whatever she wanted to throw at me, I could fucking take. But I could never handle being frozen out like this because I knew it came from the kind of devastation that crushed a soul. And I never fucking wanted to crush her soul.

I closed the distance between us, slid my hand around her waist and backed her up against the wall. Ignoring the widening of her eyes and the way her hands pressed against my chest, I growled, "We need to get one thing straight, and one thing only. I'm not walking away from this."

Her throat worked hard as she found her words. With her hands still pushing against me, she blurted out, "I don't know what you think *this* is, but as far as I'm concerned, there isn't anything for you to walk away from."

I moved my free hand to her neck, gripping her there and

circling my thumb over her throat. Bending my face to hers, I said, "That's bullshit and you know it. Stay mad at me. Stay fucked off. Yell at me, scream at me, fucking hit me, but don't you fucking shut down on me."

She sucked in a sharp breath. And then she found her fighting spirit. "This isn't something you can fix, King. You can't just swoop in and demand I forget what you did. I needed you and you just left." She pushed hard against my chest, forcing me backwards. "You hurt me, and I won't allow you to do that again."

There she was.

Fucking beautiful.

"Good," I said, my entire body blazing with heat. I could work with what she'd given me.

"*Good*? What the hell does that mean?"

Fuck, if only she knew how much her fight turned me on. "You're not done either, Lily. I don't expect you to forget what I did, but you'll move past it. This pull between us is too fucking strong for you not to."

"My God, you're arrogant."

"No, I'm honest."

"You're fucking presumptuous is what you are."

"We can stand here all fucking day slinging words at each other, but that would only prove I'm right." I moved into her personal space again, unable to stop myself. Fuck, I wanted this woman. Tracing my finger over her lips, I added, "If you didn't still want me, you would have ended this conversation before it even got started."

Her lips flattened and she pushed me away again. Moving past me, she snapped, "You tell yourself that, but don't ever presume to know my thoughts again. You are so wrong it isn't funny."

I watched her walk into the waiting room and sit with Skylar. Not once in our conversation had she brought up her ex. If she were committed to trying again with him, she would have thrown that at me. Not that I'd let him get in my way when it was clear she wanted me, but she hadn't mentioned his name once, signalling that was bullshit, too.

Eric Bones eyed me with hesitation. "You're stirring some shit up, King. You sure you wanna do that?"

I leaned back into the booth where we sat in the darkened corner of the dingy pub I reserved for these kinds of meetings. Crossing my arms over my chest, I said, "I haven't been so fucking sure of something for a long time."

"Fucking hell," he muttered. "It's throwing a lot of heat my way."

"And?" Did he think I gave two shits?

"Look," he said, angling forward and resting his arms on the table, "I'm just sayin' that Sydney hasn't seen any major trouble for a long time. Well, besides what went down with Silver Hell. You've mostly kept the peace with everyone. Don't force a war on all of us just because of the shit you've had going on."

"I'm done with keeping the peace when it's not warranted. It needs to be known that if a line gets crossed, Storm won't take it. I'm just letting everyone know this'll be how it is in the future."

"Yeah, well some people don't like it."

"I don't give a fuck what people like."

His face morphed into a pained expression. "I hope you know what you're doing."

This conversation had been a waste of my time. Standing, I said, "I don't do shit I can't stand behind. You wanna fucking cry over it in future, do it with your sisters. I don't have time to waste talking it out."

As Hyde and I exited the pub, my phone sounded with a text. After I read it, I looked at Hyde, every cell in my body alive with the crazy energy I welcomed. "We have an address. Call the boys. It's fucking on."

This moment had been too fucking long coming. Romano's blood would finally dirty my hands.

7

King

If, as claimed by some, the two most powerful warriors were patience and time, I was a motherfucking warrior when it came to Romano. He'd evaded me at every turn over the last few weeks, and before that, he'd fought a war against me in the shadows. I'd had to be more patient with him than I'd ever been with anyone. That had only intensified my hunger for his blood.

Axe's guy had come through with the goods, and after my men had surrounded the secluded property on the outskirts of Sydney and fought their way through the security guarding Romano, I finally stood in front of him.

"And so we meet," he said, his attention firmly on me. He ignored Hyde, Nitro, Cole, Nash, and Axe who stood behind me. He knew his time was up. Knew there was no point trying to find a way out of this.

"You had to know that was inevitable."

"I wasn't convinced you had it in you. I've been coming at you for a long time, King, and you never worked it out. So no, I didn't know it was inevitable."

Motherfucker.

I *had* missed it.

I would never make that mistake again.

My body strained to have at him, but first I needed to make sure I knew everything there was to know about this situation. Moving closer to him, I gripped his shirt and yanked him to me. "We're gonna have a little talk about that," I snarled.

He snorted. "No, we're not."

Pulling out my blade, I slowly ran it across his throat. Hard enough to let him know I wouldn't hesitate to use it, but not with enough pressure to draw blood yet. "Oh, I think we are, asshole. And while we're at it, we might as well talk about Ivy." The flare of emotion in his eyes and the clench of his jaw told me I was right in my assumption she was the key to breaking him. "Were you aware she was planning on leaving you? I'm guessing not because if you were, you wouldn't have allowed it to happen."

He jerked out of my hold. I let him go easily in an effort to get him talking. I figured I had more chance of that if I gave him some space first. "You don't get to talk about her," he spat. "Not after what you put her through years ago. You have no fucking idea of my relationship with her. I would never have treated her the way you did."

My blood roared in my ears. This guy was a piece of fucking work. It was going to take every ounce of my restraint to keep myself in check. "I know you beat the fuck out of her often enough to cause her to lose your children."

He smiled. A menacing smile. "Don't believe everything she says."

"I fucking witnessed the after-effects of her latest miscarriage, so I do fucking believe her."

His smile slipped from his face, replaced by anger. "She has ways of faking stuff."

"Jesus, what fucking drugs did you take this morning?" I shoved my face closer to his, fury heating my cheeks. "No one can fake the blood loss she had. Not to fucking mention my own doctor treated her and confirmed the miscarriage."

The glaze in his eyes told me he would dismiss anything I had to say about her. "I know my wife, King, and I know she's a lying, manipulative woman. Regardless, I love her more than you ever did."

"And yet, she left you. Says a lot about your love."

"No, it says a lot about you and how much she wanted to ruin you."

"What the fuck are you on about?"

A satisfied smile blared from him. "You met Brant, yes?"

I clenched my jaw as I nodded.

"She manipulated him into doing her dirty work. She knew he was in love with her, and she worked that to her advantage." He paused for a moment. "Ivy has carried a desire for revenge against you for as long as I've known her. I refused to humour her request to initiate an attack on you years ago, so she started in on Brant."

"I don't fucking believe you. *You* came after me using Marx. *You* killed my ex and her child. And besides, Brant is a psychopath, best I can figure. You've got shit about those two around the wrong way."

"Brant's a weak man. He's not a psychopath. Where the hell did you get that from?"

"We did some digging on him. He has a history of stalking women and murdering them."

He flinched like I'd slapped him.

I'd found something he didn't know.

When he didn't respond, I said, "He tell you she's working him or did you figure that out for yourself? And don't feel bad for screwing up on this one. We did, too." Brant had played us for fools. I imagined he'd done the same to Romano. I'd shared that sliver of information to encourage his walls down a little.

The way he glossed over it confirmed my suspicions. "Either way, it doesn't fucking matter. They're concocting something up for you. Any of the shit I've given the feds on you will pale in comparison to whatever they do to you."

And that right there was what I wanted. I didn't buy into Ivy gunning for revenge, but I *did* buy into Romano feeding the feds shit. "Ahh, Detective Ryland's told me about you singing to him."

"I don't know what you did to him, but it must have been fucking bad. The asshole can't see straight because of you."

I cocked my head to the side. "You hear they pulled him off the case? Seems he's on someone's payroll and they don't like that." I watched his reaction closely in an effort to judge if it was his payroll Ryland was on.

Confusion flickered briefly in his eyes. He attempted to cover it, but I had my answer. It wasn't Romano he'd been working with. He opened his mouth to reply, but a loud crash sounded from somewhere in the house, interrupting my interrogation.

I sheathed my knife and pulled out my gun before pushing Romano towards Nitro and ordering, "Don't let him out of your sight."

Signalling for everyone else to search the house, I stalked in the direction the sound came from. The house wasn't huge so it wouldn't take us long to find whoever it was.

It didn't.

He came charging at me as I entered the kitchen. Gun pointed at my head, he fired with one clear goal—to kill. This wasn't the fucking feds we were dealing with. This had to be Romano's crew.

My rage screamed to life and my demons raced from the far corners of my soul.

We'd been trained for moments like this from birth.

This asshole brought a gun to the fight.

He had no idea I was a motherfucking bomb.

Ducking the moment I saw him, I avoided his bullet and threw myself at him. My arms circled his body and with unrelenting force, I drove him backwards against the fridge. He hit with a thud, his head banging against it hard. His gun fell to the ground and I kicked it out of the way. I'd caught him off guard and he was slow to get his bearings.

Gripping his throat, I dug my fingers in hard as I aimed my gun at his foot. Pulling the trigger, I demanded, "Who the fuck are you?"

His cry of pain as the bullet went through his foot fed the beast inside me.

This was what I came here for today.

Blood and pain.

He scowled at me and spat, "Fuck you!"

I shot his other foot before striking him across the face with my gun as hard as I fucking could. With one last squeeze of his throat, I let him go, grasped his shirt and spun him around so I could slam him across the small room into the kitchen bench. He scrambled to get back in the fight, but he was no match for me. I closed the distance between us again and punched him. He grunted and took a shot at hitting me, but I evaded the jab and punched him again, my fist connecting with his jaw with a satisfying crack.

I was fucking manic.

Wired for hell.

I could keep going at him for hours, but all I had were minutes. Fuck, I didn't even have that. Our plan had been to get in and get out fast. I'd gone and screwed that up by taking my time questioning Romano.

I needed to get back to him. This guy wasn't going to give me answers to my questions, and I didn't have time to drag them from him, so I struck him with my fist a few more times before putting a bullet between his eyes. A lot less satisfying than what I would have preferred to do, but it got the job done.

"King!" Hyde called out as his boots thudded through the place. "We need to hurry this the fuck up."

Yeah.

I stalked back into the living room and found Axe standing over a guy, landing punch after punch on him. The guy was covered in blood and didn't have any fight left in him, but my brother's own demons had surfaced. Once they were let loose, a motherfucker had no chance against him. Axe and I were cut from the same cloth; he was just better at controlling the darkness running through his veins.

I looked at Hyde. "Did we get them all?"

He nodded. "Yeah. There were four of them. They weren't feds. I pulled this from one of them." He handed me a piece of paper.

It was a map of the area that contained scribbled notes regarding the detail that had been guarding Romano.

"Romano's men," I said.

"That's my guess."

I shoved the paper in my pocket. "Good. With any fucking luck that's the last of them."

Turning to Romano, I pulled my blade out again as antici-pation coursed through me. This was going to be over far too fucking quickly for me, but I had no choice. As much as I wanted to take him with me so I could dedicate some long days to making him suffer, what I wanted more was to make a fucking statement.

This is what happens when you fuck with Storm.

We will go to the depths of hell to find you.

And you won't be the one left standing.

My eyes locked on his.

He bucked in Nitro's hold, but we both knew this was the end of the road for him.

I called on every memory of what he'd done to my club and the people I held close.

I allowed the thoughts to swarm like angry fucking bees.

And with a roar that I dragged from the pits of my soul, I plunged the knife into his chest.

Flesh and blood and pain filled my senses as he cried out in agony.

I ripped the knife from his body and thrust it back in, twisting deep.

Pure fucking satisfaction rushed through me, but it was tinged with torment because his death would never make up for what he'd done. The lives he'd taken would never be returned. The life he'd tried to take was still in jeopardy. The suffering he'd dealt would never be eased.

I leaned in close to him and snarled through gritted teeth, "Rot in hell, motherfucker."

His head had rolled back but he dragged it up so he could look at me one last time. "I didn't kill your ex... Didn't fucking kill anyone..." He gurgled through his pain before his head lolled back again.

My mind attempted to process that, but I stumbled over it.

He did fucking kill her.

He had to have.

Because if it wasn't him, who the fuck was it?

8

King

"You think he was bullshitting you?" Nitro asked late that afternoon as we watched Kick and Nash trade jabs in the boxing ring we had set up out the back of the clubhouse.

I scrubbed a hand over my face. "I don't fucking know, brother."

This had been on my mind all afternoon, and I hadn't come closer to figuring out where I stood on it. It was fucking convenient for him to throw that out as he took his last breath. I wouldn't have put it past him trying to fuck with me from the grave. If I believed him, I had to entertain the thought we were still at risk while the killer remained free to attack again.

Fuck.

I was restless after killing Romano.

On edge.

I needed to work the high out of my body.

This shit churning through my brain didn't fucking help.

Loud cheers from the boys watching the boxing interrupted our conversation. I looked over to see Nash grinning like a motherfucker with both arms raised.

Nitro sucked back some beer before commenting, "That asshole is good for the club."

He was right. Nash was always welcome in my clubhouse. Mostly because he stepped the fuck up when we needed him, but also because he had a way of easing the tension running through the club.

Kick got up and returned Nash's grin before smacking him across the head. "Rematch tomorrow, fucker. And put your fucking dick away."

Nash's smile only grew larger as he grabbed his crotch. "You wanna see it, brother?"

Nitro chuckled, which was fucking odd for him. But that was what Nash did.

I stood, needing to get out of here. "We'll go over everything at church tomorrow."

Nitro nodded before turning his attention back to the ring.

I headed inside to check on a few things before leaving. Fuck knew where I'd end up, but I couldn't sit around doing nothing any longer.

Skylar met me as I walked the hallway to the office. "Oh good, I've been looking for you! Can you do me a favour?"

"What?" The question came out harder than I intended, but I was so fucking tense I couldn't stop it.

She frowned. "Why are you so cranky? I just asked you a question."

I worked to rein my shit in, but failed. "Fuck, Skye, just ask the fucking question."

Her lips flattened. "Fine," she snapped. "Can you drop some meals over to Lily's? Annika and Kree cooked some up

61

for her family, and I promised her I'd get them over to her today."

I stilled, my shoulders rocklike. It wasn't a good idea for me to see Lily in the state I was in. Not when I was wired for sex. Not when all I wanted to do was wrap my hands around her neck and fuck the hell out of her. When what I needed to do was fuck the dark shit out of my head.

"Get Devil to do it."

The scowl she directed my way let me know what she thought of that. "Why are you being such an ass about this? Like, is it so hard for you to do something nice for her after everything she's done for us?"

"I've got shit to do. Ask Devil. And if he can't do it, find someone else."

"No," she said with force. "I think you should do it. I want this to come from our family, not from the club."

I stared at her for a long few moments, warring with myself over this decision. I wanted to do it. Wanted to see Lily. Fuck knew she was the only woman on my mind. While I always used sex to come down after a day like today, I wouldn't go looking for it with anyone else tonight. But no fucking way would I show up looking for it from her when she was dealing with her sister in a coma. Doing what Skylar asked of me would put me in dangerous territory. I wasn't convinced I could be near Lily and hold myself back.

I never did the right thing, though.

"Jesus fucking Christ, okay," I barked.

"Good. They're in the fridge. You should go now," she said, lifting her brows, daring me to argue with her.

I ignored that and continued on my way towards the office, my mind already focused on what I had to do. I wouldn't be going now, that was for fucking sure. I'd give myself a few hours to get my head together before seeing her.

"And stop being a dickhead," she called out as I rounded the corner of the hall.

The women in my life would be the fucking death of me.

I entered the office, my phone ringing in my pocket as I did so.

"What's up?" I answered it after seeing Hyde's name flash across the screen.

"Where are you? There's a fed out the front to see you."

And so it all fucking began again.

"I'm on my way."

This was the first we'd heard from them since discovering Ryland had been removed from the case. I wondered if the new guy would be as determined to see us go down. At least this time we weren't distracted by Romano. This time I could dedicate my attention fully to the motherfuckers.

I made my way out to the front gate, slowing as I laid eyes on the new fed I was up against.

She stepped forward, her gaze full of steel, her features schooled into an unreadable blank canvas. "Mr. King, we finally meet. I'm Detective Stark."

I levelled a harsh expression on her and crossed my arms over my chest. The sooner she got her ass off my property the better. "What do you want?"

"Just wanted to stop by to say you left us a hell of a mess today."

I'd only just met the bitch, but my first impressions of people were usually spot on. This one had brass fucking balls. "I've been busy today, so I have no fucking clue what mess you're talking about."

"We can agree on one thing—you *have* been busy."

"Now that you've said what you came here for, you can leave."

"I also wanted to tell you that Romano was the least of

your worries." She took a step away from me. "Strap in. We're in for some fun now."

I watched her leave, my mind going crazy with a million thoughts. A million fucking more than were already in there. As she drove away, I pulled out my phone and dialled Bronze.

"You find Brant yet?" he asked as he answered.

"No, but we've dealt with Romano. That's not why I'm calling, though. I've got a question for you."

"What?"

"You ever work with Detective Stark?"

He whistled low. "I haven't worked with her, but I've heard of her. She's a ballbuster."

"Yeah, that's what I got from her. She ever had any dirt on her hands?"

"Not that I know of. I'll do some digging."

"Don't fucking put yourself at risk, Bronze. Axe has a contact we can use."

"I've got nothing else to fucking do," he muttered.

"Yeah, you do. Get the hell out of town and never look back."

He ignored that. "I'll call you if I find something."

After he hung up, I looked at Hyde. "She's gonna prove more difficult than Ryland."

He nodded. "Yeah, brother. My thoughts, too."

I jerked my chin at him. "Do whatever you need to do tonight to get your head focused. Tomorrow we make a new plan. No fucking way are we lying down for these feds."

9

Lily

"Call me if you need me, okay?" Adelaide said as she exited the house, stepping out into the dark of night. We'd had a downpour of heavy rain earlier. A cold wind lingered, reminding me we were heading into the time of year I wasn't a fan of. I didn't mind autumn; it was winter I wished we could skip every year.

I reached for her arm and pulled her back so I could hug her. When I finally let her go, I said softly, "Thank you for today. I promise I'll call you if I need you."

She smiled. "I wish I could take tomorrow off, too. I'm not far, though, so call and I'll come as soon as I can." The sound of a car pulling up drew our attention, and Addy said, "Good God, it's almost ten o'clock. Who would be stopping by now?"

I squinted into the dark trying to see who it was, but I knew the only person who would come by at this time of night was the one person I really didn't want to see. *King.* My belly fluttered, betraying me, the bitch. She'd done the same thing this morning when he'd dropped by the hospital.

I was a mess over this man.

Completely confused and flustered.

"Oh no he doesn't," Adelaide muttered as she saw King approaching. "What the hell makes you think it's okay to come here at this time of night?" she snapped at him.

His scowl was unmistakable as he walked up the stairs onto the front porch. My gaze dropped to the casserole dishes he held. Odd. My attention, though, was quickly drawn back to his face as he looked at me and said, "Skylar asked me to bring these over."

It was totally King not to bother answering her question about why he'd chosen to come so late. And as hurt and angry as I still was with him, I couldn't move past the way he watched me with concern blazing in his eyes. It was so unlike anything he'd given me at any other time.

Shit.

Addy started in on him again. "Well, you can give me those and turn around—"

I placed my hand on her arm. "It's okay, babe, I've got this."

She spun her head to look at me, eyes wide with disbelief. "You're not seriously going to let him in?"

"No, but I'm not going to stand here and get into another argument," I said, giving her the look I reserved for when I needed her to let me fight my own battles. Adelaide was the kind of bestie every girl needed, always going into battle for her friends. Sometimes, though, she didn't know when to back away. This was one of those times. King and Addy both had strong personalities. If I let her continue her tirade, God knew where we'd end up.

We stood making eyes at each other for a few moments,

the kind of eyes best friends made when they were trying to communicate "are you sure" and "yes, I'm sure" and "I don't think you are" and "I promise you, I am." Finally, she took a deep breath and glanced back at King. Pointing her finger at him, she said, "You hurt her again, you'll have me to answer to, buddy."

The intensity with which he looked at her and nodded his agreement took my breath away. What was going on here? Three days ago, he'd told me we were done. Now he seemed determined to disregard that decision, so much so that he took Adelaide's warning without argument. This wasn't the demanding man I knew.

After giving me one last questioning glance, Adelaide left us and walked to her car. I watched her in silence, refusing to give King my attention straight away. I needed a moment to gather my thoughts. God, I needed more than a freaking moment, but I knew he wouldn't give me that.

As she pulled out of the driveway, he moved closer and said, "I'll put these in your fridge."

I turned my face to his, trying hard not to trace my gaze over his skin. The man was far too good-looking, though. Or maybe it was those eyes of his that did me in. They revealed the depth to him I knew was there. The things I'd desperately wanted to know about him, but hadn't had the time to learn.

He remained quiet while I examined his face and then his neck. I lost myself for a beat, remembering how his mouth had felt on me, how his lips had grazed my skin, how his eyes had tracked my movements making me feel more desired than I ever had. Making me feel like the woman I'd always wanted to be.

Oh God.

No.

I could not go there with him again.

"Lily," he rumbled at the same time my mother joined us.

"Lily, I want to call the priest," she said, her words as disjointed as her actions had been since Brynn was shot.

I frowned at her. "Why?"

She looked at me like I'd asked a silly question. "I want him to give Brynn the Sacrament of the Anointing of the Sick."

Her words winded me. I struggled to breathe as they worked their way through me. I understood what she said, and I understood the significance of asking for that, but my world spun at the thought of my sister being close enough to death to call on a priest.

She isn't going to die.

We do not need that sacrament.

"Lily," Mum said again, cutting through my fog. "Can you please get me his number?"

"No, we don't need him," I snapped. "Brynn's not dying, Mum."

My outburst caught her by surprise, and her eyes widened. But she came back with, "You don't know that, and I want to make sure—"

"No! Don't you dare say that!"

I was wild.

Livid.

I would not entertain the thought my sister was at death's door.

Mum stared at me and then without another word, she turned and walked back inside. This conversation wasn't finished, though. Not by a long shot. I stalked after her, ranting as I went. "Do not walk away from me when we're in the middle of a conversation!"

She ignored me and continued moving towards her bedroom.

I followed. "Mum! Stop. We need to discuss this."

Finally, she spun around to look at me. The agony lining

her face killed me, quieting me long enough for her to get a word in. "Lily, shhh. You will wake the children."

That was what she was worried about? I knew I should have thought about that, but the only thought in my mind was that I was nowhere near ready to give up on Brynn.

"Brynn isn't going to die, Mum. You can't call the priest. The doctor said they are weaning her off the ventilator. That has to be a good thing."

Her beautiful face crumpled into the kind of sadness that tore at my heart. I hated watching her struggle for the past few days. No mother should have to go through this. "We don't know what will happen when they do that. Brynn needs this."

Pain cut straight through me as I allowed her words in.

I didn't want to think about my sister not being around anymore. Not being my person.

I need a person.

And I don't want anyone but Brynn.

I had never experienced pain like this. It was an ache that sat sharply and deeply in my body. It felt like a knife had sliced a line from my heart down to my toes. I wanted to cry every second of the day. I wanted my anguish to be ripped from me so I didn't have to feel it ever again, because surely one jagged tear like that would never hurt as badly as this.

This pain was merciless.

It felt like it could literally kill me.

"Lily," Mum said, her voice softer, "you must understand I'm doing this to help her heal."

I swallowed hard, trying to find my voice. "Yes," I choked out, "but I can't get behind it, because to me, it feels like you're saying you agree she might die. I never want to agree with that."

The silence consumed us as we each stayed rooted to the spot, unable to talk, and unable to move. At a time when we desperately needed the other, we had nothing to offer. I wondered how long it would take for my sister to wake up. I prayed it would be soon, because I wasn't sure how we would survive this otherwise.

Mum turned away from me and walked the few feet to her bedroom. I stood alone in the hallway as she closed the door, shutting me out. I wished I had it in me to reach out and provide her some comfort, but I didn't. Instead, I had to carry on with life. Had to get through the day, so I made my way back outside to where I'd left King. He wasn't there, though, so I went in search of him.

I found him in the kitchen, rifling through the fridge.

He straightened, his gaze roaming over me before settling on my face. "I made room for them in here and pulled out some shit that looked like it had gone off."

I eyed the bench where he'd placed two containers. "Thank you." Such a simple gesture, but it meant something to me. At a time when life was so messed up, it was the little daily tasks that helped me focus. That helped me breathe.

Closing the fridge door, he came to me, eyes searching mine. I willed him to stop, but he didn't. He did what King always did—he forced his way into my space and then some. By the time he was finished, he had me backed against the kitchen bench, his hand on my hip. "Talk to me," he bossed. "How's your sister?"

He had been right this morning—I did still want him. God, how I wanted him. The pull I felt toward King wasn't something I'd ever experienced before. It scared me because he'd already cut and run once, had already hurt me, and that was after only a few weeks of knowing him. How could I trust he wouldn't do it again? How could I trust him with my heart?

"Lily," he ordered, "Talk."

I looked up into his eyes and shook my head. Placing both

hands to his chest, I pushed him away. It surprised me that he allowed that, but he did. "I told you this morning that I wouldn't do this with you again, and I meant it. I appreciate you bringing food over, but—"

Something I said or did triggered a shift in his mood, and a dangerous glint flashed in his eyes. There was heat there, too, and that caused desire to pool in my belly. Before I had time to process that, he came at me again, this time a ferocious energy blazing from him.

Crushing his body to mine, his hand came to my throat as he growled, "Tell me you don't want this." He ran his other hand down my body, over my breast, to the button of my jeans. Mouth against my ear, he said, "Tell me you don't want my hand in your pants, or my fingers deep inside your cunt."

I moaned. It fell from my mouth before I could stop it. And God, if my pussy wasn't throbbing with the need for everything he'd just said. I was wet for him, and he hadn't even moved past the button on my jeans.

He ground himself against me and popped the button. His hand tightened around my throat as a grunt sounded from deep within him. Cutting some of my air supply off, he rasped, "I'm wound so fucking tight for you I can hardly think straight, and while I didn't come here to fuck you, just laying eyes on you is enough to snap any restraint I have." He lowered the zip on my jeans. "Tell me you fucking want me as much as I want you."

He practically had me panting. Everything he said and did turned me on to the point where I wasn't sure I could say no to whatever he wanted. All he had to do was slip his hand in my pants and I would cross the line of no return. I had to stop him from doing that.

I gripped his hand that held my zip. "I don't want you."

He gripped my throat harder, and when he spoke, his tone had turned harder. Edgier. "You're lying to me." Before I knew what he was doing, he lifted me onto the bench, took hold of my hand, and guided it into my panties. With his hand over mine, he pressed my finger to my clit and rubbed it.

It was too much. Felt too good. A whimper escaped my lips as my head fell back. I was his to do what he wanted with, and there was no denying it.

His mouth claimed mine in the kind of kiss I craved. Brutal in his intensity, King reached deep into my soul, arousing the side of me I'd never known until he came along. He was savage and demanding, and I gave him what he wanted.

I kissed him back with everything I had.

My moans matched his growls, and when he directed our fingers inside my pussy, I grasped his bicep with my free hand and dug my fingers in hard.

Oh God.

Fuck.

He'd lit me on fire, and I would burn from his heat.

He tore his mouth from mine and found my eyes. The ferocity in his should have scared me, but it didn't. I may have been scared he would walk away from me again, but I was never scared *of him*.

Working our fingers inside me, he commanded, "Tell me, Lily. Tell me you want this." His voice deepened. Grew more forceful. "That you want me."

I bit my lip, not wanting to give him that. Admitting it gave him all the power. And yet, we both knew the answer. I was dripping for him. Would have been begging for him if he pulled his finger from me. It was clear just how much I wanted him.

"I want you."

Approval flashed in his eyes and his mouth crashed down onto mine again. He was like a crazed man, kissing me and stroking our fingers deeper and harder inside me. The pleasure became almost too much. I was so close to coming. It was divine and urgent and amazing and *too fucking much*.

"Oh my God… oh… *fuck*…" As I came, and as the words tumbled from my lips, he covered my mouth with his hand to muffle it.

I swore I stopped breathing. It was like I was floating, not breathing, unable to think. And as my orgasm shattered through me, I found King watching me with a level of heat I hadn't seen from him before. It was like his eyes hid a storm of need and fury.

He pulled our hands from my pants, and with his gaze firmly on mine, he sucked my fingers into his mouth. Licking them clean, he grunted his pleasure and said, "You can lie to me as much as you want, but the truth is plain to see in your eyes. I'm not going anywhere. You will be mine."

He then let me go, stepped away, and with one last look, he walked out of the kitchen and out of the house. He left me in a state of need like no other I'd ever been in. And I knew he would get what he wanted. Because if I stopped lying to myself for even a second, the truth was right there to see and feel.

I wanted King just as much as he wanted me.

10

Lily

I'd never spent much time thinking about death. Having never lost anyone close to me, grief wasn't something I'd ever experienced. Brynn being shot brought up a lot of new emotions I had to work through, but up until last night when my mother talked about calling a priest, I'd pushed away thoughts of death every time they came at me. Today, that was proving difficult. Today, my mother was hell-bent on getting the priest.

As she made plans for him to come this morning, I dialled Adelaide and put the phone to my ear waiting for her to pick up. Sitting on the chair in the far corner of the intensive care waiting room, I bounced my leg up and down, mentally begging Addy to answer. I didn't understand my response to all of this. All I knew was I had to get out of here. And I didn't want to be alone with my thoughts.

The call went to messages. I ripped the phone from my

ear, muttering, "Shit," as I searched for Quinn's number. I shot her a text to see if she was working this morning. Georgia definitely was, so there was no point asking her to come rescue me. She worked with brides. No way would they understand if she cancelled on them so she could help a friend out in her hour of need.

Quinn rang. "I'm so sorry, babe, but I can't get out of my shift today."

My heart sank. "It's okay. It was a long shot."

"Shit. Is Addy working, too?"

"Yeah."

She didn't bother mentioning Georgia. We both knew she was a workaholic. "Okay, I'm gonna try to find someone to do my shift. I'll let you know how I go."

"I love you, girl, but honestly, I'm just being dramatic. I'll be fine." Even I didn't buy that as the lie fell from my mouth.

"Yeah, no. Hang up so I can go look for someone."

We ended the call and I scrolled my phone. Skylar's name appeared, and my mind went straight to King. It wasn't the first time I'd thought of him today. He'd been on my mind from the minute I woke up. And as soon as Mum had brought up the priest again this morning, I'd thought of calling both him and Adelaide at the same time.

I gripped the phone harder.

Do not call King.

That would send the absolute wrong message to him.

Just like I had last night.

My legs squeezed together as the memory of him finger-fucking me filled my mind.

Of him bringing food for my family.

Of him cleaning out my fridge.

King didn't say a lot and he certainly didn't make apologies, but his actions meant more than words.

Yeah, like that time he walked away right when you needed him.

I closed my eyes and slowly exhaled in an effort to calm myself. Sometimes people made mistakes. God knew, I'd made many. If I was really honest with myself, I knew the feelings of confusion and hesitation that went along with the early days of a new relationship. Maybe King felt that way. Maybe that was why he did what he did. I just had to answer one question now that he was back and making it clear what he wanted—could I understand and give him another chance?

I could hold onto my hurt and keep my heart closed to something I wanted, or I could choose to let that hurt go and embrace the possibility of a relationship that may grow into something I cherished. That's what life ultimately came down to—the choices we made. I'd always believed clinging to hurt and suffering wasn't productive. And had always chosen forgiveness over holding onto stuff.

That I was being stubborn about this only told me just how much King meant to me already. It told me I'd found someone who had the power to hurt me, and that spoke to how much I wanted this relationship.

I opened my eyes and looked down at my phone.

I took a deep breath and called King.

He answered almost immediately. "Lily." His voice rumbled through the phone, gravel and grit. It was the trace of concern it held, though, that affected me the most.

My heart raced. "What are you doing right now?"

He didn't hesitate for even a split second. "What do you need?"

"You."

"You're at the hospital?"

"Yes."

"I'm on my way."

He didn't give or wait for a goodbye; he simply disconnected the call. And got on with business. He did exactly what I needed him to do. And for the first time in days, a hush fell over the chaos of thoughts in my head.

King arrived at the hospital twenty minutes later. That told me he'd hustled to get here. He found me sitting alone in the intensive care waiting room. His eyes held the same concern I'd heard in his voice on the phone. Taking the seat next to me, he said, "Talk to me."

I gave him a small smile as I placed my hand on his leg. "For a man who doesn't talk much, you seem to want to do a lot of talking lately."

His serious expression didn't change. "Your mum called the priest."

With those five words, my heart opened.

I nodded and gripped his leg. "I need you to take me away from here. I can't be here when he comes."

He searched my eyes before nodding. When he stood and held his hand out for me, I knew I'd made the right choice calling him.

I'd already told Mum I was leaving, so I followed King out to his bike. He handed me a helmet and waited for me to put it on before settling himself on the bike. Motioning for me to get on behind him, I extended my leg over the seat and slid onto it. King grabbed hold of my legs and showed me where to place my feet. He then took my hands and placed them on his hips.

He turned his head to the side, half facing me. "Grip me with your knees, soles on the foot pegs rather than your heels. Keep your weight centred and watch for turns. If I'm turning right, look over my right shoulder and keep your body in line with mine. Do not lean out of a turn. Keep your front pressed to my back and do not wiggle around at a stop."

I heard every word he said and took it all in. This was my first time on a bike, so I was a little nervous. If I hadn't been in a state over Brynn and the priest, I would have been a whole lot more nervous. And a whole lot more turned on. Because, holy fuck, sitting on the back of King's bike with my body pressed against his and my hands on his hips was hot.

He fastened his helmet in place and took off. I clung to him, my hands sliding around from his hips to circle his waist. I wasn't sure if that was okay, but he didn't respond in any way to let me know it wasn't, so I kept them there. I wasn't scared of the ride or lack trust in King, but I did feel a little unsure of what to expect. Holding onto him for dear life eased some of my jitters.

We rode for a long time. Well, it felt like hours, but when we finally stopped, I discovered it had only been just over an hour. It didn't take me long to settle into the rhythm of the ride. The steady vibration of the engine calmed me. It was almost hypnotic.

King took us out on the highway, along the Old Road to Cowan where he pulled into the Pie In The Sky café. The scenery along the way soothed me just as much as the bike did. By the time I hopped off, I felt a thousand times better than I had before the ride.

I removed my helmet and passed it to King with a smile. "Thank you," I said softly. Being so close to him on the bike, legs and arms around his body, combined with the way he watched me now, had my tummy in a flutter. I wasn't nervous with him, but my feelings were definitely heightened.

He jerked his chin towards the café. "You want a drink?"

I nodded and followed him inside. My eyes were firmly on his ass, because no one filled out jeans quite the way King did. They fit snugly against the hard muscle he'd packed onto his body, and I found it difficult to drag my gaze away. I was so engrossed that when he came to a stop at the café counter and turned to face me, I ran into him.

My hands went straight to him as we collided, grasping his leather jacket. His arm came up and around me, and he pulled me close to steady me. His scent hit me, stirring the butterflies in my belly. King smelt like leather and sandalwood and something else I couldn't quite put my finger on. It wasn't overpowering, but it was completely him, and it aroused my memories of the times he'd made me come.

I gripped his jacket harder and attempted to push those thoughts from my head. I mean, they were good thoughts, amazing thoughts, but right now was not the time for them.

He looked down at me, still holding me close. "You good?"

I nodded and let him go. Moving out of his embrace, I said, "Yeah, I just wasn't watching where I was walking." Heat stained my cheeks as I thought about what I *had* been watching.

Good God, why did he make me so flustered?

It wasn't like I was a freaking virgin who'd never had sex before or who'd never seen an ass before. And yet, here I was, my cheeks turning red just thinking about having sex with the man.

I was sure he noticed, but full points to him, he didn't mention it. Instead, he asked, "What do you want to drink?"

Happy for an excuse to concentrate on anything but him, I turned my attention to the menu board. "Ooh, I'll have that chocolate milkshake with extra ice-cream and Oreos. And I'm gonna want extra chocolate syrup on top, too, please."

His eyes flared with what looked like heat, but he didn't

say anything.

"What?" I asked. King was so damn guarded with his thoughts, and I wanted to know them all. I knew he'd never share everything, because that seemed like the man he was, but I was going to push to get to know what I could.

Bending his face to speak against my ear, he said, "I was just filing away that chocolate obsession for later use."

My core clenched with need, and not just because of what he said. With King, it was so much more than that. It was the way his voice always seemed to have that growly tone, and how he exuded masculinity like no other man I knew, and how he just said what he wanted, regardless of how bossy or filthy it was.

King blazed with sex and a wild, untamed side I was helpless to say no to. It wasn't just a glimmer or a flash here and there; he walked and talked it every second of the day. To me, it was magnetic and irresistible.

Being with him distracted me from Brynn. Every time he came near, my focus shifted, and for the time we were together, I was able to put the worry aside for a while. I couldn't decide if I felt guilty about that or if I welcomed the distraction.

He ordered our drinks and guided me to a table in the back where we had some privacy. It was still early in the day, so there weren't many people here yet.

Once we were sitting, he eyed me with that intense gaze of his. "How's your sister today?"

Not wanting to have this conversation, I glanced down and fiddled with the salt and pepper shakers on the table.

King rested his arms on the table and leaned forward. "Lily." He uttered just one word, but delivered it with his signature bossiness. I wondered if he ever stopped being bossy, but quickly dismissed that thought. King only knew one way in life.

Looking up, I found his eyes again. "The doctors are weaning her off the ventilator." I wrapped my arms around my body, suddenly chilled. "That's why Mum was so intent on calling the priest. She's scared that won't go to plan, but she fully believes God will make everything okay." My tone made it clear where I stood on that, but he asked me anyway.

"You don't?"

I swallowed my Catholic guilt. "No, I don't. I stopped believing in God a long time ago." I paused. "Well, that's not true. I didn't stop believing in God. I just don't think he makes everything okay, and when people like my mum rely on him to do something he can't do, I get a little cranky." I cocked my head to the side. "Do you believe in God?"

He slowly shook his head. "Fuck no."

I didn't know what compelled me to ask, but the question popped out without thought. "Did you ever?"

He shifted, resting his back against the chair, contemplating that. "If I did, it would have been at an age I have no memories of."

"That makes me sad." Because it told me he hadn't been told not to believe, but rather, someone had stolen that from him.

A dark look crossed his face. "Yeah," he said gruffly.

I studied him silently for a few moments, curious as to the things he'd lived through, but not ready to quiz him on it yet. Finally, I said, "Thank you for today. I needed to get out of there, and it turns out I love being on the back of a bike. It was exactly what I needed."

The waitress brought our drinks out, cutting into our conversation, but I did notice the hint of a smile on his lips at what I said.

After the waitress left us, I watched King sugar his black coffee. "You don't drink milk?"

"Yeah, but not in my coffee." At my questioning look, he added, "Skye had to give up dairy for a while when she was a kid, so I didn't have it in the house. Got a taste for black coffee from that."

"Skylar lived with you when she was growing up?"

He drank some of his coffee before answering my question. "Our foster mother died when she was eight. She came to live with me after that."

This gave me an insight into their relationship that had been missing before. It was a piece of the puzzle that made up King. And goodness, it revealed so much about the man sitting across from me. "How old were you?" My guess was he couldn't have been much past twenty, which if true, amazed me even further.

"Twenty-three."

"So you were her father figure," I murmured, my mind spinning at this new information about King. He'd done for his foster sister what my own father hadn't done for me, and I had so much respect for him for that.

He glanced around the café, seemingly uncomfortable with this conversation. "You could say that."

I drank some of my milkshake, a smile dancing across my face.

At my smile, he said, "What?"

I picked up the Oreo biscuit from my drink. "I don't think I've ever seen you like this, where you don't wanna discuss something. I kinda like it, because it shows me a different side to you."

His intense expression returned. "What kind of side?"

"You're always so in control and demanding and directing the conversation and what we do. But here, just now, you let your guard down for a bit and you allowed me to run the conversation." I leant forward, my gaze pinned to his. "And even though you didn't seem completely comfortable talking about that time in your life, you still answered my question and shared something personal with me. You showed me a little bit of vulnerability, and I liked that."

He remained guarded for a couple of moments longer before giving me something unexpected. "Our foster mother was the only mother we each had worth a damn. There was no fucking way I was putting Skye back into the foster system when Margreet died, so I raised her like she was my own child. She gave me far more than I ever gave her."

I reached my hand across the table and covered his. "That's the blessing of children, and if parents are too fucking stupid to cherish that or their children, they don't deserve them."

He glanced down at my hand over his before meeting my gaze again and nodding. "That's the fucking truth."

We stayed like that for a beat before I pulled my hand away. To me, we'd shared something meaningful, and I hoped it meant something to King, too.

"So," I said, "changing the subject, how often do you get out for a ride?" It was the lightest thing I could think of asking him. I had so many other subjects to broach with him, but I didn't want to throw them all at him today. I figured with a man like King, who didn't like to talk a hell of a lot, I had only a small window of opportunity to get him to open up here, so I ran with the option I felt he'd be most willing to discuss.

He drank some more of his coffee. "Not fucking often enough lately. Used to be weekly, but not these days."

"Well, just so you know, I'm up for a ride again whenever you want to get out. I loved it."

Heat flickered in his eyes. "I plan on getting you on that bike soon."

Lust whooshed through me, because I was fairly sure

King wasn't referring to a long bike ride. "That sounds like fun."

He arched a brow. "Fun?" It was a growl. A sexy-as-fuck growl.

I grinned and changed the subject again. Otherwise, this was about to go down a path that would get both of us worked up in ways we didn't have time to take care. "So who introduced you to your first bike?"

He moved from subject to subject with ease. Something else I liked about him. "The father of one of my schoolmates had a Harley and taught us how to ride. I was seventeen and fucking obsessed with bikes after that. He had his own business fixing bikes and taught us how to fix them and rebuild them." His eyes lit up as he continued. "There's nothing like getting your hands dirty and losing your time to a bike. I worked for him for years, learning from him and saving cash so I could buy parts. Built my first bike when I was nineteen."

"And your second?"

The smile in his eyes couldn't be mistaken. "Six months after that."

"How many have you built since then?"

His eyes dulled a little. "Two." He drank some coffee. "Life got in the way."

My phone rang, and I pulled it out to see it was Mum calling. And just like that, I was thrown back into real life. My distraction from worry ended.

"Hey, Ma," I answered.

"Lily! Brynn is awake! Hurry and come back!"

A huge wave of emotion engulfed me and tears streamed down my face. "She is?" I managed to get out in between sobs.

"Yes!"

"I'm on my way."

King had already stood. "She's awake?"

I smiled through my tears, an emotional wreck of happiness, relief, and adrenaline. "Yes."

He took two steps toward me, reached for my hand, and strode out to his bike with me in tow. Within a few minutes, he had us both on the bike and on our way back to the hospital. This was King back in charge, and I couldn't deny that I liked him like this. After years of me having to take on most of the responsibility for my family, it felt good to have a man help me in this way.

11

King

I eyed the clock as I scrubbed a hand over my face. It was just past 8:00 p.m. and I still had a few loose ends to tie up here before I could check on Lily. After her sister had woken up this morning, I'd stayed at the hospital with her for a couple of hours before she'd kicked me out and told me to get back to work. I fucking appreciated a woman who had the sense to ask for help when she needed it and then the strength to deal with shit on her own later. She'd called me just after six to let me know she was heading home for the night and that I should drop by when I was done with work. That she'd put some dinner away for me in case I was hungry. My gut had tightened at that. It had been years since a woman had put dinner away for me.

"Johnny called," Axe said, entering the office. "He's agreed to your terms."

"Good. Keep on him for that info. We can't afford to drop the ball on this."

Axe's contact in the feds, Johnny, was now Storm's contact. We'd put him on our payroll in exchange for names of any witnesses the feds had in relation to the case against us. I'd pay those motherfuckers off to keep them quiet, or if warranted, something a little more permanent.

"Also, Zane and Griff have started pulling more surveillance of the area from the day of Jen's murder like you wanted." *To see if Romano had been bullshitting me about not having a hand in that.*

"And Brant?"

"Still looking, but nothing yet. He's an evasive motherfucker."

"Yeah." I narrowed my eyes at my brother. "You look like hell."

He nodded. "We both do."

"Justine giving you grief at the moment?"

He rubbed the back of his neck and stretched it. "When isn't she?"

"Fuck," I muttered. "That bitch has a lot to fucking answer for, brother."

"She also has my child in her belly, King, so I can't just fucking walk away."

This was an old, recurring argument of ours. Me telling him to leave; him telling me he loved her. Except he was right—he now had his child to consider, and my brother had the same convictions I did, so he would never walk away from that responsibility.

I jerked my chin at the door. "Try to get some sleep tonight. Or find someone to take the edge off." At his scowl, I said, "Fuck, she screwed around on you and fucking walked out. You don't owe her any loyalty."

I knew his stance on this, though. If I considered myself a

loyal bastard, Axe was a motherfucking nun when it came to this shit. Women threw themselves at him, fucking begging him to let them suck his dick. Not once had I ever seen him so much as look at them if he was with someone.

"I'll see you in the morning. And I'll check in with Johnny first thing. Hurry him along."

After he'd gone, I thought about Justine. She'd had her claws in my brother for five long years, and just when I'd thought he was finally rid of her, she'd announced her fucking pregnancy. Axe had wanted a child for as long as I could remember, so he'd been over the fucking moon. And then he'd discovered her infidelity. I hadn't thought I'd ever see my brother lose his shit, because Axe was the guy who held himself together when everyone around him couldn't. Fuck, if there was an apocalypse, Axe was the one I'd want in my corner. But he had lost it for a while there and had only recently pulled through that.

A text came through, distracting me from my thoughts.

Lily: If you're coming over, I need milk please.
   Me: On my way soon
   Lily: Thanks.

I stared at the messages, at the simple and uncomplicated way with which Lily acted. She'd put up a fight when I'd told her we weren't done, but I'd expected that. I'd anticipated that would continue longer than it did, but something had shifted in her since last night, and she appeared to have let it go. I'd fucking make shit up to her for what I did, but that she didn't play games or screw me around meant a fuck of a lot.

I left the clubhouse an hour after she'd messaged me about the milk, grabbed some on the way over, and arrived just after she'd had a screaming match with Zara. I knew this because she yanked the front door open with the force of a crazed woman, eyes wild, stepped outside, and dragged me onto the front lawn before producing a cigarette and begging me, "Do you have a lighter on you? Zara may be fucking pregnant, which may mean I'm about to kill some fucking teenage boy who should not have chosen my daughter to mess around with. And I need a fucking smoke to deal with this, which means I will have to kill that little fucker twice, because I'm supposed to be quitting cigarettes, and if he got my kid pregnant, I am most definitely not quitting cigarettes."

I eyed her, trying like hell not to smile. Lily had a way of lighting my fucking world, just by being her. She didn't have to do shit for me or work any special magic. All she had to do was look at me or smile at me or go on about the shit she was dealing with, and I felt better than before I saw her.

Pulling out my lighter, I said, "That's a fuckload of fucks, woman." It was unlike Lily to swear so much, which only told me how worked up she was over this.

She ripped the lighter from my hand, still crazed as fuck. "Yeah, because they are *necessary!*" Lighting the smoke, she sucked nicotine deep into her lungs.

"What's going on with Zara? You know for sure she had sex?"

"No, she won't confirm it, but I read some texts on her phone from that little shit, and I'm almost completely certain she has."

Lily was fucking hot when she was worked up like this. I had to work harder than usual to drag my mind from thinking about the shit I wanted to do to her. "Right, so you get through tonight, and then tomorrow you force a pregnancy test on her."

She pulled a face as she took another drag of her smoke. "You have to wait a little while before those tests will work accurately. God, unless she had sex weeks ago, and I didn't know. Fuck."

In an effort to take her mind off her daughter, I said, "How's Brynn?"

Her shoulders lifted and then dropped as she let out a long breath, almost like she'd been holding it forever. "She's confused and not really with it." She gave me a small smile. "But she's awake and that's all that matters."

"Yeah," I agreed, because that really was all that fucking mattered.

She reached for the milk after she finished her smoke. "Are you hungry? I put some steak and veges in the oven for you."

I closed the space between us and grabbed her around the waist. I needed my hands on her. Hell, I needed a lot more than that, but it was what I had to settle for. "I'm fucking starving."

She stared up at me, aware I wasn't referring to food. Her eyes flared with the same heat running through me. She surprised me when she said softly, almost hesitantly, "Are you sure this is what you want?"

I tightened my hold on her. "Never been more sure of anything in my life."

Continuing to watch me with uncertainty, she said, "I've only ever dated a handful of guys in my life, and have mostly been with Linc, so I'm not experienced in this whole relationship thing, but I will tell you one thing—I don't do games. I'm not saying that's what you're doing, at all, but I *am* saying, the idea of you walking away again hurts. It hurt the first time you did it, and I don't wanna go through that again. So if you're—"

I put my finger to her mouth. "I don't like games either, and I don't engage in them. I'm not going anywhere, Lily. And if you ever mention those motherfuckers you dated again, I'll put you over my fucking knee and spank that out of you." Bending my head, my lips grazed her ear as I growled, "You're mine now, and I don't fucking share."

Her hands found my face and she took hold of it so she could direct my mouth to hers. Her grip was hard, determined, and when our lips met, she kissed me with an urgency and passion she hadn't yet. This kiss was hot as hell, and all I wanted to do was rip her clothes off, lay her the fuck down, and slam my dick inside her.

I gave her a minute longer with my lips than I should have before tearing myself away. Jesus, it had been hard enough not having her last night—I had no fucking idea how I'd make it through tonight without getting my fill of her.

"Fuck, woman, don't kiss me like that when I can't do anything with it," I rasped as I took a step away from her.

She watched me, breathless and just as aroused as I was. "Well don't tell me I'm yours and that you don't fucking share. That shit is hot and makes me wanna climb you."

Jesus fuck.

"We need to move this inside," I muttered as I put my hands to her hips and spun her around.

"You do realise that manhandling me only gets me hotter, right?" she threw over her shoulder as we walked inside.

I ignored that and focused on getting us inside so I could eat my dinner and take my mind off screwing the hell out of her. There was only so much a man could take when he was as hard as I was, and I'd reached my limit. At this point, I was calling on divine fucking intervention, and that was saying something, because like I'd told Lily today, I didn't believe in that shit.

Robbie came screaming into the kitchen as we entered, irritation plastered across his face. After a quick glance at me, he grumbled, "Mum! Zara won't get out of the bathroom, and I want to have a shower."

Lily looked at her son. "She only just hopped in the shower. You need to give her some time."

His eyes widened. "But I need a shower *now!*" He'd worked himself up into a state over this and looked like he was about to completely lose his shit.

Lily wrapped her hands around his biceps and bent so she could look him in the eyes. "Baby, take a deep breath." When he refused and simply stared at her, she said, "Robbie, we've talked about this. Being part of a family means we have to make allowances for each other, and learn to compromise and share. Just because you're ready to have a shower right now, doesn't mean you can. Sometimes our plans don't fit with each other's, so we have to rework them. You understand that, right?"

His lips flattened as he stared at her. He seemed caught in that place where kids know they're wrong but don't want to admit it. Finally he nodded. "I do, but I don't like it."

I fought back a smile. I liked his style. I also liked her patience with him.

Lily stood and pressed a kiss to his forehead. "Yeah, buddy, I get that. There's a lot of things I don't like, too, but that's life and we just have to learn to work with it."

He grumbled something I couldn't figure out as he stomped out of the kitchen.

Lily sighed as she watched him go. She then turned to me and said, "You want a beer with your steak?"

"You drink beer?"

"No. I picked some up on the way home. I figured you

probably drank it and might want some. I mean, I have no idea if you do or what you'd prefer, but the guy in the shop told me which ones were his bestsellers so I ran with one of them." She paused for a moment, thinking, before adding, "Mum probably has some whisky in the house if you want that instead."

Fucking hell, this woman.

I jerked my chin. "I'll have a beer."

"You don't want me to look for some whisky?"

I shook my head. "I'm good with beer."

Something I said, or my tone, caused her to slow down and hit me with a smile that shot warmth to my gut. "Okay."

She then busied herself heating my dinner, grabbed a beer from the fridge, and brought it all to the table for me. I sat on my ass and watched her every movement, paying special attention to her ass and legs that were painted with those tight-as-fuck jeans she liked to wear. As hard as I tried, I failed at not allowing my mind to wander back to last night when I'd had my hand in her pants. She hadn't wanted to admit how much she wanted me. I'd known it wouldn't take long to break her down though, because it was clear as fucking day that she wanted my hands on her.

"What are you thinking?" she asked as she placed my meal in front of me.

I hooked my arm around her and pulled her onto my lap. She came easily, sliding into place like she was made to be there, arm around my neck, tits pressed against me, smile blazing just for me. Moving my free hand to her throat, I ran my fingers over her collarbone and said, "I was thinking about our fingers deep inside you and about how much I need to taste you again."

She bit her lip, and fuck if that didn't hit my veins with a craving I knew wouldn't be satisfied tonight. "I've never been with a man who has a filthy mouth like yours."

My grip around her neck tightened. "Pretty fucking sure I told you never to mention another man to me again," I growled, shocked as shit at the possessiveness sitting deep in my gut.

Heat radiated from every inch of her and she brought her mouth close to mine. "It needs to be said that you're hot when you're jealous." As the last word fell from her lips, she kissed me, her tongue tangling with mine in ways that made me think of it on my dick.

Fuck.

Lily had me all worked up to the point I could hardly fucking think straight. Dragging my mouth from hers, I smacked her ass and ordered, "Off. I need a moment without you wiggling that pretty ass of yours all over my dick."

She raised her brows, her lips twitching with a smile. "If I'm not mistaken, it was you who pulled my ass onto your lap, so stop your whinging and bitching."

She did as I said, though, and sat next to me, watching me with amusement, and heat, and care all rolled into one. I'd never met a woman like her, and maybe that was half of my attraction to her, but the way she nurtured had a lot to do with it as well. Lily might have been gentle, with a softness I didn't often see in my world, but she was also solid, and there for those she loved, and *that* was something that called deeply to me.

I took a swig of beer before asking, "When are you moving back home?"

"Oh God, I've hardly thought about that. Soon. The kids need to get back into a routine, and I do too."

"It'll be a mess, Lily. I can organise for the boys to clean it up for you."

"Linc already cleaned it. Well, he said he did. I haven't been over yet to inspect."

"I'll go over and make sure. Fingerprint dust is a bitch to

fucking clean and there may be some shit that needs to be repaired or thrown out, depending on..." I pulled myself up —she didn't need to hear or think about her sister's blood splatter. "I'll check it out and clean up anything that still needs it."

"Thank you," she said softly.

I eyed her mother who had entered the dining room, and Lily turned to greet her. "Hey, Ma. You okay?"

Hannah sat next to her and threw me a smile before answering her daughter. "I'm just tired, that's all. I think I might go to bed now."

Exhaustion lined her face. Hell, it lived and breathed all over her. She was far from the woman I'd met who talked my ear off.

Lily reached out to hug her. "Do you want a sleeping pill or do you think you'll be okay without one?"

Tears pooled in Hannah's eyes as she nodded. "Yes, I think I need one, darling."

Lily jumped up. Glancing at me, she said, "I won't be long."

I jerked my chin. "Don't worry about me."

She ushered her mother out, speaking soothingly to her as they went, leaving me in silence. I sat and ate the best damn meal I'd eaten since the last time I'd had Lily's cooking. The peace and quiet in this house was fucking music to my ears. And yet, it wasn't completely quiet because I could hear the kids arguing over something. But without the tension I was used to being surrounded by daily, this was peaceful. Calm.

I finished my dinner and beer, and had just finished washing the dirty plate and cutlery when Lily walked into the kitchen. She moved next to me, placing her hand on my hip. "Thanks for doing that."

I didn't know if it was the need I had for her, or the gratitude I heard in her voice, or the softness in her eyes, or what the fuck it was, but one of those things drove me to reach for her waist, lift her onto the kitchen counter, and crush my lips to hers.

She moaned into my mouth as her legs and arms circled me. By the time we finished with the kiss, we were both a mess of frantic desire. Problem was, we couldn't do anything with it. Not with her family in the house.

Gripping my hair, she panted, "God, I want to fuck you."

"Jesus," I rasped, "I need to get out of here."

She pulled her head back to look me in the eyes. "You're not staying the night?" Her disappointment couldn't be mistaken. It was written all over her and bled from her voice.

My fingers dug into her hips. "There's no fucking way I can sleep next to you tonight without having my hands all over you and my dick inside you."

"So do that."

She didn't know what she was saying. "Lily, your mother and your kids are in the house. You do not want me—"

She pressed her lips to mine and claimed another kiss from me. "Maybe I do."

"Fucking hell." I slid my hands around her ass and yanked her hard against me. "The level of need I have for you isn't the kind that can be satisfied with a quick fuck, and it sure as hell won't be quiet. There is no way I'm fucking you tonight."

She squeezed her arms and legs around me even tighter, like she couldn't get close enough to me. Bending her face to my neck, she kissed me there and murmured, "I'm sorry I'm being needy. I just really want you to stay and cuddle me tonight."

"I don't fucking cuddle, Lily."

Her mouth moved along my collarbone as she continued kissing me. "Yeah, you do. It's nice."

Hell, no one had ever called the shit I did nice. And just like that, I changed my fucking mind. I let her go and took a step back. "Get your ass in the bedroom."

Her eyes lit up. "You're staying?"

"Yeah, I'm fucking staying."

12

King

"See, you do cuddle," Lily said early the next morning when she woke. "You're like a big bear, all arms and legs around me."

I tightened my embrace and ground my dick against her ass. The night had been hell sleeping next to her. I put my mouth to her ear. "What time do your kids wake up?" I'd stuck to my word last night and hadn't fucked her, but I wasn't a fucking saint—I couldn't restrain myself any longer.

She wiggled and twisted until she faced me. Reaching for my dick, she said, "We've got at least an hour, I'd say."

Before she knew what was happening, I had her under me, naked. Raising her arms over her head against the headboard, I pressed firmly on her wrists and ordered, "Keep them there."

The change in my tone caught her attention and her eyes flared with the same excitement they did every time I had her. That always increased my desire, and today was no different. But fuck, after the past couple of days, the need I had for Lily had stirred some dark shit in me, so what I felt now had me on the edge of danger. I was fighting with myself not to take her too far, not to fucking break her. And that in itself was a whole other mindfuck, because caring whether I forced a woman past that edge wasn't something I'd experienced for a long time.

I ran my gaze down the curves of her body, taking my time with this because it helped focus the erratic thoughts in my head. When I was this wired for sex, my mind ran in a million different directions, imagining every last fucking thing I wanted to do. Some fucked-up shit drew me down dark alleys in my brain, demanding release. Driving my actions. Sometimes I acted on these thoughts, other times, I managed to control myself. Today, I was working like fuck to get a handle on my shit. It seemed that wanting a woman as much as I wanted Lily, heightened my dark desires.

Fuck.

"King."

Her voice snapped me back to attention, and I reacted with a hand around her neck. "Don't talk," I rasped, my gaze pinned to her throat. I'd come back to her neck, but first I needed to taste her.

I bent my face to suck one of her nipples into my mouth as I cupped a hand around her tit. Lily's breasts were a perfect fucking handful, and if we weren't on a time limit today, I'd dedicate some serious time to them. Since we were low on time, I made do with a few minutes sucking and biting before continuing down to her pussy.

She arched her back as I let go of her neck and gripped her hips. And when my fingers dug into her soft skin, a moan fell from her lips. Before I buried my face in her cunt, I glanced up to find her head turned to the side, eyes closed, mouth parted while she took shallow breaths.

Fucking hell, she was beautiful.

My need raged through me at the sight, and I forced her legs wide, slid my body down the bed, flat to the mattress, and finally took the taste of her I'd been craving for days.

She was wet for me, and within a few moments of running my tongue through her, my beard was fucking coated in her. Gliding my hands under her ass, I lifted her slightly so her pussy was in line with my mouth. And then I ate her out, my rhythm rough and hard.

It was all lips and tongue and teeth, a little brutal, completely possessive. This was me stamping my fucking ownership of her cunt. And she fucking loved it. Lily writhed and moaned and pulled my hair while I made her come. As her orgasm took hold, our eyes met and I licked slowly along her pussy, lapping her cum up.

"Oh fuck, King... Fucking hell..." Her head fell back as she arched up off the bed again and shuddered through the orgasm. Her body was a quivering mess, and seeing her lose herself like that got me harder than I already was.

I moved off the bed, stripped out of my boxers, and grabbed a condom before coming back to her. Dropping it on the mattress, I reached for her legs and yanked her down to where I stood at the end of the bed. She'd barely recovered from her orgasm and my rough movements appeared to bewilder her as she attempted to bring her complete attention around to what I was doing. She was fucking hot with her flushed skin, messy hair all over the place, and those lips of hers slightly parted while she watched me to see what would come next.

When I had her sitting on the end of the bed, I grasped her cheeks with one hand while slowly wiping her cum from my beard with my other hand. She stared silently up at me, just like I'd told her. Taking hold of my dick, I ran the tip of it along her mouth. "Open up and suck me in. I wanna feel your throat," I growled.

Keeping our eyes locked, she placed one hand over mine, wrapped her lips around my cock and took it into her mouth. She did as I said and sucked me back to her throat. As I shifted my hand away, her fingers laced through mine and she gripped me firmly keeping our hands together, eyes still holding mine. She worked my dick with long and slow sucks. Her rhythm wasn't my usual preference, but fuck if I didn't want anything but what she gave. Her tongue slid over me with the same slow style her lips did, and a low moan came from deep within her, signalling how fucking turned on she was. It vibrated along my dick, and her lips pulled up a little as the hint of a smile touched them, revealing her pleasure.

Everything she did quieted the frenzy in my mind. It was as if by her slowing this down, she slowed my brain down. She pulled all my thoughts into a straight line, helping me focus on the one thing I wanted rather than allowing those thoughts to shoot out in a thousand different directions. It was clarity like I'd never experienced, and fuck, the pleasure was intense.

I needed to be inside her cunt.

Needed her heat.

Her wet tightness around me.

Now.

And while I'd intended to have her from behind, the need to fuck her while looking into her eyes overwhelmed me. I had to fucking watch as she took my dick. As she took everything I had to give her.

I pulled out of her mouth and reached for the condom. After I tore it open, she grabbed it from me and said, "I want you to fuck me bare. I'm on the pill."

I always made a point not to fuck without a condom. I

didn't wanna put kids out there on the street without a father if the woman fell pregnant and didn't fucking tell me. I also didn't wanna have kids with the whores I'd fucked. Lily was different. It was fucking beyond my understanding, but I trusted her. I didn't hesitate for a second when she asked me for this.

Jerking my chin at her, I directed, "Move back up the bed."

She did what I said, lying with her head on the pillow, watching and waiting. So fucking ready for me.

I put my knee to the mattress and made my way to her. Placing my hands on her thighs, I spread her legs and bent my face to take another taste of her. I licked her clit before pushing my tongue inside. Fuck, I needed hours with her cunt. With my mouth to it. My tongue inside it. But that would have to be another time. We had that fucking time limit hanging over us, and even more than that, I needed my dick deep inside her.

Kneeling with my legs spread and my ass to my feet, I gripped her and pulled her to me. I positioned her legs over mine, her feet flat to the bed behind me, and without wasting another second, I slammed inside her.

"Oh God," she cried out, arching her neck while her eyes fluttered closed.

I put my hands to the bed either side of her and bent for a mouthful of tit. As I sucked and bit her, she took hold of my shoulders and gripped me hard. I grunted as her nails dug sharply into my skin, and bit her harder. Lily loved it rough and returned it to me. She reached her hands around to my back and clawed my skin there. That shit hit my veins and my mind at the same time, drawing a savage response from me.

I tore my mouth from her breast and found her eyes as I curled my hand around her throat. Applying enough pressure to steal some of her breath, I thrust hard inside her and growled, "You like that?"

She nodded, her need for me unmistakable, her nails digging into me again.

Her answer stirred my animal side further, and I finally succumbed to it. I allowed my needs to take over fully and pounded into her with unrelenting force. With both hands around her neck, I watched her take everything from me. Nothing escaped my notice. Not the way she bit the inside of her lips, or the way her breathing sped up, or the way her mouth parted and her tongue curled as the pleasure consumed her. I saw it all, and I fucking stored that shit in my mind. I didn't want to forget any of it.

She came, eyes closed, hands gripping my biceps, squeezing hard enough to leave bruises. I followed her over the edge a moment later, burying my face against her neck to muffle my roar. I stayed there until she let go of my arms and reached her hands up to the back of my neck and threaded her fingers through my hair.

Something about that caused my gut to tighten, and a feeling so violently demanding and unexplainable filled me. It rushed at me, claiming my attention unlike it had been in a long time. It wasn't just one feeling; it was many intertwined, but together they equalled one.

Mine.

Lily was mine, and I would do whatever the fuck it took to keep her.

13

King

I eyed Zane. "So, you're telling me it *was* one of Romano's guys who killed Jen?"

"No, I'm telling you we've traced a car caught on the surveillance the day of the murder, to him. On top of that, we can't trace any of the other vehicles in the area to anyone of significance to you. There are a couple we can't track at all, but if I had to give you an opinion, I'd put it at around 95 percent certainty it was Romano."

I leaned back in my office chair and exhaled the breath that had been trapped inside me for weeks. It had to have been Romano.

Zane didn't wait for a response before continuing. "As for Brant, he's left Sydney, and as best we can make out, he's back in Melbourne. We had a hit on his credit card there last night. Still can't confirm if Ivy is with him or not."

"Keep tracking him. Winter was supposed to head down there tomorrow. I'll move that up, and he can go today."

"Will do."

After he left, I sat for a moment thinking about all the shit we'd been through over the last few weeks thanks to Romano. While we still had stuff to work through, a weight had lifted off my shoulders. Now we could direct all our efforts to dealing with the feds and then Gambarro. That motherfucker still had to be taken care of.

I exited the office and headed out to search for Hyde. He'd arrived back at the clubhouse about half an hour ago after helping Nitro take care of a cleaning job that had been called in early this morning. Business was almost back to normal on all fronts. We just had one thing left to deal with before club life could go back to normal.

I found Hyde in the kitchen with Scott. Glancing up at me, he said, "Just got a call about that meet with Black Deeds scheduled for Monday. They wanna push it to Thursday. You good with that?"

"Yeah, but let Zero know we won't push it again." Looking at Scott, I asked, "You boys pulling out tonight?"

He nodded. "We'll leave around eight. You sure you don't need us anymore?"

"Zane's just advised me he believes Romano was behind the shit that went down, so yeah, I'm sure." To Hyde, I said, "Let everyone know they can move their families home."

"It's about fucking time," he said, echoing my thoughts. It really fucking was.

Leaving them, I made my way to Annika's room. I figured she'd be in there trying to get the kids to have an afternoon nap. I was right. She looked at me as I pushed the half-open door all the way open, and put her finger to her lips in a silencing motion.

I jerked my chin at the hallway and she nodded, holding up a finger to let me know she needed a minute.

While I waited for her outside the room, a text came through.

Lily: It's official, I'm going to prison.
    Me: Why?
    Lily: Zara's boyfriend just gave me lip. I really am going to kill the little shit.
    Me: I could have a word with him
    Lily: To save me from prison?
    Me: Yeah
    Lily: You really like fucking me, huh?
    Me: I like a lot fucking more than that

She didn't come back straight away, and I took a moment allowing it to sink in just how fucking much I liked hearing from her in the middle of the day.

Lily: You like roast chicken?
    Me: Yeah
    Lily: I'm cooking it for dinner. You should come. 6pm.
    Me: I'll be there. Don't commit murder before I see you

Annika stepped out into the hallway as I sent the last message. Closing the door softly behind her, "What's up? And why do you look all smiley?"

"What the fuck does all smiley mean?"

She pulled her head back, inspecting my face. Waving her finger at me, she said, "That look in your eyes. You might not actually be smiling with your mouth, but your eyes are."

Another text sounded and I glanced down at my phone.

Lily: You should sleep over more often. I'm liking this side of you.

Lily: I mean, I know there would have to be some hot sex to go with that sleeping over, but just sayin' I'm down.

Lily: BTW you give good head. I'm always down for that.

Fuck.

Me: Stop texting me. I'm busy

Lily: I wish you were busy with me.

Lily: OK, OK, I'm stopping now. I'll get you some more beer on the way home. Just let me know if you prefer something different to last night.

I shoved the phone back in my pocket and met Annika's gaze.

She lifted her brows at me and crossed her arms. "Okay, brother, what gives? Who is this woman and when do I get to meet her?" When I didn't answer her, she said, "It's clearly a woman. The only other time in your life that I've seen you smile like this was when you were first dating Ivy. You may as well tell me before Skye figures it out. You know what she's like when someone in the family is dating. I can save you from her if I'm prepared."

She was right—Skylar had a way of forcing herself on the people we dated. I hadn't been subjected to it for a long time, but I'd watched as she'd done it to Axe and Nik over the years. Skye was too much for some of the people they dated, but I had a feeling Lily would be okay with her.

"It's Lily, Skye's physio, so I think we're good, Nik."

Her eyes widened. "Oh my God, I never saw that coming." She grinned. "I like it."

Shifting the conversation back to what I came for, I said, "I came to let you know you can take the kids home."

"Really?"

"Yeah, really. I can take you when they wake up if you want."

A smile spread out across her face. "This is the best news you could have given me. The department called me offering me some days, so I'll be able to say yes."

Annika was a primary school relief teacher. She'd taken time off when her dickhead ex-boyfriend had talked her into letting him support her. I'd argued with her over the wisdom of that, but she'd been so infatuated with him she hadn't been able to see straight. That, and she had a burning desire to be at home for her kids, which I understood. In the end, he'd shown his abusive side and I'd gotten her out of that shit. What I couldn't get her out of was her inability to find a job that worked in with her kids. I was fucking over the moon to hear the education department had called her.

"Let me know when you're ready to go," I said. "I'll be around the clubhouse all afternoon."

"Thank you," she said, like I'd given her the world.

I shook my head. "Don't thank me, Nik. I put you and the kids in this position, and I fucking hate that I had to."

Her smile lingered. "You really need to stop giving yourself a hard time over stuff. It's not like you intentionally cause bad things to happen."

"No, but I've made my choices in life and now I have to live with them. And unfortunately, they affect you guys."

She placed her hand on my arm. "We might bitch and

grumble at you, but deep down we don't mean it. You have *always* been there for us, and the shit you've done to help won't ever be forgotten. That's family, right? We get each other through the crap, regardless of any bad decisions we might make along the way. God knows you've stood by me through *all* the bad choices I've ever made. I love you, big brother."

I took all that, letting it sit in me. She was right—that *was* what family did.

Reaching for her, I curved my hand around the back of her head and pulled her to me so I could press a kiss to her forehead. Letting her go, I said, "Yeah, Nik, that's family."

She shooed me away after that and I headed towards Skylar's room to give her the good news. After that was Kree, but I knew I was in for an argument there, so I chose to visit her last.

Right before I made it to Skylar, another text hit my phone.

Lily: You didn't let me know about the beer.
Me: There's plenty still there. You don't need to get more

She took a moment to reply.

Lily: Oh ok. I just thought I'd keep the fridge stocked for you, but that's fine if you don't want more.

In my experience, women only used the word *fine* when they were shitty about something.

Me: Are you pissed at me?

Lily: I'm fine.

Something was off here, so I called. Fucking texts did my head in.

"Hi," she said, short with me.

"Have we got a problem?"

Silence for a beat. "No."

"Lily, don't fuck me around. What's wrong?"

"I'm not fucking you around," she said sharply. "There's nothing wrong."

I scrubbed my hand over my face. This was the shit I didn't deal well with when it came to women. The not fucking understanding them or the bullshit that came out of their mouths. "You asked me if I wanted more beer. I didn't. And then fuck me, you're shitty about something. What gives?"

"I got the wrong impression, that's all. Can we just drop this?"

"What fucking impression did you get that was wrong?"

She huffed out a breath. "God, King, why are you being so difficult? Just let it go. It doesn't matter."

"Something you need to learn about me right now is that I don't ever let shit go. Start fucking talking so we can fix this."

Silence again, and then she finally started talking. "Fine. I thought that you coming over last night and again tonight meant you'd be around more. That made me think you might like some beer in the fridge. And I know there are a few bottles still in there, but I wanted to stock up for you so you don't run out."

"Jesus, woman, I'm not seeing the fucking problem here."

"Well clearly you don't plan on coming over as often as I

thought if you think there's enough beer in the fridge, so now I feel like an idiot for even mentioning it, okay?"

Fucking hell, this woman.

"First, let's get something very clear between us—I do plan on coming over a fucking lot. Do not read between lines or twist shit I say in your head or do any of that overthinking bullshit women do. I plan on being at your dinner table and on your couch and in your bed as often as possible. Second, I'll bring my own fucking beer. I appreciate the fuck out of the shit you do for me, but *I* take care of *you*. You don't take care of me. We clear?" When all I got was the sound of her breathing, I growled, "Lily, are we clear?"

"Yes, we're clear, but just so you know, if I wanna buy you some beer, I'm gonna buy you some fucking beer."

Jesus fuck.

"I'll be over at six."

"Okay." This came out a lot fucking softer than everything else she'd said, and it hit me in the gut. Lily's brand of sweet was everything I'd never had, but exactly what I fucking wanted.

14

Lily

It was funny how, in the blink of an eye, life changed, and then in another blink of an eye, it changed again, and although some bad stuff had happened in there, I was running around with a huge smile on my face. Even while ranting at my kids on a crazy Saturday morning. Only one week had passed since Brynn was shot, and yet, so much had happened.

"Why can't you just let me make my own choices for once?" Zara yelled at me as we stood in my bedroom arguing over her spending the day with her boyfriend.

I was half-naked, wearing only my bra and panties since she'd barged in while I dressed. Story of my life. "Zara, you are fourteen and lately you haven't been showing me you're capable of making good decisions. On top of that, how do you expect me to handle the messages I read on your phone from Sam when you refuse to enter into a conversation with me about them? They don't encourage me to allow you anywhere near him."

She scowled. "I told you those were private. You shouldn't have snooped."

"Yeah well, I'm your mother, so expect me to snoop. And I don't care what everyone else's mother does, I'm not changing. I take parenting very seriously and will do whatever it takes to keep you safe."

"Ugh," she groaned, "you are so annoying! I just wish you could remember what it's like to be my age." With that, she stomped out of my bedroom, her shoes thudding all the way to her room before the sound of her door slamming rang in my ears.

Frustration and anger ran through me. Why were teenagers so damn difficult to deal with? I wasn't convinced I would make it through to see her become an adult. I would probably drink myself into an early grave before then at the rate we were going.

I rummaged in my suitcase for something to wear. Thank God we were going home today. Living out of a suitcase at your mother's home was only good for a very short time.

The bedroom door closed, causing me to jump. I'd been lost in my own little world, and the sound snapped me out of it. Turning, I found King standing at the door, watching me with that intense stare of his I loved. It stirred butterflies in my tummy and made me go weak at the knees.

He'd come for dinner last night, charmed my mother, and engaged my kids, all before fucking me for the second time that day and exhausting me completely. I'd woken this morning wrapped in his arms and legs again. King could swear all he liked that he didn't cuddle, but the man freaking cuddled.

"I fixed the light in your mum's bathroom, so you don't need to worry about her falling over in there anymore. No fucking clue how she hasn't fallen yet. That light was too dim for that room," he said, making my heart speed up a little. He had no idea what it meant to me when he did little things like this for my family. Mum had made a casual remark over breakfast about the light and he'd taken it upon himself to go out and get a new bulb and change it.

I turned the T-shirt I held so it was the right way out to put on. As I lifted it to put it over my head, King closed the distance between us and stopped me. His nostrils flared as he dropped his eyes and ran them down my body. Holding my shirt in one hand, he placed his other one on my breast, sliding his thumb under the material of my bra, and stroking my skin. "You got the kids this afternoon?"

Staring down at his thumb, it struck me that King had never been this gentle with me. I liked his rough ways, but I really freaking liked his gentle.

When I took my time answering him, he growled, "Lily," as his touch turned a whole lot less gentle. He then gave me his signature style of rough when he reached further into my bra and squeezed my nipple while adding, "I need your cunt again, and I want a plan for when that's gonna happen."

King was the crudest man I'd ever met, and I couldn't get enough of his filthy ways. I wasn't a fan of the c word, but coming from him? I was going to hell because of how much I liked it on his lips.

Putting my hands to his chest, I tried to push him away, because I needed a moment and the space to think. He got me all flustered when he bossed me while talking dirty. When he refused to move, I said, "King," with the kind of tone that told him I wanted him to move.

As per usual, he took no notice, and instead, took it as a signal to move further into my personal space. His hand snaked around my waist and he forced our bodies together. "I've got some club shit to take care of this morning, and then I'm heading over to your place to clean it. I know you're taking your mum to the hospital and Robbie to karate, but what else have you got on?"

"Well, for one, I'm trying to keep my daughter from getting pregnant. But in answer to your question about the kids, Linc is picking them up from here at three. I've got the night to myself."

The way his eyes flashed with heat told me he liked that answer. And when he bent to kiss me, as roughly as he usually did, I knew he really liked that answer. Letting me go, he moved out of my space and said, "Lock this afternoon in."

I took my T-shirt when he passed it, and put it on. I then found a pair of jeans to wear, and my boots. King stood silently and watched me as I dressed and brushed my hair, his eyes greedy for my every movement. By the time I was ready to walk out of the bedroom, I was actually more ready to lock the door, strip, and beg him to fuck me. Good God, this man only had to look at me and I was a mess. I wasn't sure how I would get through life now he was in it. And yet, I did know, because having him by my side was a whole lot better than not having him there.

King called me at one and told me my place was clean and ready for me and the kids to move back in, so I bundled them up and moved us back home, arranging for Linc to pick the kids up from there instead of Mum's. I'd spent the morning at the hospital with Mum and Brynn. She was starting on her road to recovery, much less confused than two days ago, but still not completely herself. I knew it would take time. I was just relieved and happy she was still with us.

Robbie wasn't feeling well, so he hadn't gone to karate, and I was concerned about sending him to his father's while sick. Linc wasn't the best at coping with the kids when they were like this. Zara was still mad at me, refusing to talk to me. Holly had thankfully moved past the stress she'd felt earlier in the week and had given me no hell today. She'd tried to talk her sister around, but had no luck. I was resigned to the situation with Zara getting worse before it got better. I based that on the way I'd acted at her age. Turned out karma was a bitch.

By the time King showed back up at my place, it was almost three. That concerned me. It meant he was around for Linc's imminent arrival. I was already stressed about seeing Linc for the first time since our fight the other day; King being here only added to my worry.

He entered the house, beer in hand, and dropped a kiss to my mouth as his hand slid down and around my waist. It was a quick kiss and then he continued on his way to the kitchen. I smiled as warmth filled my belly. This felt good. And right. Like it was meant to be.

I listened while he and Holly had a conversation about motorbikes. She'd taken to him in a way I'd never imagined she would, and loved hearing about the rides he'd been on. They'd talked over dinner last night for a good twenty minutes about his trip across Australia to Perth. I'd found her later, searching the Internet for the places he'd mentioned. When I'd jokingly said, "You gonna get a bike, Hols?" she'd shrugged and said, "Maybe." That had completely surprised me, but when I'd mentioned it to King, he'd shrugged, too and said, "Better prepare yourself now. When bikes get in your blood, there's no getting them out."

I lingered, listening to them for a while before going in search of Robbie. I found him lying on his bed staring up at the ceiling. Entering the room, I sat next to him and asked, "You okay, baby?"

Turning to face me, he said, "I don't know."

I frowned. "What's going on? Is your tummy still not feeling well?"

"It's okay." He paused for a moment, and when he spoke again, his eyes shimmered with tears. "I miss Dad."

With those words, my heart cracked a little more than it already had every other time we went through this. Robbie had been five when Linc and I split, and he'd struggled a great deal with the break-up. He'd been okay for the last six months, though, so I thought things were better for him. But as I sat watching him, I knew deep in my gut where these emotions were coming from.

King.

I'd dated since Linc, but not one of the men had meant as much to me as King did. Robbie was a sensitive soul; I figured he'd picked up on my feelings for King. And while he appeared to like King, I understood how confused he must be about everything.

Running my hand over his forehead, I said, "I know you do."

I felt out of my depth with this, but that was a recurring feeling in my life. Marriage and parenting didn't come with a how-to manual, and it sure as heck wasn't easy to navigate a family break-up. I'd stumbled and fumbled my way through it all. Some days I felt invincible, like I could take on the world. Most days, I felt how I felt right now—completely lost and desperate for the answers that told me how to not screw my kids up any more than I already had.

"I want him to move back home."

Oh man.

I should never have allowed Linc to stay with us at Mum's this week. I could see that it had confused Robbie, and now we'd have to go through another round of him coming to terms with the fact his parents would never be together again.

"Robbie, we've talked about this before. You know that Dad has his own home."

His face crumpled. "Why does he have to? Why can't he live with us?"

"Sometimes mummies and daddies can't live together anymore, buddy. Do you know how Dad and I fight a lot?" At his nod, I continued, "Well, we just aren't very good at living in the same house. It makes us just as sad as it makes you, but at the same time, we are happier when Dad lives at his house. That doesn't mean we don't love you. We love you very much, and will always make sure you get lots of time with both of us."

He listened to everything I said, and then he rolled over and faced the wall. That was his sign he was done with the conversation, and previous experience told me it was best not to push him to talk more. Robbie was a deep thinker; he just needed time to process it all.

With a heavy heart, I left him and made my way to the kitchen looking for King. I had the overwhelming need for his arms crushed around me in a hug. When I didn't find him there, I kept searching until I found him on the couch in the lounge room watching television.

His eyes came to mine the second I stepped foot in the room, and his shoulders tensed as he watched me walk to him. He reached out his arm, grabbed my shirt at the waist, and pulled me onto the couch next to him. As his lips brushed my cheek, he asked, "What's wrong?"

I curled my legs up under me and snuggled against his warm body. God, he felt good. Like home. Wrapping one arm across his chest, I looked up at him and said, "Robbie's all confused over his father again."

"Over what?"

I sighed. "He doesn't understand why Linc doesn't live with us. He goes through these phases, but it's been a good six months since the last one. I guess having his dad stay with us for a couple of nights this week messed him up."

King was silent for a few moments while he thought about what I said. "And having me around would be confusing to him, too."

"Yeah," I said softly, not wanting to admit that, but having to.

"You want me to go? Give you guys the night?"

That he put himself last and did so without hesitation meant the world to me. I moved my hand to his face, placing it against his cheek. Shaking my head, I said, "No. Don't you dare leave. I need you."

Heat flared in his eyes, and with a growl, he bent his face to mine and kissed me. When he was done, he said, "Fuck, there's nothing like a woman telling you she needs you."

My tummy practically somersaulted out of my body at his honesty and the way he willingly shared it with me. Gripping his face hard, I said, "And there's nothing like a man who speaks the truth."

His eyes searched mine for a good few moments before he tightened his hold on me while simultaneously shifting his hand to rest on my ass. He then turned his attention back to the television and continued watching the sport.

My man wasn't one for a lot of words, but the ones he did give were worth every breath he took to say them.

15

King

"The fucking feds are back on us," Kick said as he took the barstool next to me late Monday afternoon. "Devil and I were just tailed by two of the assholes on our way back from Brian's."

I threw some beer down my throat and scowled. "Yeah, I had a tail today, too." The motherfuckers hadn't let me out of their sight for the three hours I was out on club business. It had made it fucking difficult to get shit done.

Kick eyed me, concern etched into his face. "They aren't the least of our problems, though, are they?"

I shook my head. "No."

"Fucking hell," he muttered, shoving his fingers through his hair. "You want me to do anything? Start putting some precautions in place?"

"Get eyes on him, but don't do anything yet. We'll see how this plays out first. Hell, if we weren't able to find

Moses, I'd like to fucking see the feds find him. And the link to D'Amato isn't obvious so they may not have even connected it." The fact the link between Storm and D'Amato existed pissed me off. He had his fingers in a lot of shit in Sydney, and we didn't need a problem with him. This fucking Moses bullshit meant that was possible, so all we could do at this point was watch and wait. Because if he didn't know anything about Moses, I sure as fuck wasn't gonna bring it to his attention.

A cheer erupted from the back corner of the bar, drawing Kick's attention. "They're celebrating hard."

I glanced over at them. "Yeah, brother. You gonna stick around?"

The club had been celebrating since Friday—since they'd been told they could move their families home. Devil had organised a get together for tonight to bring everyone together, and members had started rolling in an hour ago. It was getting rowdy in here.

He nodded. "Evie's mum is having Elizabeth for the night so she can come."

Hyde cut in as he joined us. "Just got word from Winter. He's checking out a lead on Brant. Will let us know what he finds. And he's found some premises to operate out of down there."

Sending Winter had been a good decision. He was an attention-to-details guy and would get shit done efficiently. His military background made sure of that. "You got any ideas of who we should send down there to work with him?"

"I've got a few names on my list."

"We'll go over it tomorrow."

His gaze turned serious in the way it did when he had shit to tell me that he knew I wouldn't like. "Also, Ghost's release is scheduled for this week. We gonna find him a place to stay?"

That was the last fucking thing I wanted to do for that cunt. "No."

"You might wanna reconsider, brother. We've got a lot riding on Ghost keeping his mouth shut."

I motioned for Kree to get me another beer before turning back to Hyde. "We think we need to keep him happy to keep him from talking to the feds, we may as well put a bullet in his head and call it a fucking day. If Ghost has forgotten the meaning of loyalty, he can learn the fucking meaning of dead." Fucking hell, just thinking about the motherfucker caused my head to stir with the beginning of a headache.

"Yeah, I get that, King, but Ghost disappears right after he gets out, the feds are gonna be looking in our direction."

Kree placed a beer in front of me, a blank expression on her face. She'd made it pretty fucking clear all day what she thought of our new arrangement, and I was fucking over her attitude. I made a mental note to bring that shit up with her before she went home.

I took a long swig of my drink before looking back at Hyde. "I couldn't fucking care less, Hyde. We start running on fear, we may as well surrender to those assholes now."

"Fuck," he muttered. "I hope you fucking know what you're doing."

I was back running on gut instinct after allowing outside forces to interfere with decisions, and my gut was telling me to trust very few and eliminate all threats I couldn't control.

Kree placed a Coke in front of Hyde, eyes on me as she did so. "King's flying by the seat of his fucking pants, Hyde." Without waiting for a response from either of us, she stalked to the other end of the counter to serve Mace.

"What the fuck's going on there?" Hyde asked.

I moved off my stool, shoulders rock hard with tension, gaze pinned to Kree. "She's pissed I've put eyes on her and added some security to her place."

He frowned. "The cameras?"

"Yeah. She gave me some bullshit about an intrusion of her privacy."

"Jesus, she gets the threat her ex is, right?"

I stretched my neck trying to loosen my muscles and shake the headache building. "I don't fucking know. She says she does, but I think she's under some illusion he won't ever hurt her." She looked up and I caught her eye. Jerking my chin at her, I barked, "Kree. A word."

"Go easy on her, brother. She's probably confused as fuck," Hyde said.

She glared at me but walked my way. I turned and headed toward the office so we could have this chat in private.

When I had her in there, door closed, I said, "Wanna tell me what the fuck is running through your head?"

Her brows lifted. "You know, I don't really care at this point that you're my boss or that you think you're helping me, King. I really don't like the way you've taken over my life and have started controlling everything I do."

"I don't give a fuck if you don't like it, I'm doing it for a good reason." I narrowed my eyes at her. "Do you have any idea what men like your ex do to the women they can't have? Because I can fucking tell you some stories if you don't."

"Of course I know what men like Don are capable of, but Zane has told me he's got a handle on the situation, and I'm choosing to put my faith in my cousin. Having said that, I told you I'm okay with the men you've got watching me. Thankful, too. But those cameras in my home? No fucking way. I want them gone."

"The cameras are staying."

She stared at me for a long few moments, her anger growing. "I'll pull them out."

"You fucking won't."

She straightened, pulling her shoulders back defiantly. "I fucking will."

"Fuck, Kree." I rubbed my temple. "I've got enough other shit to deal with—"

"So deal with it, and I'll deal with mine." She exited the office after that, leaving me angrier than I was before we talked.

Yanking my phone from my pocket, I called Griff. "You dug up anything on Don yet?"

"Only that he's a fucking asshole when it comes to his kids and ex. I'm still going through everything trying to connect dots. I'm getting the sense, though, that he's tied up with the Vinzani family somehow, and if that's the case, shit ain't good for anyone."

"Let me know when you have something," I said and disconnected the call.

Stalking out of the office, I found Kree and pulled her aside. "There's shit going on that you don't know about, so the cameras stay," I said with force. "Am I clear?"

Her silence roared between us, and I figured I'd have to be harder on her to get what I wanted, but in the end, she said, "You fucking exhaust me," before walking away.

"Kree, answer the fucking question."

She stopped and faced me again. "Yes, we're clear."

Thank fuck.

I reached for my phone again and called Zane. The call went to messages. "Zane, where the fuck are you? I haven't seen you for days. We need to talk."

If Kree's ex was tied up with the Vinzanis, and if he fucked shit up with them, it wouldn't matter what Don had planned for her, because what they'd do would be far worse, and they'd get to her first. The time had come for me to take charge of this situation, because Zane's refusal to use whatever force necessary wasn't going to cut it anymore.

16

Lily

"Lily! I'm so glad you came," Skylar said when I arrived at her place after work Monday afternoon. She'd texted me during the day to ask if I could drop by and check on her progress. I'd said yes, because Linc had the kids at his place tonight, and after I'd checked in on Brynn, I drove to Skylar's.

I followed her inside, taking note of how well she used her crutches. "You're doing great with those." She was clearly doing her exercises, which made me happy. Some patients became a little complacent with their recovery, which slowed it down, but if Skylar kept this up, she'd go from strength to strength fast.

She led me into her lounge room and we settled on her long couch. I instantly felt at home here. That probably had more to do with the fact I genuinely liked her, but her home was so cosy and inviting with the colour she had splashed here and there, and the plants scattered around. Not to mention, the framed prints on the wall that held a mixture of positive quotes and gorgeous artwork.

"I knew I liked you," I said with a smile as I read one of the framed quotes. "I need to get some of these for my place."

"They're from a market. When I'm walking better, I'll take you."

"Thanks, babe." I nodded at her hip. "How's it all going?"

She rattled off the work she'd been doing on her rehab and the challenges she'd faced. She also detailed for me the concerns she had now she was back home and living alone. Her list wasn't too long, though, and it contained challenges I could easily help her address.

We spent about twenty minutes going over everything, and when we were done, she exhaled a long breath and smiled. "I'm so glad I called you. I was kinda worked up over all this, but you've put my mind at ease that I can manage this on my own with just a little help. Thank you."

I reached for her hand and gave it a squeeze. "I'm just a call away, okay? Don't hesitate to reach out."

"I know, but I don't want to intrude on your time when your sister is in hospital. And I know you're busy with the kids and work."

"Skye, it's all good. Brynn is doing really well. I just visited her before I came here. They've moved her to a ward, and the doctors think she'll likely be home by the end of the week. And even though my ex is being a dick because of King, he's being more hands-on with the kids, so I have some free time. Also, besides all that, and besides the fact King paid me a lot of money to manage your rehab, I want you to know I'm here for you because I feel like we're friends now."

"Wait, go back. What do you mean your ex is being a dick because of King? Have I missed something there?"

"Oh," I said, my mouth forming an *O*.

"Oh what?"

I suddenly felt a little nervous about having this conversation. I wasn't sure if King would be down with me discussing our relationship with his sister.

She nudged me with her hand. "Spill, Lily, and don't leave anything out."

I made myself comfy, and as I crossed my legs, I said, "King and I are seeing each other."

Her eyes widened as a huge smile landed on her face. "Oh my God! This is the best news! Tell me everything."

I laughed. "Ah no. That would just be weird. He's your brother. And honestly, I'm not sure he'd be happy to know we're having this conversation."

She frowned. "Why wouldn't he be?"

"He might have preferred to tell you himself."

"Look, I think we both know my brother isn't a big talker. He wouldn't give a shit that we're having this conversation, because it saves him having it with me. But on top of that, let me just tell you one thing—King hasn't dated for years. I think it's probably been like seven years since he was in a relationship. You must mean something to him if he's, umm, how do I put this without sounding crude… If he's been back for more." She cringed. "Sorry, that sounds awful, but that's King."

"Don't be sorry. We are who we are, right?"

What she told me caused a rush of fluttery goodness in my belly. King and I hadn't discussed past histories except for him laying down the law about me never mentioning another man to him again. I figured it wasn't something he wanted to get into, and honestly, I wasn't the type of woman who wanted to think about his past either. But I couldn't deny that this new information Skylar had shared made me feel all kinds of happy.

I stayed chatting with her for another half hour before she

said, "You should go. It's not often you get a night to your-self. You need to make the most of it."

"Yeah, I'm looking forward to a long bath with a couple of glasses of wine and no kids harassing me."

Her brow lifted. "Are you shitting me? Wouldn't this be the perfect night to spend with King?"

I tried not to laugh. "Is this weird for you? I mean, discussing your brother's sex life has to be weird."

She shook her head. "No." Shrugging, she added, "Sex isn't something we've kept secret or never talked about. Hell, King was the one who had to give me the birds and bees talk when I was twelve. Annika was too busy with her boyfriends to do it. I remember him sitting me down and shoving me that *What's Happening To Me* book before giving me the rundown on penises and vaginas and periods. He also took me shopping for my first bra, but Nik did come for that, too. He drew the line at talking me through my first period, though. He made Annika handle that. And let's just say that he wanted nothing to do with discussing the loss of my virginity. I think he was ready to take a gun to the guy I was dating in year twelve."

It was both funny and touching hearing how King had manoeuvred his way through that time in Skylar's life. Funny because I knew the difficulties a parent faced when explaining puberty to their child, and from what she'd said, I imagined King had felt a little out of his depth, and that wasn't something you often saw with him. But I was far more touched than entertained by her story. It peeled back more layers to the man I couldn't stop thinking about. Layers I really, really liked.

By the time I made it to my car, I'd decided to call him. We hadn't made plans for tonight because he'd said he had club stuff on, but I just wanted to hear his voice.

"Lily," he answered the call in the way he always did

when I rang. God, how I loved the sound of my name from his lips.

"Hey you," I said, feeling all fluttery again. "I just wanted to call and say hi. See how your day has been." It struck me that he never called me during the day to check in with me, but it didn't bother me. I knew he was busy. And I was busy, too. King definitely wasn't a man who was about needless interruptions.

He blew out a long breath. "It's been long. Busy. Yours?"

I frowned at the exhaustion I heard in his voice. "Are you okay? You sound tired. And stressed."

"I'm good. Tell me how you are."

"Liar," I murmured before answering him, "I'm really good. My first day back at work went well. Brynn's doing great, and I just stopped by to see Skylar, and she's doing well, too. And the best part of my day is that I now get to go home and enjoy the peace and quiet of no freaking children. Just me, a bath, and some wine. The only thing that would make it better was if you were in that bath with me."

"Fucking hell," he muttered. He didn't say anything else, but he didn't need to. I may not have known a great deal about King yet, but I'd worked out the inflections in his tone and his body language. And while I couldn't see him, I could hear the desire in his voice.

"You busy right now? I could stop by for a few minutes if you aren't. I won't stay long." My tummy knotted a little as the words fell out of my mouth. I didn't want him to think I was trying to force my way in and steal his time when he was busy with the club. And I certainly didn't want to come across as a needy woman who always had to be with her man, but damn, I really wanted to see him.

"I'm never too busy for you. Get your ass over here."

And holy shit just like that, he caused an almighty whoosh of lust deep in me. He might have said a lot of filthy stuff to me, but he also had a way of saying exactly what I needed to hear sometimes.

"Okay," I agreed softly and hung up.

He's never too busy for me.

Oh God.

This man.

17

Lily

The club was partying tonight. It was unlike anything I'd ever seen. There had to be at least twenty guys and just as many women here, drinking and laughing as they celebrated something. I wondered if it was someone's birthday, and then my mind jumped to the fact I didn't know when King's birthday was. There were a lot of things I didn't know about him yet, and suddenly I wanted to know every last one of them.

A couple stumbled out the front door as I entered. His hands were all over her; they barely noticed me there. That was the kind of passion I'd always wanted in my life, and I smiled as I thought about King and how he'd given me that.

"Lily."

I glanced up to find Devil standing in front of me, watching me with a smile that lit his face. "Hey, Devil, is King around?"

"You mean you don't wanna hang out with me?" He

winked as he said that. I also didn't miss the slur in his words.

I grinned, liking this fun side to him. "I'm sure you've got someone willing to do that."

His smile grew and his eyes flashed with happiness. "I do," he said, turning to point towards a group of women. "She's right over there." I struggled to hear him over the beat of the music, but I didn't miss the happiness in his voice that matched what I'd seen in his eyes.

I also didn't miss seeing King who sat at the table next to the one the women were at. He was with two other guys, leaning back in his chair, beer in hand, legs stretched out in front of him, causal in a way that wasn't normal for King. His eyes were firmly on me, watching with an intensity that was anything but casual.

Without another word to Devil, I drifted across to King, my mind and body completely focused on him and him alone. Being here in his clubhouse with all his people around him, and none of mine, nerves fluttered in my chest. Or maybe that was simply because of the way he watched me. I wasn't sure. But I needn't have been, because he put me at ease the moment he snaked an arm around my waist and pulled me onto his lap. The kiss he claimed eased any remaining nerves.

I shifted a little in his embrace to make myself more comfortable before grasping his face and saying a little breathlessly, "I like it when you do that."

His hold on me tightened and he took a swig of his beer as his eyes dropped to my chest. "You wore that to work?"

I looked down at the V-neck blouse I'd worn today and then frowned at him. "What's wrong with it?"

"It's fucking see-through for one. And for two, it's hanging so fucking low every asshole can get eyes on your tits."

I arched a brow as I pulled away from him a little. "Whoa

there, it's not hanging low. And no one has had their eyes on my tits, thank you very much."

It was his turn to lift a brow. "Of course they fucking have." He ran the bottom of his beer bottle over the swell of one of my breasts, pushing the blouse to the side. The cool, wet glass left drops of water on my skin. It did little to cool the heat between us, though. "Your top falls to the side like a fucking hooker's legs fall open. You bend over with a patient like you did with Skylar, and he cops a fucking eyeful."

"I can assure you that does not happen."

"Bullshit, Lily. Only a fucking gay man wouldn't take an opportunity like that."

"So you're telling me this is what you did while I worked with Skylar in the hospital?"

"I didn't get the chance. You didn't wear this top."

I narrowed my eyes at him. "I can't tell if you're shitty about this and trying to lay down the law about what I wear —which, for the record, if you are, don't—or whether you're just telling me how you feel about this, or whether you've had a few drinks and are simply sharing your thoughts as they come to you. I mean, I don't think you're shitty. You don't really seem it, but help me out—tell me what's going on here."

"I'm not telling you what to wear. I'm just telling you your top is see-through and hanging low."

"Seriously? That's all that was?" I couldn't work out if I was disappointed there wasn't more to it, or if I was relieved he hadn't tried to boss me about my clothes. And that made me feel like a crazy freaking woman. I mean, what woman wants to go to battle with their man over the clothes they choose to wear?

He shifted positions swiftly, catching me off guard. Sitting up straight with his body to mine, he reached his hand into my blouse and cupped my breast as he growled, "I don't like anyone's eyes on your tits but mine. Wear whatever the fuck you want, but I catch a motherfucker copping a look, he'll wish he didn't."

I gripped his biceps, heat rushing through me. King's possessiveness turned me on so damn much, and that was completely unexpected. On top of that, his public display of sticking his hand down my top also freaking turned me on. I'd never been with a man who did that kind of thing, and I decided then and there, I was all for it.

"King!" Someone called out to him, and he slowly turned to see who it was. It was like he didn't want to take his eyes off me for even a second.

I dropped my gaze to his neck, inspecting the tattoos there. King's body was covered in them, and each time I looked at them, I saw something extra. Today I realised the eagle tattoo on one side of his neck was layered with a skull and dream catcher underneath. I traced my fingers over it, admiring the beauty in the design.

King lifted his chin at the guy speaking to him before smacking my leg and saying, "I need to go have a conversation. I'll be back soon."

I moved off his lap so he could stand, and he strode purposefully out of the bar without another glance my way. I decided a drink was a good idea. I wasn't an extrovert, and being surrounded by all these people I didn't know was a little intimidating, so I made my way to the bar and waited a few minutes for the woman behind it to serve me.

The dark-haired woman met me with a smile. "What can I get you?"

"A Jack and Coke, please."

Her smile grew as she pulled a glass out. "I'm impressed."

I frowned. "With what?"

She slowed her movements and met my gaze with a serious expression. "The woman King's dating has manners."

I wasn't sure what to make of that or of her. "What does that mean? Why wouldn't I? And what makes you think we're together?"

She grinned again and made my drink. Sliding it to me, she leant across the bar a little and said, "I've never seen King like that with a woman. Never seen him give his complete attention to one the way he just did with you. Everyone noticed, babe, because none of us have seen that. And let's just say, King's manners leave a lot to be desired, so I'm fucking impressed he managed to score someone who knows her pleases and thank-yous."

Deciding I liked her style of honesty, I returned her smile. Lifting the drink, I said, "How much do I owe you?"

She shook her head and shooed me away with a flick of her hand. "Nothing. I'm pretty sure my boss would want your drinks on the house."

A red-headed woman arrived at the bar, moving in between me and the man to my right. "Hey, Kree, two Jäger-bombs please, honey." Then turning to me, she hit me with a huge smile and said, "One of those is for you by the way, so don't go anywhere."

"For me?"

She nodded. "Yeah. I wanna have a drink with the woman who made King smile." Before I could say anything to that, she reached for my hair and pulled a few strands to the side, and said, "Goodness, you need to tell me what products you use on your hair. It's so silky. I do so much shit to mine that I swear it's gonna start falling out."

And just like that, this woman made me feel welcome and put me at ease. "Thanks for the drink. I'm Lily by the way, and I'm not sure I actually saw King smile today so you may be wrong there."

She laughed. "Oh honey, you are gonna fit right in here. And yeah, your man totally smiled. You just missed it because you were too busy being all flustered by his hand down your top."

I took the Jägerbomb Kree placed in front of me and lifted it up with a questioning look at the woman. "Two questions. What the hell is in this? And what is your name? I mean, by the time I'm finished with this drink, I may not remember it, but I'm gonna give it a good shot."

She lifted her drink, too. "It's Jäger and Red Bull, and just drink it down in one go, okay? Like, trust me on this. And I'm Monroe, but you can call me Roe."

I eyed the drink. "Am I gonna make it to work in the morning?"

Another laugh escaped her lips. "Honestly, what's one day in the whole year with a hangover?"

A blonde woman joined us and said, "Not that my cousin only ever has one day a year with a hangover."

Monroe glanced at her. "Oh shush, Tatum. I've almost found a Jäger buddy. Don't ruin this for me when none of you bitches will drink it with me."

"Wait," I said, looking at Tatum, "is this gonna taste bad?" God, the woman was beautiful with her long, blonde hair, stunning features, and gorgeous tattoos. I decided I wanted to be Tatum when I grew up.

She pulled a face and nodded. "Yeah, it's fucking awful."

"Shit," I muttered. And then to Monroe, I said, "Okay, let's do this." And with that, I took her advice and downed the drink in one go. She did the same, and when she hit me with a questioning look afterwards, I pulled a face and said, "I agree with Tatum—it's fucking bad—but I'm willing to go another round to see if it improves."

"Fuck, yes!" Monroe said as she looked at Tatum and wrinkled her nose while grinning at her. She then called out to Kree, "We need another round, Kree. Before Lily changes her mind."

Being with these two reminded me of being with Adelaide and the girls. By the time Kree had served up two more rounds of Jägerbombs and I'd drunk them, as well as the Jack and Coke I'd originally ordered, I was a little tipsy and unsteady on my feet. Monroe was in the same state, and between us, we'd become a little loud. Hailee, the woman Devil had referred to earlier as his woman had also joined us, along with another old lady, Evie. I knew nothing about club life, so I hadn't even known what an old lady was, but they started my education, filling me in on a few things, all while getting drunk.

King was gone for ages, but I hardly had time to miss him. The girls had me laughing over stories of the funny stuff they'd done together, and I realised they must have spent a fair bit of time with each other to have all these stories. I liked the sisterhood that it felt like they had. I'd always been drawn to having friends who liked to get together often, and I hoped this might be the beginning of some new friendships.

"When are you and Nitro getting married?" Evie asked Tatum.

Tatum sighed. "We've put it off for now, while everything has been so up in the air. Honestly, at this point, I'm just glad to have him home again."

"But you guys are still getting married, right?" Hailee asked.

"Yeah. We'll just wait for the dust to settle."

I wasn't sure what they referred to, but it sounded like she and Nitro had been through something recently. I wasn't the kind of person to pry, so I didn't ask any questions.

A dark-haired man who was built like an I-don't-know-what-except-he-was-freaking-huge joined us at the table where we'd relocated. With his gaze glued to Tatum, he said, "Vegas. You ready to go?"

Her eyes snapped to his and her body reacted to him. She

nodded and stood. Glancing at me, she said, "It was great to meet you. I'm sure Roe will organise drinks or something soon, so I'll see you at that." She then moved into the man's embrace, their bodies connecting like they were made for each other. He had to be Nitro. I wasn't sure I'd ever seen a couple so in sync before.

As they left, King entered the bar and caught my attention. He made his way over to us, and I stood to meet him. Something had happened in between him leaving me and now returning. Gone was the relaxed King, and in his place was the wired King. His face was a mask of intensity and determination as he placed his hand on my hip and said, "I have to head out to take care of some shit."

"Okay. I've had a few drinks, so I'm gonna call an Uber. It's okay if I leave my car here, right?"

"Yeah," he said, looking around the room. "I'll get one of the boys to run you home." He called Mace over and organised him to do that before turning back to me. "Depending on whether I get shit done tonight, I might be over later."

With that, he left. No goodbye kiss, no other words exchanged. But I didn't care, because each passing day with King in my life showed me that sometimes those things weren't what mattered. The backbone of a relationship came down to more than displays of affection and fancy promises; it came down to actions that showed respect and care. Sometimes those actions consisted of words as well as deeds, but sometimes it was mostly the things we actually followed through on and did that meant the most.

18

Lily

"How much have you had to drink?" Adelaide asked me on the phone later that night when I told her about something weird that had happened to me during the day.

"I swear to you this happened. I'm not saying it because I've been drinking. And besides, most of the buzz I had is gone now. The guy looked like a younger version of John Travolta, and he watched me leave the hospital and then followed me to my car. I thought he was going to stop me and tell me something, but he didn't. He just kept walking."

"And he was there yesterday, too?"

"Yes! I remember him because he was sitting outside the ward Brynn is on, and as I walked past him, I thought about how much he looked like John Travolta. You know how much I love *Grease*. Anyone who even kinda looks like John catches my attention."

She laughed. "Was he wearing tight black jeans and a leather jacket?"

"Ugh. If you were here right now, I would poke my freaking tongue out at you."

"Lil, he was probably visiting someone at the hospital, too," she said, her voice softer, less amused at me. "I think you need about a week's worth of sleep at the moment. Go to bed now and get an early night."

"Well, King might be coming over, so I might wait up in case he does."

"Text him and tell him not to come."

Adelaide still wasn't on Team King. I knew she was just being a good friend and waiting for him to prove himself after he hurt me, and I didn't blame her, but I also didn't pay any attention to the cooler tone she took when she mentioned him. I had confidence he'd prove himself over time and that she'd come around. And I was glad to have a friend who looked out for me.

"I'm going to take a bath. If I fall asleep before he comes, I fall asleep." I didn't tell her King still had a key to my place from when he'd cleaned it for me.

"Good. And what about Linc? Is he still being a dick?"

I headed out of the kitchen to walk into my bathroom and get the bath started. "Yeah. I figure he's gonna be a dick until old age and then some. I've decided to ignore his bullshit. Especially since I'm trying to quit smoking again. That's hard enough to do without having to also be thinking about Linc."

She chuckled. "How many times are you up to now?"

Sitting on the edge of the bath, I flicked the taps on. "Shut up and don't be mean to me."

This was an old argument between us, and Addy never let up about it. She knew I was way into double digits on this. She also knew my attempts were only half-assed, because smoking was something I really didn't want to give up. I knew I had to, and the smart side of my brain knew I was a freaking idiot for not having made more of an effort, but what was hard to explain to someone like Adelaide, who'd never smoked, was the enjoyment I got from it. That first drag of a cigarette was like the first hit of caffeine in the morning or the first bite into a warm, fresh doughnut. It made me smile and it helped take the edge off from all the stress and pressure I felt being pulled in a hundred directions between work and family. I liked smoking. And who wants to stop doing something they love? That was the switch in my brain I had to flip, but I knew that would only happen when I was ready and wanted to. I also knew that until then, I'd have to put up with Addy giving me a hard time.

"You know I'm never gonna shut up about this, Lily. I want you by my side in the nursing home, and I worry you won't be around for that if you keep smoking."

"I know, babe."

"Okay, enough of that tonight. Go have your bath. Get your meditation on. I'll call you tomorrow to see how you're going. Love you, girl."

"I love you, too. Talk to you tomorrow."

After the call ended, I lit the candles in my bathroom, set my phone up with my guided meditation open on my Spotify app, and stripped. Five minutes later, I was immersed in the warm water, hair up in a messy bun, eyes closed, meditating.

Perfect.

I chose a forty-minute meditation, and it was almost finished when a text came through from King.

King: I'm letting myself in.

I smiled. Mostly because he was here, but also because it

appeared he realised I would freak out if I heard a sound I wasn't expecting. Closing my eyes again, I listened to the last few minutes of the meditation. When I opened my eyes again, King stood resting against the doorjamb, arms crossed, watching me.

"Hey, you," I said, not shifting from under the water. It was warm and cosy in the bath, and I wasn't ready to get out yet. Not even for King.

He didn't speak, but rather moved to the bath and sat on the side of it. As he watched me, I took in the fierce energy blaring from him. From the hard set of his shoulders to his tight jaw, to his eyes that flashed with a storm of emotion, King was wound up. On edge. And from previous experience, I knew that when he turned up like this, he wanted the kind of sex that would wear me out in the very best ways.

Shifting his attention to my body, he dipped his hand into the water and found my stomach. As he reached down to my pussy, a low growl came from him, and when he pushed two fingers inside me, he met my gaze again and held it steady while finger-fucking me.

Arching my back, I bit my lip and closed my eyes. His touch relaxed me in ways no meditation could, but at the same time, it excited me to the point where I couldn't get enough from him. With King, I wanted him to hurry the hell up and make me come already while also wanting him to take his sweet time and send me over the edge in a complete and utter mess of bewilderment and frantic need.

"Lily," he rasped, "Give me your eyes."

They fluttered open, and I gave him what he wanted, which he liked, because it caused him to reach deeper inside me and work me harder. His strokes were demanding, and with each one, the heat between us intensified.

He bent forward and curled his free hand around my neck. Fingers digging in hard, he pulled me to him and kissed me. It was savage, and while mostly it pushed me into a desperate state of need, I wondered at the back of my mind, what caused him to become so fiercely aroused.

He ended the kiss, but he didn't let my mouth go fully. His teeth nipped at my bottom lip while his fingers continued fucking me, and he growled, "It doesn't fucking matter how often I have you, I can't fucking get enough. Your cunt, your body"—he bit my lip harder—"this mouth... You're in my head twenty-four-fucking-seven."

I couldn't stop myself. I moved without thought, just feeling. Pure need. It was like a frenzy of arms, legs, and water as I scrambled to my knees so I could take hold of his face and kiss him. I didn't even care how uncomfortable it was to be in this position; I needed King's mouth on mine, his face to mine, his breath in me. I needed to get closer to the core of him, to his soul, and right now the only way I knew how to do that was to kiss the hell out of him.

I may have started this kiss, but he took charge of it. His tongue became as demanding as his fingers had been inside me. I wasn't sure I'd ever kissed anyone the way I kissed King. It was like we were forcing each other to go deeper, to give more. It was hard and rough and violent. Neither of us wanted it to end; we just kept pushing for every last piece the other had to give. When he finally tore his mouth from mine, his eyes flashed with a level of desire I'd never seen in a man. And when he scooped me into his arms and carried me into my bedroom, I craved him in ways I'd never imagined possible.

Dropping me on the bed, he yanked his clothes off before gripping my ankle and pulling me to the end of the mattress and off the bed. A shiver ran over my skin as I watched the muscles in his arms flex. I didn't care that I was still wet from the bath; I didn't want anything slowing this down.

Positioning me in front of him with my back to him, he

placed one arm around me, his hand splayed across my stom-ach, fingers so hard against my skin it felt like he might gouge holes in me. His other hand slid around my hips and he took hold of my pussy, his whole hand covering me, his fingers curling under. He held me so tightly against him I felt like we were fused skin-to-skin.

He then did something unexpected. He swept my hair to the side, bent his head, and pressed his mouth to my shoul-der, kissing me. The pressure was the complete opposite to that applied to the lower half of my body. He moved along my shoulder slowly, trailing kisses as he went. His beard tickled me, and his tongue licked me, and holy hell if the slow, steady way he moved didn't turn my legs to jelly.

He covered both my shoulders with kisses and then began making his way down my back. Letting go of me, he glided his hands around to take hold of my hips, grasping me there until his mouth found the dip of my body right above my ass.

His kisses turned rougher, and his teeth joined in. The slow moves disappeared as he found the rough rhythm he favoured. Straightening, he ran his hand up my back to my neck. Taking hold of me there, he forced me to bend forward, placing my hands on the bed. At the same time he nudged my feet wide apart.

"Do you want my mouth on your cunt?" The gravel in his hard tone hit my core. God, how I wanted his mouth there.

"Yes."

He squeezed my neck, his body to mine, his mouth against my ear. "Say the words, Lily—I want your mouth on my cunt."

With that order, King stripped another layer between us away.

I had never uttered words so dirty to a man before.

"I want your mouth on my cunt."

He grunted. It was such a deeply masculine response, and it drew an equally feminine one from me.

I moaned. It was long and loud, and a sound unlike any that had ever escaped my lips.

Everything he said and did felt so good.

"Fuck," he rasped. "Say it again."

I spread my fingers out and clutched the sheet as I arched my back and pushed my ass higher in the air. When I gave him the words he wanted, they practically purred out of me. "I want your mouth on my cunt."

His restraint snapped.

He crouched behind me, taking hold of my ass, and buried his face in my pussy. It seemed to be one of his favourite places to be, and I wasn't complaining, because King knew what the hell he was doing. He knew his way around that part of a woman. Hell, he knew his way around a woman, full stop. But he had skills when it came to using his tongue. And his beard only heightened the pleasure. I couldn't get enough of it.

I lost track of time while he brought me to orgasm. It was one of his specialties. Being with King, I shut off all my thoughts and feelings, and simply clung to him for the ride.

As my release shattered through me, I lost the ability to hold myself up, and my arms gave way. King moved swiftly, standing and catching me. He then flipped me over and pushed me onto the bed. Without giving me a moment to get my bearings, he spun me so I was almost parallel to the end of the bed with my ass at the corner. He positioned himself with his feet planted wide either side of the corner, a hand around my throat, the other hand on the top of my head gripping it, my legs up in the air hooked over his while he bent over my body and slammed his dick inside me.

He fucked me with brute force, his hands firmly holding me, not letting go. There was no slow and steady to his pace at all; he thrust in and out with increasing speed and force. His face was near mine, his mouth and beard grazing my skin, his grunts filling the air around me. Everything about it overwhelmed me. All my senses were in overdrive. I tried to take hold of him, but his arms had mine pinned down with such strength I could hardly move. In the end, I held my hands against his biceps and tumbled down into the dark abyss of pleasure he created.

As he inched closer to orgasm, his grip around my throat tightened, cutting off most of my airflow. It intensified every sensation coursing through me, and I madly tried to grasp his arms. My nails scratched him as I did so, and he lifted his head to look at me. Our eyes locked until his were drawn to my mouth when I gasped for air. That pushed him over the edge, and he thrust into me one last time and came with a roar. His grip loosened on my neck and he let go of me as he moved his arms to rest on the bed beside me. I wrapped my arms around his body and searched for that one last bit of friction that would make me come. As the orgasm hit, I squeezed my arms around him hard and arched my body up off the bed.

"Fuck," he growled, his body almost squashing me, his face buried in my neck.

I didn't care that his body was crushed to mine. I liked it there. I felt close to him there. Keeping my arms around him, I tried to catch my breath. When he started to pull away from me, I pushed my hands down onto his back, keeping him in place. "Gimme a minute," I said. I wasn't ready for the loss of contact yet.

He settled there and lifted his face to look at me. "You good?" I didn't miss the trace of concern in his eyes or his voice.

I smiled and nodded. "Yeah. I just like you there."

He watched me silently for a few moments before

bending to kiss my collarbone. After another few moments, he murmured, "I fucking like me here, too."

It was these unguarded moments with King that meant so much to me. He didn't give them to me often, which only made them more special. But when he *did* give them to me, the whole world opened up with bright light. I was the happiest I had ever been in my entire life.

After we had a shower, where King fucked me again, I was too exhausted to go on. He'd been ready for another round, but I just didn't have it in me, so he'd bundled me into bed and wrapped his arms around me while we lay facing each other.

I reached up and ran a finger down the scar on his face. "How did you get this?" I asked softly. It was so jagged that I knew it had to have hurt him, and that caused my heart to hurt. It was crazy, because King was so strong and capable, and seemed unbreakable, but that scar reminded me that even the toughest men could be hurt.

His features darkened. "My father."

It felt like he didn't want to give me more than that, but I was at the point where I wanted more. I hadn't pushed him for anything yet. This, I would push for. "How old were you?"

His jaw clenched. "This is old shit that doesn't need to be rehashed."

"It's not old to me, King. I hardly know a thing about you. I know you're bossy and moody and demanding and giving, and that you love your family and your club." I put my hand to his chest, to his heart. "I want to know what's in here, too."

He stayed silent for a beat, and then after exhaling hard, he said, "I was eight and I pissed him off one Saturday afternoon when I didn't steal the right tins of spaghetti for him from the supermarket. He took a knife to me, letting me know how badly I'd screwed up."

I stared at him with my heart in my throat and tears at the backs of my eyes, unable to comprehend a parent doing that to their child.

When I didn't say anything, because I was lost for words, he said, "My parents were the fucking scum of the earth, Lily, and I don't wanna get into a conversation about them, but for what it's worth, they both went to prison for kidnapping, raping and murdering teenage girls. She lured the girls, he did everything else. I fucking had to listen to and watch some of that shit. And yeah, he slashed my face and beat me up and burnt his fucking cigarettes into my body, but I refuse to give that cunt another fucking thought, so don't mention him to me again."

I wiggled closer to him and placed my hand on his cheek. "He's responsible for the scars on your back, too?"

He nodded once but didn't say anything.

I wasn't the kind of person who hated people. It was such an extreme emotion, and I didn't feel it was a useful one. But I hated King's parents. And I hated what they'd done to him physically and emotionally.

I pressed my lips to his and kissed him. It wasn't one of our usual kisses, more of a softer, quick kiss. He didn't push for more, and I didn't give more. When I ended it, I said, "Thank you for sharing that part of yourself with me. I won't bring them up again, but if you ever wanna talk about stuff, I'm always here. I just want you to know that."

His eyes searched mine for the longest time. He didn't respond to that, but I knew he took it in. Finally, he said, "Roll over and go to sleep. You're tired, and I have plans for this body in the morning."

I rolled over.

I also wiggled my ass against him, loving the grunt that came from him when I did that.

He tightened his embrace and hooked a leg over mine, pinning me in place.

I loved every second of being in this bed with him.

And I was already ready for his plans for the morning.

19

King

"Kree still giving you hell?" Hyde asked late the next afternoon when he got back to the clubhouse after taking care of some club business.

I placed my phone down on the office desk after just having finished a call I'd rather have avoided with Eric Bones about some bullshit I'd have to take care of tomorrow, and stretched my legs out in front of me. "Yeah. I've got Havoc taking care of her ex. Just waiting to hear back from him when it's done, and for Griff to then confirm she's safe before I rip those fucking cameras from her house." I jerked my chin at him. "You heading home?"

"No, I'm on my way over to Monroe's shop. She's got some renovations for me to take care of."

I stood and met him at the door. It was time for me to leave, too. Lily's oven was playing up, so I'd told her I'd take a look at it. I'd just opened my mouth to reply to Hyde after stepping out into the hallway when a fist came flying at me. Having not seen it coming, I stumbled backwards, hitting the wall hard.

Zane came at me with another punch, but I was ready for him this time and blocked him. Grabbing hold of his fist, I shoved him back and bellowed, "What the fuck, Zane?" In all the years we'd known each other, we'd never had a problem between us.

He yanked his hand from mine, fury rolling off him in waves. "I fucking told you I had the Don situation under control, and you went ahead and stuck your fucking nose in it anyway. And caused Kree a major fucking problem in the process."

Anger surged from deep inside me, and every inch of my body tensed. "What the fuck did you just say to me?"

"You should have stayed the fuck out of it, King. I was handling it."

"No, you fucking weren't. You were fucking tiptoeing around trying not to fucking upset anyone. Fuck that shit when your cousin is at risk."

"You wanna know what you managed to do by sticking your nose in? You alerted the Vinzanis to the connection between Don and Storm. They did a little digging and discovered Kree works for you, discovering, in the fucking process, that she now lives in Sydney. They didn't fucking know that before, King." He jabbed his finger at me. "That shit is on you."

His words became a jumbled mess as they each made their way into my brain.

What the hell had I done? I'd been so fucking sure of what we needed to do to fix this shit.

"What's Don's tie to them?" I asked as I tried to shake the anger out of my system. Problem was, the anger was now directed at myself for fucking this up. And that was a whole lot fucking harder to shake than any anger I ever felt towards someone else.

He continued glaring at me, his chest pumping furiously with his own anger. "He got tied up running a dog fighting ring for them when he was trying to make some cash to pay off his gambling debts. I paid off his debts in exchange for him leaving Kree alone, but it turned out he had information about those dogfights stashed on a hard drive somewhere that the Vinzanis want. He took off after I covered the debts, and they couldn't find him, so they've been threatening his family and friends in an effort to draw him out."

"So you have no idea where he is?"

"I said *they* couldn't find him; I found the asshole yesterday and put a fucking bullet in his head like you wanted me to do. I then delivered the hard drive to the Vinzanis and told them to leave Kree out of this shit." He paused for a moment before adding with another jab of his finger, "But you put her at risk for a while there, King, and you need to learn to take a fucking step back when I tell you I have shit handled. Or else you and I are gonna have some big fucking problems going forward."

I scowled at him. "Perhaps in fucking future you could give me the whole fucking story."

He shook his head at me. "Don't twist this to suit your-fucking-self, King."

We stood glaring at each other, neither wanting to back down, when Hyde stepped into the argument. "Let's call this shit a day," he said, glancing between us. "No one's in the wrong, it's just a fucked-up mess. However, we're all on the same fucking side, so let's walk away and mark it as handled."

Neither Zane nor I budged until eventually he blew out a long breath and ground out, "Yeah," before stalking away from us.

As he left, Devil came striding down the hallway towards us, a look of determination on his face. When he reached us, he said, "You know how I spoke to Lily's neighbours and none of them had seen anyone suspicious the day her sister was shot?"

I nodded, not liking where this was going. "Yeah."

"Well, turns out one of the neighbour's sons has been away and just returned home, so she asked him if he'd seen anything. He did, and the description he gave me matches Brant."

The anger Zane had stirred exploded like a fucking volcano spewing lava. I turned to Hyde. "We heard anything more from Winter today?"

"Nothing yet."

"Fuck," I roared, my chest tight with fury. "We need to get down there." I looked at Devil again. "And I want two guys at Lily's place within the next half hour. Keep eyes on her and the kids until we have Brant."

He nodded his agreement and left us.

"Fucking hell," Hyde said. "How the hell did we fuck shit up so badly with Brant?"

"At this point, I don't fucking care how. All I care is that you and I find him and rip him the fuck apart so he can't get at anyone else."

"Yeah, brother. Agreed."

"I'm gonna head over to Lily's and give her a rundown of what's going on. I'll be back so we can leave at ten. I need you and Axe to figure out how the fuck we can shake these feds so we don't have a fucking fan club follow us to Melbourne."

"Will do."

"Zara! Have you seen my necklace?"

I rested my ass against the kitchen counter in Lily's kitchen and watched silently as she tried to make dinner while she also attempted to load the dishwasher, clear old shit out of the fridge, and search in weird fucking places for the necklace. I'd arrived fifteen minutes ago, and she'd been going on about it from the moment I stepped foot inside the house. She was worked up over losing it, and Zara was ignoring her each time she called out about it. Those two had a fucking fiery relationship, completely different to the one she had with Holly. Some days I thought Lily would completely lose her mind over the shit Zara did.

"Fucking hell," she muttered, rifling through her handbag. "I could have sworn I put it in here."

I pushed off from the counter and moved to her. Attempting to take the bag from her, I said, "I'll look for it. You finish the casserole."

She clutched the bag, refusing to let it go. "You don't know what it looks like."

"Fuck, Lily, it's a fucking necklace. I know what they look like."

Her eyes widened. "Don't you take that tone with me."

Jesus fuck. I'd had a headache before I got here, and it was only getting worse. "Pass the fucking bag."

She scowled and pushed past me so she could dump the entire contents of the bag on the counter. After a quick inspection, she shook her head. "It's not there." A moment passed before she said, "Oh shit, maybe it's in the laundry." She then bolted out of the kitchen, presumably to head into the laundry.

"Just ignore Mum," Holly said, joining me in the kitchen. "This happens all the time with that necklace. She always finds it."

I couldn't recall ever seeing Lily wear a necklace. "What's the importance of it?"

Her eyes met mine, a sad expression in them. "It was her grandmother's necklace. They were close, and she freaks out in times of stress if she can't find it." She shrugged. "I don't know why. It makes no sense to me, but that's Mum for you. She can be a little crazy sometimes, you know?"

I nodded. I was getting a feel for that side of Lily.

I followed her into the laundry and found her madly going through a jewellery box. Seemed like the oddest fucking place for one of them, but what the fuck did I know? Moving behind her, I placed my hand over hers and halted her progress. I brought my other hand to her neck, wrapping it around her throat. Meeting her questioning gaze in the mirror on the wall, I said, "What's going on? Why are you stressed?"

She jerked her hand out from under mine and snapped, "You're slowing me down. I've got a million things to do tonight, so please just let me find this necklace so I can get back to my freaking to-do list."

"Stop," I growled, turning her to face me.

She winced, tensing under my grip of her neck. It drew my attention there, and being the bastard I was, her pain turned me on.

Without easing my grasp of her, I demanded, "What the fuck is going on? When I left here this morning, you weren't like this."

"Yeah well, when you left here this morning, I hadn't had a shitty day at work, or a son who isn't really talking to me, a daughter who skipped school to hang out with her boyfriend, or a missing necklace. On top of that, I just discovered I have to bake ten freaking cakes by Thursday for a bake sale I didn't even know was on because not one of my children told me about it. And I am no freaking expert when it comes to baking cakes. I would have preferred time to practice the cakes they want me to cook." She reached for my hand around her throat. "And can you please let me go. I'm all for your hands on my neck when you're fucking me, but right now, not so much. Right now I just need to be able to breathe a full freaking breath so I can get my shit together."

I stepped closer to her, forcing my body hard against hers. She had me fucking hard for her with the bullshit she just threw at me. The urge to spin her around, bend her over and hold her down while I slammed inside of her overwhelmed me, so I was hanging on by a fucking thread here. Gripping her neck harder, I said, "None of that shit is the real reason why you're in a fucking panic, so stop bullshitting both of us and start fucking giving it to me straight."

She drew in a ragged breath as she curled her fingers around mine at her neck and tried to prise them off. I gave that to her because I wanted her to talk. When I let go, she said, "I'm not bullshitting you, King. That stuff stresses me out. Some days it feels like I'm drowning. Like I literally can't breathe under all the stuff I have to deal with." She glanced down for a moment, turning silent, before meeting my gaze again and placing her hand to my chest. "I'm also feeling a little overwhelmed by you, I think. Like, not in a bad way. It's just a lot so soon, you know? A month ago, I didn't even know you, and look at us now."

"So you bring that to me when you're feeling like this. You don't ever shut that shit down and hide it from me. I'm not a fucking mind reader, Lily."

Her brows shot up. "Are you fucking kidding me, right now? I just laid my feelings out for you, was as honest as I could be, and you give me that? And for the record, I wasn't trying to hide it from you. I was trying to process it all myself so I didn't have to worry you with it. I know these feelings are just because this is so new and so fast."

I gripped her waist. "My job is to worry. Your job is *not* to fucking worry. I don't care if what you've got to tell me will rip shit apart, because I will put that shit back to-fucking-gether. So in future, you bring me your feelings and anything else you've got, and hand them to me." I bent to growl into her ear. "My job is to take care of you, and I don't give a flying fuck how long I've known you, you are mine now, and I will go to the fucking ends of the earth for you."

When I pulled my head back, I found her staring at me. This lasted for a good few moments, and then it was like a switch had been tripped. Her hands landed on my cheeks, and with the kind of force that caused my gut to tighten, she dug her fingers in and pulled my face to hers. Our lips smashed together, and she kissed me with wild fucking reck-lessness. She wrapped one leg around my body and used it to fucking climb me, adding her other leg until she'd positioned herself where she wanted to be, arms and legs encircling me, mouth still kissing the fuck out of me.

I dragged my lips from hers. "You wanna kiss me like that, you need to be prepared for me to fuck you," I rasped. This was not the fucking time for sex. Nor the place. But hell if I would be able to stop myself if she continued down this path.

She squeezed her legs around me. She was fucking panting with lust. "Lock the door. You can be quick, but fuck, I need you inside me right now."

I ground my teeth together. "Your kids are right the fuck out there, Lily. You really want them to hear me fuck you?"

"King, for the love of all things good, just fuck me already. I guarantee you they all have their headphones on. Most of the time that pisses me off, but I'm starting to think it might not be such a bad thing."

I was no fucking saint. With her clinging to me, I took the few steps to lock the door before sitting her on the washing machine that was shaking its way through the spin cycle. She reached for my jeans and madly pulled my cock out, like a fucking starved woman. That shit only got me harder. Pulling her off the machine, I spun her around, forced her down over it, shoved her dress up, and yanked her panties down. And as the machine vibrated and shook, I grabbed her hair and pulled her head back while pounding into her so fucking violently that she would feel me for days.

It didn't take either of us long to come. I couldn't recall any time in my life that I'd orgasmed so fast. That was the effect Lily fucking had on me.

As she pulled her panties up, her eyes met mine. "When I said I was overwhelmed by you, I just meant that I wasn't looking for a relationship when you came along. And you aren't like other guys. You're intense and fast. It's not a bad thing, though. I like that you're always here and that it feels like I've known you forever even when I know hardly anything about you. I mean, I can't even explain it—I just feel like this is so right, this thing between us. Like it was meant to be. God, and now I'm rambling and—"

I put my finger to her mouth to quiet her. "I have to go away, and I'm not sure when I'll be back. Might be a day, might be a few. While I'm gone, I'm gonna have some of my guys watching you and the kids. And before you give me hell over that, there's some shit going on with my club that has put you in danger. I don't want to scare you, but you need to why I'm doing this."

Concern flickered in her eyes. "How bad is this? Like, how worried do I have to be for the kids? You're freaking me out here."

"Remember when I said it's my job to worry?" At her nod, I continued, "Let me do my job. All you need to do is go about your business like normal. I'll handle the situation, and then I'll come home and shit will go back to normal."

"You're not going to tell me what's going on, are you?"

I shook my head. "No. You need to learn to trust me when shit like this comes up."

She watched me silently, processing that. I waited for an argument, like all the females in my life liked to give me, but in the end, she nodded and said, "Okay."

Fuck.

Some of the tension in my shoulders eased.

How the hell had I been blessed with a woman like Lily?

She finished straightening her clothes as I zipped myself up. When she was done, she asked, "Are you staying for dinner, or do you have to leave straight away?"

"I'm not leaving until ten tonight. I'm here till then."

A smile settled across her face. "Good. I've got some jobs for you. And also, prepare yourself to watch re-runs of the royal wedding." At the arch of my brow, she lifted hers too and said, "Trust me, Harry gets me hot. You're gonna want me to watch those re-runs."

Fucking hell, this woman.

I jerked my chin towards the door. "Go. Get your list of jobs for me." After she hit me with one last smile and turned towards the door, I said, "And Lily?" She looked at me. "I will never be like other men. When I know what I want, I don't fuck around. I make sure I get it. And while I may have fucked up with you once, that shit won't happen again. You take whatever time you need to wrap your head around this relationship. I'm not going anywhere."

20

King

I eyed the house Hyde, Winter, and I stood outside as the cold Melbourne wind whipped around us. Motherfucking winter had come a few months early. Not only were we dealing with wind, but rain had poured down on us at least once every hour since we'd arrived in this fucking city about six hours ago.

Melbourne and I were not friends. Never had been. I'd tried to avoid coming here after a crazy African motherfucker had attempted to cut my head off years ago. The assholes down here pulled some shit I wasn't a fan of. However, now that I'd decided to set up shop here, I figured I needed to get over my shit and find some fucking joy in the place. Today didn't look like it would be the day for that.

"You ready, King?" Hyde asked.

I pulled out my gun. "Yeah, brother. Let's shake some

fucking shit up." With that, I drove my foot into the back door of the joint and kicked it in.

The heavy metal blasting through the house assaulted every one of my senses. That and the smell of weed filling the place. Winter had come through with this address after digging through all of Brant's known associates and visiting them one by one. Hyde and I had tagged along to two other places so far today, and I was really fucking hoping this would be our last stop. I was always down for some fun, but this fucking weather did my head in. I wanted to deal with Brant, get Ivy out of this shithole town if she was with him, and get back to the woman who had settled herself deep in my soul.

We made our way towards the voices we could hear, and when we entered the dining room where a guy and a girl sat smoking pot, I pointed my gun at them and said, "You're having a fucking party and forgot to invite us."

The guy shoved his chair back, stood, and pointed his gun at us. "And who the fuck are you motherfuckers?"

Before he had a chance to pull the trigger, Winter had him in a chokehold. "Put the gun down, asshole. We just wanna chat."

As the asshole attempted to fight Winter off, the girl made a grab for my gun. I saw her coming and reached my hand out to push her back down into her chair. "Stay the fuck down unless you want a bullet through your fucking head," I snarled.

She spat at me. "Fuck you!"

Jesus, I didn't need her shit today. We'd come for one reason today and it didn't concern her. Aiming my gun at the wall behind her, I shot at it, over her shoulder. The intent was to frighten the fuck out of her so she'd sit down and stay quiet. I didn't achieve my goal. The dumb bitch lunged at me instead, so I found myself in a fucking wrestling match with her.

"Fucking hell," I roared as I wrapped my arms around her and barrelled her backwards into the wall. When I had her there, I grabbed her around the neck while pressing my gun to her temple. "You want this?" I demanded. "Because I'm not fucking above killing a woman if she gets in my way."

"Carly!" the guy yelled out. "Stop!"

Her eyes flicked to the guy, and whatever she saw there did the trick. Her body went limp and she stopped fighting me.

I kept my gaze trained on her. "You done?"

Her lips flattened, anger surrounding her, but she nodded and said, "Yes."

Dragging her back to the chair, I shoved her down before turning back to the guy. "Now, can we agree to have a chat or do you need some further encouragement?"

Winter eased the pressure around the asshole's neck when he nodded, but didn't let him go completely.

"You had a visit from a guy called Brant this morning. Presumably, you sold him a gun. And after doing a little digging, we've worked out that you two have done business together before and have spent some time getting shitfaced with your favourite strippers. So what I want from you is every-fucking-thing you know about him and an address for where I will find him today."

He stared at me. "You're joking, right? Like I fucking know where he's gone today."

I stretched my neck to one shoulder and then the other. I also inhaled deeply and then exhaled while I contemplated how best to deal with him. Wasting time wasn't high on my priority list for the day, but the idea of drawing this out had woken my monster, and now I wanted to dedicate some time to getting blood on my hands.

"I never joke," I said, moving closer. Putting my gun away, I flexed my hands before making a fist and jamming it in his face. As he grunted and lifted his eyes back to mine, I said, "You wanna try answering my question again?"

His lip pulled up angrily. "Nah."

"Fuck," Hyde muttered as I took another swing at him.

Adrenaline coursed through me as my body hummed with the dark thrill the sight of blood gave me. I jerked my chin at Winter, indicating he could step away.

"Last opportunity, motherfucker. After that, I'll beat the information out of you, and you'll wish you just started speaking a whole lot sooner."

"Go to fucking hell," he spat.

I grinned, the beast deep inside me screaming to life for this shit. Torture and pain were my beast's vices, and for the next ten minutes, I gave him what he craved. The asshole took blow after blow. He lasted longer than I figured him for. The crazy fucker. He was a skinny bastard with not a lot of meat on his bones, and he didn't look like he'd stand up to much of a fight, but he surprised the fuck out of me.

Ten minutes and a whole lot of blood and broken bones, though, and he was done. Lying in a crumpled heap on the floor, he begged me to stop. "He's probably at his place on Rutherford Street. He was raving on about setting up base there and that he figured his woman would like it there."

Ivy.

Thank fuck she was okay.

That knowledge released some of the tension from my shoulders and neck.

Hyde stepped in and got everything he knew about Brant from him.

I was already focused on what was to come next.

The fucking end of all this bullshit.

We still had the feds to deal with, but once Brant was

taken care of, I would breathe a whole lot fucking easier.

It was almost too easy to get into Brant's place. For a guy who'd pulled off some intricate fucking shit, he sure as shit didn't have his house well secured. It concerned me that this was perhaps a setup, but once we were inside and had spoken to Ivy, I came to the realisation we were simply dealing with someone who'd achieved his goals by sheer fucking luck.

Brant was out when we arrived. We found Ivy watching television, not a hair out of place on her head, completely surprised to see us. And pissed off that we'd forced our way into the place.

"Was it really fucking necessary to break the door down and scare the absolute shit out of me?" she demanded, glaring at me. "You could have just knocked."

"Not if Brant was in here we couldn't."

She frowned. "Huh?"

"He's not a good guy, Ivy. He shot a woman tied to the club and left her for dead. Where is he now?"

Her eyes widened. "Umm, I don't know. He said he had some stuff to take care of."

I glanced at Hyde. "You and I will wait until he gets back. Winter can take her now."

"What? Take me where? You can't just come here and boss me around again," she said, her shoulders pushed back like she was ready for a fight.

"You're not fucking safe here, Ivy."

"I don't—"

I cut her off. "You need to get your shit together and leave with Winter. We don't have time to fucking stand around arguing over this."

Before she could respond to that, the sound of the front door opening and closing filtered through to the lounge room, and Brant called out, "I'm home, Ivy. Where are you?"

I put my finger to her mouth to silence her and jerked my chin at Hyde. He took the few steps to position himself behind the wall near the entry to the lounge. Winter also moved out of sight. When Brant stepped through the entry-way, his eyes came directly to me, darkening with displeasure as they did.

"What the fuck are you doing here?" he asked, glancing between Ivy and me. "If you've come to get her, she's with me now."

I pushed Ivy behind me. "No, asshole, she's with me."

He advanced our way, his face a storm of hatred. "You're a smug fucker, King, but this time you're wrong. This time, Ivy chose me, not you. She finally woke up to the fact you treated her like shit all those years you were together. And she realised I would never treat her that way."

"Until the day she changes her mind," I snarled, "And then you'll just stalk and murder her, you sick fuck." At the surprise on his face, I said, "Yeah, we know who you really are, Brant, and we know your history with women. I haven't had a chance to tell Ivy yet, but once I do, you really think she's gonna choose you?"

Ivy inhaled sharply and stepped from behind me to face Brant. "Is that true?"

His face twisted into an ugly canvas of malice. "They're lying to you, Ivy. He always lies to you."

I grabbed her bicep and tried to pull her back behind me, but she refused to budge. Instead, she took a step toward him. At the same time, he pulled a gun out and aimed it at her.

Motherfucker.

No fucking way was he getting a round off.

I lunged for her as he pulled the trigger.

The gun fired, the sound deafening as I lurched toward Ivy.

A second gunshot rang out, and Hyde bellowed something out I couldn't understand. I was too focused on getting to Ivy that I could barely make out what he was doing, but I did see him charging toward Brant.

I collided with Ivy, covering her body with mine, and we went down.

A moment later, a thud echoed on the floor next to me.

I looked up to find Winter rolling Brant over before Hyde stood over him and shot him. Moving off Ivy, I stood and eyed Brant who lay dead at my feet.

Looking at Hyde and Winter, I said, "We need to get the fuck out of here now.

Hyde nodded. "Yeah, brother. You good?"

"Yeah." The shot Brant fired at Ivy missed both of us, thank fuck.

"King."

I turned to Ivy who stood staring at me in horror. "Was that stuff true about Brant?"

"Yeah." When she didn't say anything to that and just kept staring at me in shock, I reached for her. "You need to pack a bag, and we need to leave. And if you try to fucking argue with me, I'll put you over my shoulder and carry you the fuck out of here."

She blinked and then nodded. "Okay."

Ten minutes later, we were on our way to the premises Winter had found for Storm to operate out of. Romano was out of the picture, Brant was out of the picture, and Ivy was safe. We would finalise some plans with Winter for what he had to do going forward, and then we'd go the fuck home. And once we'd taken care of the feds, life could get back to fucking normal.

21

King

I stood in the doorway and watched Ivy at the kitchen table talking with Brian. I'd brought her to the women's shelter that he ran for us yesterday and she hadn't been happy with that decision. She'd argued with me for a good half hour over it until I'd had enough and told her to pull her head in. I'd left not long after that, hoping like fuck she stayed. It had been a long night of little sleep while my thoughts thrashed about in my head.

I'd come to the decision I couldn't force her to do something she didn't want to do. Fuck knew, I'd forced enough upon her in the years I'd known her. And not all good things. It was up to her what she did now. I would help her in whatever way she asked, but I had to take a step back and let Ivy live her life to her own plan.

Brian glanced my way and stood. "King, we were just wondering what time you'd come by."

I entered the kitchen, my eyes meeting Ivy's. There was still resentment there, but it had eased a little. To Brian, I said, "Can you give us a minute?"

He nodded. "Sure."

After he exited the room, I pulled out the chair next to Ivy and sat. Resting my arm on the table, I turned my body to face her. Taking in the tired lines on her face, I said, "You didn't get much sleep either?"

She shook her head and reached for the mug in front of her. After she took a sip, she said, "I think I managed two, maybe three hours. I was thinking about you all night."

"Me?"

"Yeah. What a prick you can be."

"Because a prick would fucking rescue you from the motherfucker you put your trust in, and find you a bed to sleep in while you get your shit together." Fuck, even when I didn't wanna argue with her, she managed to get under my skin and rile me up to the point where I fucking found myself arguing over stuff I gave zero shits about.

"Fuck you, King."

I scrubbed a hand over my face while I forced myself to take a moment and think about what came out of my mouth next. We could sit here and argue our way to lunchtime or I could lead the conversation in a better direction. Blowing out a harsh breath, I said, "Why did you say no yesterday when I suggested I drop you over to Bethany's?"

She averted her gaze, refusing to look at me while she turned silent.

"Ivy," I pushed. "What's going on?"

Another few moments passed between us in silence before finally she looked back up at me. "I haven't spoken to her in five years. We had a falling out, and she refuses to talk to me now."

"What happened?" I didn't like the woman; I didn't like

that she turned her back on family.

She fiddled with the tablecloth as a tear slid down her face. "She didn't like Tony. We'd argued over him for a long time, and after one of my miscarriages, she told me to choose between them. I chose my husband."

"So she did the same thing to you over him that she did over me?"

"Yes."

I hated that a mother could do that to her child. But as much as I disliked the woman, the fact remained she was Ivy's mother, and I could see Ivy's pain over losing her. "You should call her, tell her what's happened. She might surprise you with her response."

"And she might not." She looked at me through her tears. "I don't know if I could handle that." Her voice cracked, slicing through my heart. This conversation threw me back to the past, to the time in our lives when so much shit was going down and bad decisions were being made. It fucking dredged up old hurts and a fuckload of anger that I still carried with me. I'd tried to let that shit go, but because it was all tied together in my mind with Margreet's death, I'd failed.

I chose not to push her on it yet. Instead, I said, "You heard about Tony?"

"Yes." Her voice held relief. "The lawyers are helping me sort through everything, but there won't be much left over when all is said and done, so I just need to pick myself up and start over."

"Brian can help you with that. He's got contacts everywhere. He'll help you find a job, and you can stay here for as long as you need."

"Does he owe you for something? Is that why he's okay with me staying?"

"No. We manage this place together. I front the cash, he

runs it."

She wiped her tears away while she studied me for a beat. "For an asshole, you do good things sometimes."

"Just trying to help the people who need it. That's all."

She slowly shook her head. "No, that's not all, King. I may have hated you for a long time, and been angrier with you than with anyone else in my entire life, but even I can acknowledge when you do something nice. I've met the two women staying here at the moment. Their lives were unimaginable, worse than mine with Tony, and what you've given them is hope."

My chest squeezed with heaviness. This place may have helped numerous women, but the one woman I should never have turned my back on sat in front of me broken because of my actions. "I should have kept an eye on you after you married Tony."

"No, that wasn't your burden to carry."

"Fuck, Ivy, if I hadn't—"

Her shoulders slumped and she sagged in her chair as she cut me off. "Don't blame yourself for the choices I made in my life once you were no longer part of it. Sure, while we were together we both made some shitty decisions, but after that"—she shrugged—"my choices were all mine. And some days, like today, when I'm honest with myself, I can see I'm a fucked-up mess. Maybe if you stop by tomorrow, I'll be back to thinking you're an asshole and hating you for the part you played in it. But today, I just think you're an asshole who tries to help people and sometimes gets it right."

As I listened to her, a rolling movie of memories filled my head. All the years we'd spent loving each other and fucking each other up. We'd never had a chance. Not with the shit we'd each been through before we even met.

When a puzzle was missing pieces, it would never be complete. It would always be lacking. Ivy and I never had a shot at making that damn puzzle come together because we were missing pieces all over the place and the pieces we did have didn't slot together in the right ways.

Sometimes two people just weren't meant to be together.

Sometimes there was more hate than love, more war than peace.

Sometimes love wasn't enough.

I stood. "You've got my number. Use it if you need something."

There was one more thing I could do to help her, and as much as doing it would put me back in front of someone I wanted to forget, I would do it. Because even though Ivy and I would never be together again, I would never stop wanting the best for her.

"You shouldn't have come here, King," Bethany said to me through her screen door an hour later.

I'd left Ivy and taken my sweet fucking time coming here. It was unlike me to hesitate to do the shit I needed to do, but just thinking about this woman threw up all kinds of red flags.

I squared my shoulders. "We need to talk about Ivy."

"What about her?"

"Fuck, Bethany, what the fuck do you mean, *what about her*? You say that like you don't even fucking care about her—"

Her lips pursed. "I'm not interested in standing here listening to you swear. If you have something to say, say it, but do not use that language with me."

If her appearance was anything to go by, the years hadn't been kind. She stood hunched over, her frail hand gripping the door to steady her. Lines wrinkled her face, grey hair sat in a mess of a bun on her head, and breaths wheezed out of her. Mostly, though, she looked defeated by life. And the way her face pinched, she appeared to be full of resentment and bitterness.

"Open the door and let me in," I demanded. "Your daughter needs you, so you need to hear me out."

She debated about allowing me in for another good minute before finally unlocking the door and swinging it open.

I entered the house and walked into the kitchen, doing my best to ignore the onslaught of memories. Fuck, they were like a hundred motherfuckers coming at me all at once. Fucking stabbing me all over.

"Tony Romano is dead," I said, facing her.

I would have expected a reaction to that statement, but all she gave me was an arch of her eyebrows.

Fucking stunned, I said, "That's all you have to say when I tell you your daughter's husband is dead? You're a fucking piece of work, Bethany."

"Watch your mouth," she snapped.

"You care more about a fuck coming out of my mouth than the fact your daughter is alone in this world?" This woman made my fucking blood boil, and I regretted coming here. Ivy was better off without her.

"I care more about being subjected to your presence than the words out of your mouth. As for Ivy, she made her bed years ago. In fact, she made it the first time with you, and I should have known she was incapable of making better decisions, but I fell under her spell again for a while there."

"You fell under her spell? What the hell does that mean? She's your *child* for fuck's sake. What kind of parent talks about their children like that?" *Fucking hell.*

Her displeasure plastered itself over her face, but I ignored it. I didn't give a flying fuck if I upset her. "She's not my blood. I tried to help her, and look what I got in return—nothing but heartache."

My breaths came harder. Heavier. They carried my fury as I let loose on her. "There's a reason you weren't blessed with children of your own. Heartache is part of love, and when you choose to bring a child into your life, you choose all the things that go with love. You can't fucking have love without pain. As a parent, it's your job to teach your child how to deal with both so that they can go out into the world and stand on their own two feet and weather the fucking storm of love. If you weren't ready for that job or to accept that sometimes those you love will tear pieces of your heart out, you should never have taken Ivy in. Because the very word mother means unconditional fucking love. It means protection. It means safety. And while you knew how to make cookies and decorate a house so it looked like you were a mother, you never had a fucking clue how to give any of those things."

My tirade angered her to the point where she finally gave me the kind of emotional response I felt this conversation deserved, but it wasn't the response I'd hoped for. Pointing at the front door, she snarled, "You've said what you came for and now you can leave. And don't ever come back here. You are never welcome here again."

I had no intention of ever coming back here. I wasn't sure why I thought this had been a good idea to begin with.

Anger and disappointment punched through me as I stalked out to my bike. Thank fuck I hadn't told Ivy I was coming here. Bethany's rejection would have killed her.

Thoughts of Bethany filled my mind for the rest of the day. As much as I tried, I couldn't get her out of there. A headache settled in at lunchtime and intensified to the point where I wanted to rip my fucking head off by 6:00 p.m. I called Lily to let her know I wouldn't be over tonight. Fuck knew I was in a mood, and she didn't need to be subjected to it.

"Hey you," she answered with a smile I could hear all the way over here. "I've just put dinner in the oven, and the best news of the day is that Linc took the kids, so we have the place to ourselves."

Fuck.

"I can't make it tonight." I was a fucking bastard, but the choice was made for her, and as far as I was concerned, it was the right one.

She went silent for a beat. "What's wrong, King? You sound off."

I rubbed my temple. "It's been a shit of a fucking day, and trust me, you do not need me there tonight."

Silence again, and then softly—"Okay so while I get that, here's something for you to consider. Maybe when you have a shit of a fucking day, coming to see me is exactly what *you* need. That's what relationships are about, right? Sometimes you give, sometimes you take. Let me give tonight. And if all you want is to sit in front of the TV in silence, I'm good with that. We can just *be* tonight. We don't have to *do*."

Somehow I knew that when Lily made an offer or promise like this, she meant it and would make good on her word. I also knew this was her telling me she wanted to be the one to help me. And while I had never been big on people helping me, because mostly they just fucking let me down, I also knew I'd finally found someone I wanted to allow in to help. Lily wouldn't let me down.

"I'm leaving now," I said gruffly. "You got beer?"

"Yes," she said around another smile I figured they could fucking see from Mars, "I have beer."

22

Lily

Monday night, I sat outside on my back patio, grabbing as many quiet moments to myself as I could while my kids and mother fussed over Brynn inside. I leaned back in my seat and stared up at the dark sky while trying not to think about the fact I wasn't smoking. I'd given it up again this morning. I was sure I was already nearly dead from that. Everyone told me smoking would kill me; I figured *not* smoking might be more dangerous to my health. My mental health at least.

I shifted my thoughts to King and the weekend we'd just had together. He'd shown up Friday night all screwed up by something that had happened that day. I hadn't asked him what. He hadn't offered. I'd learnt that King didn't like to discuss shit, and I was okay with that. I mean, I wanted to know everything about him, but I refused to try to change him to be someone he wasn't. King had a lot of baggage, but he didn't want or need someone to carry it for him. He just needed someone to take the trip with him, and I liked the views his journey offered, so I was all on board.

He'd worked my body so hard that night that there hadn't been any more sex for us on the weekend. I'd taken care of him, but he hadn't tried to fuck me again, and I hadn't asked for it. Jesus, the man was brutal in bed, but I couldn't get enough of him. King put a smile on my face simply by breathing. All it took was a thought of him, and I was smiling like a loon.

Adelaide had asked me on Friday why I wasn't fearful of getting involved with a man like King, a man who ran an MC. I'd told her she didn't know his heart, which meant she didn't know anything. When I met King, I saw two things—that he had the kind of looks I was attracted to, and that he was a bit of an asshole. Then I saw how he cared for and looked after his sister. Then I saw a moody bastard who liked to boss people around, but who also helped people when they needed it. Through all of that, I saw a man trying to handle his business and look after those he cared for. I didn't see the biker or club president with a dark streak that Adelaide would have run a mile from. By the time I saw King's club and all that entailed, I'd already fallen for his heart. And for me, everything in life was about the heart.

I had been worried when he'd told me the kids and I may have been in danger. I'd definitely spent some time running through scenarios in my mind of what he could possibly have been referring to. I had also thought long and hard about what this meant for my life going forward. In the end, I'd decided to put my faith in him and his men to protect us. At the core of the matter was my heart. I couldn't change who it led me to. And King had mine. Now he had my complete trust, too.

"Lily."

I turned my face to find King walking towards me. Standing, I met him halfway and looped my hands around his neck. That was after I took the time to run my gaze over his body, appreciating the way his muscles filled out his clothes. My belly fluttered as I thought about those muscles. His powerful thighs straddling me, his strong arms holding me, his firm ass that I couldn't get enough of.

After I caught his lips in a kiss, I said, "I was just thinking about you."

He snaked his hands around my waist and settled them on my butt. "Your mother told me you've been sitting out here for a while now. You good?"

I liked how he always had a way of taking in the stuff I said to him without feeling the need to comment on it or engage in conversation about it. Because honestly, sometimes I rambled. King let me do that without complaint.

"I'm good. I'm taking advantage of the kids being occupied by Brynn and Mum." I leaned in close and inhaled his scent. "Oh God, you smell so good." At his frown, I said, "I quit smoking again today. I can smell the cigarettes on you, so you should expect me to be smelling you a lot going forward."

His lips twitched and he brought his mouth back to mine. He then kissed me so thoroughly and for so long that I got lost in it and missed him as soon as he pulled away. "Maybe I'll smoke more and kiss you more, just so you can get the taste," he rumbled.

I tightened my hold on his neck as I cocked my head to the side. "Is that you being playful?"

His eyes flashed with heat. "That's me figuring how to get my hands and mouth on you as often as I fucking can."

I let go of his neck and slowly dragged my hands over his shoulder and down his chest and stomach. Stopping when I reached his jeans, I said, "Baby, you don't have to engineer ways to do that. I'm down with you getting those hands and that mouth on me whenever and however you can."

He seemed to like that, because the heat in his eyes flashed in ways that wouldn't leave anyone confused as to what he wanted. We were interrupted by my mother, though, so the moment was broken.

"Lily, I really hate to barge in on you two, because, well, we all know that King is doing wonders for your dry spell, and I never want to do anything to stop that, but we really need to think about dinner. Brynn suggested we could order pizza. I think she's desperate for some junk after all that hospital food, but I'm not sure I can stomach it. I was thinking more along the lines of Thai if we're going to order, but that requires someone to go out and pick it up, and I wasn't sure if you would want to do that, and I certainly can't drive at the moment." She eyed me with expectation, wanting me to say yes.

"Mum, you really need to let my dry spell go. I mean, I didn't see the need to talk about it in the first place, because women are allowed to take time off sex, you know? But—"

"Oh, Lily, why do you always say that? And what woman in her right mind would want time off sex? I mean, *really*."

King positioned me in front of him with his arm around my chest, and I didn't miss the way his body shook gently with laughter.

"Maybe a woman who's taking some time to be with herself for a while," I threw out, exasperated with her.

Her forehead wrinkled as she thought about that for a moment. The idea seemed foreign to her, and in the end, she simply ignored it and carried on. "So about dinner. What do you want to do?"

"You order it. I'll go out and pick it up," King said.

Mum met his gaze and smiled. "Thank you." She then glanced at me again, still seemingly trying to wrap her mind around what I'd said. With a quick shake of her head, she turned and left us alone again.

King let me go, and I faced him, smacking him lightly on the chest. At the questioning arch of his brow, I said, "That was for laughing at me and my dry spell."

His mouth spread out in a smile. "I was laughing at your mother, not at you. She comes out with some fucking funny shit." He shrugged. "And if it's about you, I like it even more."

My mouth almost dropped open. I had never seen him like this. And I really freaking liked it. "You just like the fact I was almost a virgin again by the time you got to me."

And just like that, his sense of humour vanished and his heat returned. Yanking me to him, his mouth brushed my ear as he growled, "As far as I'm fucking concerned, you *were* a virgin when I got to you because you had never been fucked properly."

I put my hands on his chest as his possessiveness rolled through me. It hit me in all the right places and had me desperate for him. God, but now was definitely not the time for that. Pushing against him, I stepped out of his hold. "You need to stop talking, and I need to go inside and get Brynn's room set up for her."

"You need a hand with that?"

I held my hand up at him and shook my head. "God no. I need you as far away from me as possible right now, otherwise, I might start climbing you."

"Fuck," he muttered.

"Yes, exactly," I agreed. "You get to go sort dinner out with my mother."

With that, I quickly headed inside to Zara's bedroom where I was setting my sister up. I'd brought her home from the hospital this afternoon, telling her she would be staying with me until she'd recovered fully. She'd told me that King had rubbed off on me, because I was far too bossy for my own good now. I'd told her to shut up and just do what I said, to which she'd just looked at me and said, "Case in point."

The doorbell sounded, so I made a detour to answer it.

"Hi," I said to the dark-haired guy standing on the other side holding a bunch of flowers. I'd be lying if I said I didn't take a little peek at his body. Dude was built. And had the face of a god.

He smiled, and I knew by the way it was almost a smirk that he'd seen me checking him out. But full points to him for not getting all cocky about it. "I'm looking for Brynn."

"And you are?" As the words came out, though, it hit me. "Oh God, you're the fishing dude, aren't you?"

His smile turned into a grin. "I like the reference to me being the fishing dude rather than the other kind of dude. Classy. You must be Lily."

I reached for his arm and pulled him inside. Turning my face towards the lounge room where Brynn was, I called out, "Brynn! Fishing dude is here!"

He leant in close and said, "Fishing dude's name is Jamie."

I returned his grin. "Oh, I like you! You should stay for dinner. We're having Thai."

"I love Thai."

I dragged him into the lounge room and didn't miss the way Brynn's eyes lit up when she laid eyes on him. My sister liked more than just fishing with this guy.

Taking the flowers from him, I said, "I'll find a vase for these while you two catch up."

Jamie's eyes didn't leave Brynn. "We've been catching up for days over the phone."

The way he said that, and the way he watched her told me that he also liked more than just fishing.

"Okay kids, it's time to leave Auntie Brynn in peace." When they grumbled about that, I said, "Anyone still in here in one minute will be on dishes duty all weekend." With that, they all scrambled out of the room faster than I'd seen them move in weeks.

Brynn met my gaze with a smile and mouthed, "I love you."

I could be a good sister sometimes.

———

Jamie stayed for dinner. He also convinced Mum and Zara to play a game of Scrabble with him and Brynn. King and Holly ended up in front of the television watching some sport while she grilled him some more about bikes. Robbie helped me with the dishes while my heart did a little dance over all the happiness in my house.

"Dad said he'd take me to karate on Saturday if you're busy," Robbie said as he wiped the last plate clean.

"Do you want him to take you, baby? I'm good either way." I held my breath a little. This was the first conversation he'd initiated all week, and I hoped he'd spend some time opening up to me.

He shrugged. "I don't know. I just thought you might be busy with King."

I stopped wiping the counter so I could give him my full attention. "Does it feel like I'm busy with King all the time lately?"

He met my gaze, and I saw the hesitation in his eyes. "Maybe."

"I'm sorry if it feels that way, but I want you to know that I am never too busy for you. I have Saturday blocked off for karate and ice cream. I really want to take you, but it's up to you, and I promise I won't get upset if you want Dad to take you."

"If you take me, will King go, too?"

"I haven't asked him to go. I figured it would just be you and me."

"Okay. I want you to take me, unless we spend the weekend at Dad's."

Shit.

Now I was confused about his feelings over King.

"Robbie, do you like King?"

He nodded. "Yes."

"No, really, you can be honest with me. If he's done something to upset you, I want to know so we can fix it."

"I like him."

"But you don't want him to go to karate with us?"

He glanced down for a moment before giving me back his eyes. "I think Dad would be upset if he went there with us. But he can hang out here with us. I asked him about hiring *Thor* to watch again, and he said if it was okay with you, he'd hire it again for us."

Well fuck. My kid just broke my heart with his thoughtfulness and King patched it back up with his.

I nodded. "Okay, I understand what you're saying, and I think you're so thoughtful to consider your father's feelings. And I am 100 percent on board with you guys watching *Thor* again."

He grinned. "You're gonna have a bath again while we watch it, aren't you?"

I laughed. "You know me too well."

"Mum!" Zara yelled out. "We need you!"

Robbie and I exchanged looks. "When does Zara ever need me?" I whispered.

He gave me a look that said he wondered the same thing, and then we headed out of the kitchen to look for her.

We found her in the lounge room with everyone. King sat on the end of the couch with Holly next to him and Mum next to her. His arm lay extended across the top of the lounge, and his long legs were stretched out in front of him, crossed at the ankles. I wasn't sure I'd ever seen him so relaxed. Brynn and Jamie sat on the other couch, while Zara knelt in front of the coffee table. A cake sat on the coffee table. And not just any cake. It was my very favourite six-layer chocolate cake with toasted marshmallow filling and chocolate frosting.

I looked at Mum to find her watching me with love, and it almost made me burst into tears. I held my shit together, though, and asked, "You organised this? And why? It's not my birthday."

She smiled, but it was Brynn who answered. "I asked her to organise it as a thank you for everything you've done for me. It means the world to have you for a sister."

"Oh God, now I really am gonna cry," I muttered.

"I organised it," Mum piped up, "and King picked it up for me while he was out getting dinner."

My gaze went straight to him, and I found him watching me with that intense look of his I loved. While we shared a moment, the kids scrambled up off the couch and the floor, and Mum cut the cake. When the space next to King became free, I curled up next to him, wrapped an arm around him, and said, "Thank you."

He looked down at me, still with the intensity that told me he was going to fuck me just the way I liked it tonight. "I didn't do anything. This was all your mum and sister."

I smiled. "I know, but I'm still thankful you picked it up." I dropped my voice. "Maybe I'll save some of it for you to lick off me later."

His hand moved to my neck, and he swept my hair out of the way so he could run his fingers along my collarbone.

"That dirty mouth of yours will get you in trouble one day," he murmured softly enough so that only I heard.

I snuggled in closer to him. "I hope so."

He threaded his finger under my necklace that I'd finally located. "You found your grandmother's necklace."

"Yeah."

"Good." With that one word, he'd given me a taste of his soft again, and butterflies filled my tummy. I would never have enough of his kind of soft.

"Do you want me to cut you some cake, Lily?" Mum asked.

I nodded and sat up straight, still pressed against King's side, with one leg folded so it rested on his thigh. "Yes, please."

Brynn caught my eye as she, Jamie, and the kids traipsed back out to the dining room to play more scrabble. "I love you," she said.

"I love you, too, Brynny. You and me are gonna have a big long D&M before bed tonight, okay?"

She grinned, knowing exactly what I was referring to. "Yup, but I got shit to get back to now if you catch my drift."

"Oh, I catch your drift, fishing girl," I said with a laugh.

The doctors had told her she was making good progress with her recovery, and while I knew she was in pain and still had a long way to go, my sister was tough. She'd speed through her recovery and be back out there fishing in no time.

King's phone rang, and he leaned forward a little to grab it from his pocket. As he did that, he settled his other arm over my shoulders, slipping his hand under the material of my shirt so he could rest it skin-to-skin just above my breast.

"What's up?" he answered the phone.

Mum brought cake over for King and me. I noticed how

she didn't ask if he wanted any; she just assumed he would. She placed his on the coffee table and handed me mine.

"Thanks," I said softly so King could still hear the person on the other end of the call.

He'd listened silently for a few moments, and I'd just taken my first amazing bite of cake when he said, "Ivy, stop. You're working yourself into a state when you don't need to be. Ask—"

Ivy.

The woman I'd met in King's office.

An ex of his.

I wasn't usually a jealous woman, and I trusted King completely, but I couldn't deny a streak of jealousy shot through me when he said her name. She must have cut him off, because he'd been about to say something before stopping abruptly.

"No," he said.

His tone had turned a little harsh, and I decided I didn't want to hear any more of the conversation, so I attempted to stand. However, King had other ideas. He quickly moved his hand to grip my shoulder and held me tightly to him.

I turned my face to his and found him watching me closely. He gave one quick shake of his head, signalling that he didn't want me to leave.

"I'll call you tomorrow. Brian will be able to help you with this, so stop fucking worrying about nothing." With that, he ended the call in the way only King did—abruptly with no goodbye.

I shifted to sit cross-legged sideways on the couch, looking at him. I was going to broach the subject of Ivy, because if I didn't, it might just send me crazy. And too bad if he didn't want to discuss this; I needed to. "I know you told me Ivy is in the past, but I kinda need to know how far in the past. Like, is she recent and you guys are still—"

He cut me off. "I've had three relationships that mean something to me. Ivy was the first. I hadn't seen her for over a decade until recently, and now I'm helping her get back on her feet after her husband died. That's all there is to this."

"And the other two?"

"Jen was my second one. She isn't alive anymore." His eyes searched mine for a long, silent moment. "You are my third."

My heart beat a little faster and a little louder. I smiled at him and threaded my fingers through his. "You are my second."

I decided I liked King's way of discussing stuff—straight to the point with no bullshit and no dragging it out. He simply shared what he felt was important and then moved on. And he didn't ask for anything more than the same from me.

I squeezed his hand before letting it go.

I then reached for our cake and passed his to him.

We then ate in silence except for when I put my fork down halfway through my piece and said, "I'm leaving the rest for you for later," to which he muttered, "Fucking hell."

It was the best night I'd had in a long time, and my heart swelled with happiness at the thought of so many more to come.

23

King

I sat listening to what Axe was telling me, trying not to lose my shit. It had been a hell of a morning already, and now it was shaping up to be the day I'd have to take care of something I'd been putting off for too long. It seemed the feds were closing in on the club, and because of the level of secrecy surrounding their latest witness, we would have no way of silencing them. Detective Stark was proving a worthy adversary, but she was one I didn't want.

Stretching my neck, I tried to shake the tension there. Knowing we had a lot of business to take care of today, I'd woken with it. Lily had bossed me into allowing her hands on my back and neck, and while the massage had eased some of that tension, it had stirred a fuckload of other tension I'd needed to take care of.

I looked at Axe. "So confirm for me so I know I've got a handle on what you're saying. Stark has a witness that they're locking down tight. Johnny can't get at the information to find out who it is. But whoever it is will likely jam more than their dick up our ass."

"That about covers it."

I clenched my jaw as the decision I had to make worked its way through my head. "I'll take care of this today."

Axe's expression turned thoughtful. "They'll keep coming at you even if you eliminate her."

"Let them. I'll just keep coming right back. I refuse to allow them to take the club down."

"Fuck, King, do you ever think life would be a whole lot fucking easier if you turned clean instead? I don't know how you live like this, always chasing your fucking tail, putting out fires and waiting for the next one to hit."

This was an argument we'd had for years. I had no fucking clue why he kept bringing it up. This would never change for me, and he had to know that. "Maybe life would be easier, maybe it wouldn't. We'll never fucking know, because I'm not gonna step out there and try it. I'll take my chances getting shit done the only way I've ever known— kicking and fucking screaming. And at the end of the fucking day, when I lay my head down, I'll breathe easy knowing it doesn't matter what fires I have to put out tomorrow, because my club will be right there by my side putting out the same damn fire. I will never do life without my brothers."

He leant forward. "You could still do it cleaner than you are."

"No, we couldn't. This is what we know, Axe. And the world sure as fuck isn't interested in helping me today any more than it was interested in helping me when I was a kid. I won't put my life in anyone's hands but my own."

Hyde stepped into the office and glanced between us. "Hate to interrupt, but we've got a problem."

"What?" I asked.

"I still haven't confirmed what the fuck's going on, but it seems Black Deeds wanna pick a fight with us. They just undercut us on a cleaning job."

I shoved my chair back, anger forcing hard, furious breaths from me. "You and me are gonna pay Zero a visit right fucking now. And if we need to make a fucking statement to get this shit sorted, that's exactly what we'll fucking do."

Hyde nodded. "Agreed, brother."

The Black Deeds president and I had a long, hard history that I was more than ready to end if he was intent on pursuing this agenda. I hadn't forced myself and my club on Sydney only to shit myself at the first sign of trouble. Storm's reign would be enforced with this visit to Zero.

The Black Deed's clubhouse was tiny compared to Storm's, but that didn't mean it didn't house a formidable club. Zero was known for his ruthlessness, and while at times we'd been at war with each other, I gave him credit for the way he held his club together.

Hyde and I took Devil, Kick, Nitro, and Mace with us. We met some resistance at their front gate, but Zero approved our entry, and five minutes later, we stood in front of him, his VP, and a handful of his men.

He glanced between us, narrowing his eyes at me. "It's been a while since you've turned up looking like you're planning a fucking war, King. What gives?"

My muscles tensed. Every single last fucking one of them. I did another quick sweep of the weapons I could see, and made some rough calculations of each man's likely move if I shot their president. Meeting his gaze, I said, "That's because you've handled your shit, we've handled ours, and I had some fucking peace. Today, you shat all over that peace, and I'll happily begin a fucking war to get it back."

His face clouded with anger and he took a step forward, getting in my fucking face. Snarling, he demanded, "Care to fucking say that again."

I closed the tiny distance between us, adrenaline spiking in my veins. My hands fisted by my side as I threw back, "You heard it the first time."

"Yeah, I did, but whoever you got your information from doesn't know shit."

"He got his information from me, asshole," Hyde said, "And it's solid. Your club cut us out of a deal by going in at 30% less than our price. That tells me you mean business."

Zero didn't take his eyes off me. Smart motherfucker. "I don't know what the fuck he's talking about. The last fucking thing I need on my plate is to be dealing with the fallout from something like this. So fucking stand down, tell your men to stand down, and let's get to the fucking bottom of this together."

I searched his eyes. I'd always had a good feel for Zero. And he'd never fed me shit. Not once. So I was inclined to believe what he said.

Raising my hand, signalling for my men to pull back, I moved away from Zero. "Hyde, give us all the information you know," I said, eyes still pinned to Zero's. I also kept his men in my peripheral, staying aware of their every move. While we'd worked our way to this point, I trusted no fucker. Tension sat thick in the air, and I had no intention of easing it until I had what I came for.

Hyde rattled off the job details and Zero listened closely before making a call to his VP. They had a heated discussion, and from the way Zero's face twisted with anger, I figured he'd been given the information he was after.

Ending the call, he shoved his phone back into his pocket

and pulled his gun out. I'd seen that coming and had my hand on mine before he even reached for his. Within a matter of seconds, we all stood pointing our weapons at each other, the tension in the room at a whole new fucking level.

"Royce!" Zero barked, gun trained on me. "Get your ass here." To me, he said, "Steady with that gun, King. We don't want to start something here that we can't stop."

I ground my teeth together, gripping my gun harder. "In case you missed it, I'm good with starting something we can't stop. Hell, with the way I'm feeling today, I'm fucking itching to start something."

"Fuck," Zero muttered, "You're a fucking madman."

I grinned, that wave of crazy I fucking loved taking over. "That I am, my friend. That I fucking am."

He scowled. "We're not fucking friends."

"We could be if you'd stop trying to tickle my fucking balls."

"Jesus, the shit you come out with. If I was after you, I'd be doing a whole lot fucking more than tickling them."

"Yeah, I've figured that by now. You'd be clamping your fucking teeth down on them. So give me whoever the fuck did this shit and let me deal with them."

"You're not dealing with anything. I'll take care of this." He paused for a beat before barking out again, "Where the fuck is Royce?"

No one had the chance to answer him, because a gun sounded from behind him. I ducked just in time to miss the bullets coming straight at me. Hyde went into action, lunging at the asshole who'd fired it. One of Zero's men joined in, and soon we had a fucking shit-show of a brawl on our hands.

"Fucking hell," Zero bellowed, wading into the fight and reefing the guy who'd shot at me out of the fight.

When he had him, he restrained him by gripping both his

wrists together and locking an arm around his neck. Almost choking the breath out of him, he roared, "What the fuck have you done?"

The guy, who I presumed to be Royce, struggled in his president's hold, rage pouring from him. When Zero eased the pressure on his neck a little, he spat out, "This is for what Storm did to Gibson!"

"Fuck. I told you to forget that shit," Zero said.

"Yeah well, he was my cousin. No fucking way was I letting his death just sit like that. We had allegiance to him, and I don't ever forget who my loyalties lie with."

Zero spun him around and punched him, knocking him flat to the ground. Shoving his boot down on him, he roared, "Your fucking loyalty is to this club, brother. You just pissed all over that by pulling this shit."

Yeah, he had. He'd also loaded a gun and aimed it at himself.

I crouched down beside him and pressed my gun to his temple. "Gibson was a piece of shit, so it makes sense to me that you are, too. I don't play well with men like you."

"King, he's mine," Zero said.

I shook my head. "No, he's mine."

I pulled the trigger, and without a second glance, I reared up and pointed my gun between Zero's eyes. "Are we gonna have a problem, Zero?" I demanded, my body buzzing with the need to drive home the fact that Storm had control of this city. When he didn't answer, I pressed the gun firmly to his head. "Answer me! Do you understand that if you step on our fucking toes, we won't hesitate to retaliate? And when we do, we won't care whose blood flows."

He worked his jaw, his shoulders rock hard with anger. Finally, he spat out, "Yeah, I fucking understand."

I watched him for another few moments before taking my gun off him and signalling to my guys that we were done here. As I took a step away from Zero, I said, "Keep your men in check, and we won't have a problem."

He jerked his chin at me. "Fucking remove yourself from my property or else we *will* have a problem."

Axe was right—every day brought a new fire to extinguish. What he didn't grasp was that I lived for this shit. It fed my fucked-up soul. It kept me dancing with the devil rather than becoming the devil. If I didn't have my club to go to battle for, I would go out there and seek the shit out myself. And that was something I swore I would never do.

Sometimes not everything was as it seemed.

Sometimes you discovered something about a person that contradicted what you previously assumed to know, and it slanted shit in another light. And then you had to fucking reassess everything you thought you knew and make a new plan.

As I watched Detective Stark arguing with her husband on her front lawn, I got a feel for the woman and what her life consisted of. She'd presented herself as a ballbuster, and while I didn't doubt she was at work, she was far from that in her own home.

Her husband was abusive, and her fear of him bled from every one of her veins.

"You will never fucking leave me, bitch!" he yelled, gripping her face so hard I could feel her pain. "I will find ways to stop you, and if you continue to battle me, I will take Marie from you, and you will never see her again."

Motherfucker.

She tried to fight him off, furiously slapping him and pushing him, but she was no match for his strength. Finally, he let her go, shoving her to the ground. After spitting on her, he stalked to the Mercedes in the driveway and screeched out of there.

I left my bike and crossed the street. When I reached her, I jerked my chin towards her front door. "We have shit to discuss. Inside." My tone left no room for a discussion on this; we would be talking, and we would be doing it inside.

She picked herself up off the ground and hurried inside. Fear still consumed her. I suspected that had more to do with her husband than me, but I would make use of it.

I followed her and closed the door behind us. She led me into a living room, and I took note of the warmth in her home. Family photos lined walls, and flowers and art filled other spaces. Leaning in close to look at some of the photos, I saw the couple with their daughter in most of them. An outsider who had no idea of what went on in this family would assume they were a happy one.

"What do you want, Mr. King?" she asked, wrapping her arms around herself. "I'm busy and have work to do."

I drew my gaze from the photos to look at her. "How long has your husband been abusing you?"

She flinched. "I'm not about to discuss my—"

I clenched my jaw. "How fucking long?"

She flinched again, and I realised she was shaking. When she answered me, I had to work hard to hear her. "A while."

"I'm taking that to mean this has been going on for as long as you've been together. And from what I know of you after reading the notes I have on your family, that means he's been abusing you for ten fucking years." The motherfucking cunt.

Straightening, she attempted to get herself under control. My anger appeared to trigger her defensiveness. When she spoke again, she was more like the woman I'd met. "It's really none of your business, but no this hasn't been going on for ten years. He wasn't like this in the beginning. He went through some personal stuff five years ago, and that's when it started. We're working through it."

I wasn't one to judge. My anger was directed squarely at her husband, but it frustrated me that a smart woman like her couldn't hear the shit coming out of her mouth. "Isabel, I would imagine if you took a long hard look at the beginning of your relationship, you would find signs of this side of him." I glanced down at a photo of their daughter. This was where my frustration with women like Isabel came into play. Children needed to be protected at all costs. "Does he hit your child?"

When I looked back up at her, I didn't need to hear her answer; I already knew it. "Fucking hell," I muttered.

"I'm leaving him," she blurted out.

"Are you?" I demanded. "Do you have a fucking plan in place or are you just fucking thinking about it until the next time he hits you?" When she started crying, I raked my fingers through my hair and muttered, "Fuck."

She dropped down onto the couch and buried her face in her hands, sobbing. "He has power I don't have. You don't understand. He will find me wherever I go."

She was right; he did have power. The asshole had an international business spread across three continents. He wouldn't struggle to find her if she ran.

"You want him out of your life?"

Her head snapped up, and she looked at me, wide-eyed. She knew what I was asking. And with only one moment of hesitation, she silently gave me her answer with a quick nod.

I left without another word spoken between us. I'd gone there to take care of business for Storm. Instead, I hadn't fucking taken care of business; I'd taken on another job. But the life it would save was more than worth the sacrifice. Isabel Stark's daughter needed a mother more than I needed her dead. I would find another way to take care of club business.

As I left her house, Ivy called. "King, I really need your help. Brian's not here, and I have to go see a guy who just called me about a possible job. Are you able to come pick me up and take me? Please?"

I would have preferred not to get involved in this. I wanted to help her get back on her feet, but I didn't want to encourage her to rely on me all the time. "There's a bus stop down the road, Ivy. Catch the bus. I'm in the middle of shit."

Silence, and then—"Yeah, I know, but I was hoping we could go over some stuff together afterwards."

"What kind of stuff?"

"Just some plans I have that I'd really like your opinion on."

Fuck. "Okay, I'm on my way, but I don't have all fucking day for this."

"God, no need to bite my head off. I'm just feeling a bit lost here, and you know me better than anyone, so I kinda feel like you're the best person to ask."

"I'll be there."

I shoved the phone into my pocket and exhaled sharply. I'd do this for her today, but if she kept calling, I'd have to put a stop to it. She needed to move on with her life. Without calling on me all the time.

24

Lily

"Jamie's coming over tonight. I hope that's okay, Lil," Brynn said to me late Friday afternoon while we sat on my couch inhaling wine. Well, I was inhaling wine, because it had been a long day in the pits of hell dealing with shitty patients and an even shittier boss. Jackson really needed to take that holiday he'd been putting off. Brynn was on Coke because of her medication, but I was pretty sure she wished it was wine.

I frowned at her. "Why wouldn't it be okay? I love him."

"I already feel like I'm in your way. I don't want to subject you to him any more than you can handle."

I chugged some more wine. "Look, it's been a long day, and I'm tired, and so I'm just gonna say this however the fuck it comes out of my mouth. You're my sister. I love you a lot more than I even know what to do with. I would do anything for you. And like I said, I love him." I raised my glass at her as I added, "Oh, and you got me my favourite cake. No one ever buys me cake. Keep that shit up. You can do whatever the fuck you want if you buy me cake."

She laughed. "I'm pretty sure you've been spending too much time with King lately. Look at all those fucks falling out of your mouth."

I grinned. I *had* been spending a lot of time with my man. He'd had dinner here and stayed over every night for the last week, and he was coming over again tonight. "Do you like him, Brynny?"

Her face softened. "It doesn't matter if I like him. It only matters if you do."

"Yeah, I know, but you've always been a good judge of people, so I'm interested to know what you think."

"I like him. Like, I *really* like him for you. He has this way of taking charge when you need that, and then at other times, he just sits back and lets you run around like a chook without a head. You're an independent woman with a crazy streak, and King seems able to handle that while at the same time, giving it to you straight when he has a different opinion on something. And let me just say, I *really* like the way he handles Mum. I've never seen a man get her to do what he wants the way King does."

It made me happy that she liked him. I agreed with her that it only mattered if I liked him, but it meant the world to me that she also did.

"Oh, I meant to tell you I saw John Travolta again today, but it wasn't at the hospital this time. He was in the same freaking aisle as me in the supermarket, buying the same freaking cheese as me. And I swear to you he really does look like Travolta." When I'd told Brynn about this guy the first time, she'd asked me if I was hallucinating and imagining that he looked like John Travolta, because in her mind there was only one man alive as hot as him. My sister had a Travolta crush that had lasted decades, and we'd watched *Grease* together at least thirty times.

"Did you speak to him?"

I took a swig of wine and nodded. "Yes, and then we had a conversation about cheese and wine, and it was like he didn't wanna stop talking. I had to be kinda rude to him to get away from him. He's good-looking, but way creepy."

"Ugh. So nowhere near the real thing."

"Definitely not."

Mum interrupted our conversation. "Lily, why must you insist on mixing colours with whites when you do your washing?" she asked, wandering into the room holding a pair of pants of hers that used to be white. She looked stricken that they were now pink. I had to hold my laughter in, and when she saw that, her lips flattened. "This isn't funny! I was going to wear these on my date tonight."

"You have a date tonight, Ma?" Brynn asked.

"Yes, with a gentleman I met at the library today."

"No one needs to be wearing white pants on a date, Mum," I said. Shifting off the couch, I grabbed her by the arm and led her into my bedroom as I said, "I have the perfect outfit you can borrow."

"Oh, Lily, I really don't think—" Her mouth clamped shut as she eyed the dress I held up. Her face brightened, and she took the dress off me. "Well, maybe this will do."

I grabbed a pair of shoes out for her, too. "It will more than do. I guarantee that if you wear this dress and these shoes, and you let me fix your hair, this man will be doing everything he can to get in your pants."

That was my mother's language, and she practically ripped the shoes from my hands. "I need to be ready in an hour and a half. I'll call out when I'm ready for you to do my hair." With that, she exited my room faster than I'd seen her move in a long time. She must have really liked this dude.

"And I didn't mix the colours and whites," I called out. "It was one of the kids." God, I was a grown woman who still needed her mother to know when she hadn't screwed something up. That was some crazy shit right there.

"Mum," Zara said from the doorway as I closed my wardrobe. The way her voice wavered caused me to turn to her without delay, and what I saw on her face broke my heart. The minute our eyes met, tears fell down her cheeks and she rushed towards me. "Sam broke up with me."

My arms circled her, and I pulled her tightly against me. "Oh, baby, I'm sorry."

We stayed like that for a long time as she cried her heart out. Sam had been her first real boyfriend, and I remembered how I'd been crushed when my first boyfriend broke up with me. While I may have been secretly cheering on the inside that she wasn't with the little shit anymore, I hated that she was hurting.

I moved us to the bed and pulled her into my arms while we sat against the headboard. Smoothing her hair, I said, "Do you wanna talk about what happened? I'm easy either way, but if you need to talk, I'm here."

She looked up at me, tears still filling her eyes. "He's with Carmen Breen now. And I'm pretty sure they were doing stuff behind my back." With that, another wave of tears overtook her. *Little fucking shit. I should have let King have a word with him.*

I squeezed my arms hard around her, as if by holding her so freaking tightly, I could keep all the bad stuff away from her. My instinct to protect her had never been so strong. *Maybe I could lock her in this house for the next ten years.*

She and I still hadn't gotten around to having a conversation I was satisfied with over whether she and Sam'd had sex, but thankfully she'd gotten her period so I knew she wasn't pregnant at least. But as many times as I'd asked her about sex, she'd brushed me off and told me no. I suspected she was lying, and I debated whether to broach the subject now when she wiggled out of my embrace, looked at me, and said, "I did have sex with him."

Oh God.

My tummy practically cramped up with stress.

I really will lock her in this house for ten straight years.

Maybe twenty.

Reaching for my hand, she said, "Mum, it's okay, we used a condom. And we only did it once. And that was only this week."

My heart beat furiously against my chest.

She was far too young for this.

Far too young.

Where did I go wrong?

I failed as a parent.

Failed with a capital F.

"Mum."

I blinked and found her staring at me. "Zara," I started, but my voice broke and no more words came.

"You were right about everything."

I blinked again. "About what?"

"That I wasn't ready for sex yet. And that Sam's a shit. He's been trying to get me to have sex for ages, and then he told me there was no point in us dating if I wasn't going to do it with him. So I did it, and then when I told him I didn't want to do it again just yet, he broke up with me. So yeah, you were right, and I wish I'd listened to you."

"That little fucking shit. I'll fucking go and tell him what I think of him myself." God, if I could wring his neck, I would. How dare he treat my daughter that way?

She grinned. "I like this new you."

"What new me?"

"This you that just says it like it is."

"I've always said it like it is."

"Not this much. I don't know, you just seem easier about things, not as tense all the time. I mean, you could stop harassing me about studying more and stuff, but mostly you seem happier these days. I like it."

I squeezed her hand before letting it go. "So you aren't in a hurry to have sex again?"

"I don't know. I guess it depends who I date next."

Oh God, please strike all the boys down in her school. Take them all out. Hit them with lightning or some shit.

I took a deep breath. "Promise me something."

She narrowed her eyes at me. "What?"

I reached out and pushed a stray hair off her face. My heart constricted at how beautiful she was. It was no wonder the boys were chasing her. I shuddered to think about the next few years. I would be fighting them off. *No, King will be fighting them off for you. Remember he said he wouldn't allow a daughter out on a date without his eyes on her. You can make him do that in exchange for sexual favours.* "Promise me you'll talk to me about it before you decide to have sex again." When she pulled a face, I said, "I'm serious, Zara. We don't need to discuss the physical stuff unless you want to, but I want you to talk to me about how you're feeling in here"—I placed my hand to her heart—"because that's mine to protect while you're still growing and finding yourself. And I'll be fucked if I'll let any other little shit break it without me knowing to get the bandages out."

Her breaths slowed as she took that in. Finally, she nodded and agreed. "Okay." She then threw her arms around my neck and hugged me for the longest time. By the time she let me go, we were both crying. "I love you, Mum. But man, you swear a lot these days."

I wiped my tears away and shrugged. "You're nearly fifteen, and it's the language you respond to."

She grinned. "So I can start saying it in the house?"

"Let's not get too excited. I don't plan on saying it often. Just when I need to get my point across to you."

"Trust me, Mum, you get your point across just fine."

"Well, I would argue with that, because usually you're arguing with me, not sitting on my bed talking to me."

"Yeah," she said softly, "but I'm always listening to you."

I grabbed her face with both hands and planted a big smooshy kiss on her lips that she wouldn't usually allow anywhere near her. "Maybe you could give me a heads-up every now and then that you're paying attention, because honestly, I'm flailing over here some days thinking you hate me."

She moved off the bed, grinning again. "Nah, I'd rather make you work for it."

I watched her as she walked out of the room until I couldn't see her anymore. I then face-planted into my bed, feeling all kinds of weird emotions. This parenting gig was freaking hard, and I really wasn't convinced I was going to make it through in one piece.

"Lily, you in here? I'm here early to take the kids." I sat up to find Linc standing in the doorway, watching me with a frown. "Are you okay?"

"Yeah, I just had a talk with Zara about boys. I need a cask of wine now." I paused. "Wait, why are you being nice to me?" While he'd been making an effort with the kids, he'd been icy to me ever since I'd told him we weren't getting back together.

"Fuck, I'm not a bastard all the time, Lil."

"Well, you have been lately."

His face clouded with displeasure. "I had good reason. You chose that asshole over me when all I was trying to do was be there for you."

I sighed. Would he ever understand? "Linc, it wasn't a

competition. You and I weren't even on the cards. You made your choice years ago, and I've just been trying to figure out how to live with it since then. I finally have, and King came along at the right time. And while I appreciated all your help, don't do stuff for me if you're just looking for me to do stuff in return. I mean, I believe in give-and-take, but not for the sake of just getting shit out of people. I feel like after all these years, you and I should be there for each other out of respect and for the kids."

He listened to what I had to say, but all he said in reply was, "Okay, well I'm going to round the kids up so we can make it to the movie on time. Are you good with me keeping them for two nights?"

"Yes." I smiled. "I like this new thing we have going."

"What?"

"Where you want to spend lots of time with them. They love it, too."

"Yeah," he said and then left me in peace.

I had no idea if he'd really listened to what I said, but a girl could hope. And pray. Maybe I should take that up.

I reached for my phone and sent King a text. I hadn't sent him any today, and good God they were a good way to get him ready for me. He usually told me to stop sending him shit, but I had a sneaky suspicion he was starting to warm to them.

Me: Whatcha doing?

He took a good few minutes to come back.

King: Club shit

Me: Are you thinking about me?

King: Fuck, Lily I'm busy

Me: Well, for what it's worth, I'm thinking about you. And I'm thinking it would be really freaking good if we played with some toys tonight. You don't know this about me yet, but I have some. And while I know you're a man who has all the goods, I think I have some you might like.

Three minutes passed.

King: Fucking hell woman

Me: You want pictures? Gimme a minute to get some for you.

He rang. "For fuck's sake, I'm dealing with a fuckload of headaches today, and I don't fucking need you to send me any pictures. And I really don't fucking need to be thinking about you when I'm trying to sort this shit out. I'll be over in about two hours, and I suggest you have a bag packed that contains whatever toys you want me to use on you tonight. We clear?"

Oh, man, we were crystal freaking clear.

But I was just like my daughter. I liked making him work for it.

"Just one question—would you prefer—"

"I have no fucking preference on any of this. So long as I have your cunt, I'm a happy fucking man."

"Well, that was all you had to say," I said with the biggest smile on my face. Who knew bossy men who liked filthy words would get me so damn hot?

"We done?"

Also, who knew a grumpy question like that would make me smile? King didn't usually ask anyone if they were done with a conversation.

I had no idea where he was taking me, but I loved a good surprise, so I didn't push him for more on that. "We're done. I'll see you in a couple of hours."

———

He was moody when he arrived to pick me up. But I was horny as hell after our phone call, even two hours on. So he could stalk around the place throwing orders out like a general all he liked; I didn't care. Nothing was ruining my horny buzz.

I'd stopped drinking wine because the responsible side of me decided sitting on the back of a motorcycle drunk wouldn't be the best idea. But Brynn and I had spent a good part of the last two hours talking and laughing over stuff, which meant I wasn't quite ready when he rocked up.

He stood watching me in silence as I ran around my bedroom trying to locate clothes and stuff to pack. "Fuck, Lily, what have you been doing for the past two hours?"

I ignored his cranky tone and continued rifling through my underwear drawer for the exact right pair of panties that I really wanted to take with me. "Very important stuff, I'll have you know." I gave up on finding the underwear in that drawer and rushed out of the bedroom to the laundry where I did locate them. When I raced back to the bedroom, the glint in his eyes had shifted from pissed off to that intense look that got me excited. I slowed and placed my hand on his chest. "Why are you looking at me like that? Tell me what I did, because I need to file that information away for the next time you turn up here all moody and shit."

He reached for the panties in my hand and took them off me. "How many pairs of these do you own?"

"One."

"Buy more. In every fucking colour under the sun."

I smiled and pressed my body against his, looping my hands around his neck. "You haven't told me where you're taking me tonight."

His hand landed on my ass. He gripped it hard. "My place."

That answer caused an explosion of butterflies in my tummy. Threading my fingers through his hair, I said, "I like that idea."

His eyes searched mine, all the moodiness gone from them. "Yeah." He then slapped my ass and said, "Now get this ass moving."

I grabbed my panties from him and finished packing. Ten minutes later, we were on his bike heading towards his place. The level of anticipation I felt at seeing where King lived almost matched the level of need I had for him. Almost. Because nothing in this world matched that.

Traffic was a bitch, and it took us just under an hour to get to his place situated on the edge of the CBD that was, at most, thirty minutes from mine. As he pulled into the narrow lane, I glanced at the old converted warehouses lining it. Totally not what I was expecting. And that had to be one of the things about King I liked the most. I never knew what to expect. He was a constant surprise.

He pulled the bike into a garage that looked like a bike workshop with a wall of tools and parts. He also had some old couches and a bar fridge in here. An image of him kicking back with a beer and the guys filled my mind, and I wondered if he did that. So many things still to discover about this man.

Once we were safely inside, he switched the bike off,

removed his helmet, and turned his face to mine. "Come here," he bossed, his voice full of gravel. It hit me everywhere it should have, and I moved off the bike fast.

I took my helmet off, enjoying the way his eyes ran all over my body. Heat blazed from him, and I decided to give him a show guaranteed to get him hard. I slowly lifted my dress and slid my fingers down into my panties so I could lower them.

Our eyes locked as I kicked my panties to the side and moved closer to him. He held my gaze as I unzipped him and pulled his cock out. Wrapping my hand around it, I said, "You want my mouth on your dick?"

He gripped my neck and pulled me in for a kiss. Demanding and greedy as usual, he left me wanting more. When he ended it, he growled, "I want your fucking cunt around my dick."

I wanted that, too, but first I needed my lips around it. I loved King's cock. Couldn't get enough of it. Or of that piercing he had. My core clenched just thinking about how good it made sex.

Bending, I slid my mouth down over his dick, swirling my tongue around it as I went. I reached for his balls and cupped them at the same time, loving the deep growl of satisfaction that came from him. A girl could die happy knowing she'd made her man happy.

I sucked him with a slow rhythm until his hand curled around my neck and he forced my head up. His eyes burned with desire, and I knew he'd reached breaking point. He wanted inside of me, and he wanted that now.

Moving swiftly off the bike, he positioned himself behind me, bent me over the bike, and yanked my dress up. "Fuck," he growled as he thrust inside me.

I clutched the seat and held on tightly while he worked me hard. The vibrations of the bike had me wet for him, and judging by the way he slammed into me, this wasn't going to take long. I didn't care. This was just a warm-up for the real thing. If I knew King, he wouldn't let me sleep much tonight.

He came first, his fingers digging into my hips. I followed fast with an orgasm that shattered through me so completely that my legs threatened to give way. I wasn't sure I'd be able to stand, and remained bent over the bike after he pulled out.

He placed his hand on my lower back and asked, "You good?"

I shook my head. "No. You just killed me. I'm not sure I can walk."

Before I knew what was happening, he lifted me into his arms and carried me inside. The garage opened into an expansive living area that was bare except for a lone couch sitting on a large rug, overlooking a glass door that stretched the length of the room.

He placed me down on the couch, and I immediately stood, and said, "I need to use the bathroom." Glancing up at the mezzanine level above us, I asked, "Is it up there?"

He nodded. "Yeah."

I headed upstairs, taking in the exposed brick walls, polished concrete floors, and industrial-type fixtures and fittings. King's home was masculine to the nth degree, not only with all those things but also with the dark greys and browns throughout. The only thing that surprised me was the lack of furniture. He had the couch downstairs, and upstairs he had a king-size bed and another rug, but so far, that was all I could see. The bathroom had a handful of toiletries, but not many belongings. It was almost like he didn't actually live here.

I used the bathroom and made my way back downstairs, finding him in the kitchen. This room appeared more lived in, and I wondered if perhaps he was just in the middle of renovating the place, because it was amazing. I took a good look, loving what I saw. The high ceiling and large windows lent space and light to the room and allowed his use of black for the cupboards and black granite for the kitchen counters to work well. The splash of colour coming from the brick walls accented the black beautifully.

Meeting his gaze, I said, "Your home is not at all what I was expecting."

He rested his ass against the counter and crossed his arms. "What were you expecting?"

"Well for one, a lot more furniture. Other than that, I guess I just wasn't expecting a home that looked like an architect or designer had been in recently. I wouldn't have picked you for a guy who would hire either of those. Are you renovating at the moment?"

He considered that question for a beat. He then moved to where I stood and said, "I bought this place eight years ago, but I don't live here. I'd intended to renovate it and have a family here. Those plans got fucked up, and I walked away and just let it sit. I came back about a year ago to finish the work so I could sell the place, but for some fucking reason couldn't bring myself to sell it, and never did finish the renovations."

"It looks pretty good to me. You mustn't have much left to do." It looked better than pretty good; the perfection in what I'd seen showed he clearly valued attention to detail.

He looked out through the doorway to the living area. "There's still a fuckload of shit to do." Settling his eyes back on me, he added, "Figure I might get started on that soon."

The way he said that made me feel he meant something deeper by his words, but I couldn't be sure. "By the looks of what you've done so far, you've put your heart into this place, King. I can't wait to see it when you're finished."

He studied me intently, causing flutters in my tummy. I didn't know why, but there was something in the way he watched me. He didn't say anything further about it, though. Instead, he finally dropped his gaze to my breasts and said, "You see that bed upstairs?"

I smiled and nodded. Was this a trick question?

"Get your ass up there and get naked. I'll be up in a minute."

I didn't wait for any further orders.

I did as he said.

But as I went, I grabbed my bag he'd brought in and left on the couch, because I had toys and I'd be making him use them.

25

King

"Ghost isn't giving us any hell," Nitro said after church early Monday morning. "He's staying with his sister still, and his brother has thrown him some work. I'll keep an eye on him, but from what he's told me so far, he doesn't seem interested in stirring up any hell."

It had been two weeks since Ghost had been released, and I hadn't seen him or heard from him. And that was exactly the way I liked it. I'd had Nitro and Hyde lay down the law with him, making it clear Storm wouldn't hesitate to deal with him if he was even seen looking at the feds.

"Good," I said, turning my attention to Kick. "Where are we at with D'Amato?" The last he'd told me, there was nothing happening there, but my gut told me that if the feds knew about Moses, it was only a matter of time before D'Amato got wind of it, too.

"There's nothing to report. He has a routine that's more

anal than any I've ever seen, and he doesn't seem to deviate from it. Monday through Thursday is work and family. Friday is work and then boxing with his *Pulp Fiction* friend." He stopped talking for a moment, grinned, and then said, "It's the craziest shit, the guy looks like that actor from *Pulp Fiction*. And the weekends are mostly with his family. I got Zane to tap into his phone, and there hasn't been any talk about us or the feds or anything that would lead me to think he knows."

Hyde leaned forward, resting his elbows on the table. "So where the fuck are the feds directing their attention? And how fucking long are they gonna drag their feet on this? I'm tired of sitting around waiting for the shit to hit the fan."

He wasn't the only one. Axe's guy had advised me that regardless of what Detective Stark had told us, the case wasn't as tight as they'd thought. Eliminating Romano had helped with that, but also the information he'd given them had proved not as useful as they thought, because after all our visits around Melbourne and Sydney, no one was willing to talk about Storm to the feds. Also, their new witness looked likely to walk. At this point, I was more concerned about the fallout from D'Amato if they talked to him about Moses to confirm that information. And that all circled my thinking back to Stark and the fact I hadn't dealt with her like I should have.

I looked at Hyde. He was pissed I hadn't handled Stark, and had been very fucking vocal about it. "Getting Stark on our payroll is an option," I said.

"You're fucking kidding me, King. If you'd just done what you went there to do, we wouldn't be sitting around discussing one of your shittiest fucking ideas yet. You're going soft, brother."

"You'd do fucking well to watch what the fuck you say," I snarled. "Removing her from the case would only lead to them replacing her, and the body count would just keep rising."

"It'd send them a fucking message," he snapped, his shoulders squaring like he was preparing to go head-to-head with me rather than backing down.

I shoved my chair back and stood, more than ready to meet him where he was. "It'd fucking have them out for our blood more than they already are!" I bellowed, my fists clenching.

He jerked up out of his seat and came at me, fists raised. Before he managed to land a punch, Nitro had his arms around Hyde and halted his progress. "Not a fucking good idea, brother," he said as he spun him around and pushed him away from me. "We're all fucking exhausted and need to get our heads together. This kind of bullshit is what the feds want." He looked angrily between Hyde and me. "They fucking want us to fall apart and take ourselves down, and I refuse to let that happen. I am not fucking going back inside because you two motherfuckers couldn't hold your shit."

Fuck.

I blew out an angry breath.

He was fucking right.

I glared at Hyde one last time before sitting back down. "Right, this is our fucking plan going forward. I'm gonna pay Stark another visit and push her to do what we need her to do. The fact we took care of her husband should go a long way towards us getting what we want. Kick keeps watching D'Amato until we sort Stark out. Everyone else gets on with our usual shit. With any fucking luck, we'll have figured everything out *and* taken care of Gambarro by the end of this fucking week." I exhaled sharply again. *And then I can spend the weekend fucking my woman without having to think about any of this bullshit.*

Hyde hit me with a filthy look as he stalked out of the

room. I ignored it. We'd had worse trouble between us before. This shit would blow over.

"For what it's worth, I would have done what you did with Stark," Devil said after everyone left.

I nodded. "Yeah, brother." I believed he would have. We'd handled some stuff together that had shown me how similar we were in some ways.

He watched me thoughtfully. "You okay with this shit?"

I knew what he was asking. *Had it stirred up memories for me when I'd walked away from Isabel Stark? Had it reminded me that I allowed Margreet's killer to go on living after I discovered he was a single father to a daughter who needed him more than I needed vengeance?*

Devil was the only brother who knew this story of mine. He'd caught me in a bad moment one night, and after some whisky loosened my tongue, I'd shared some shit about that with him.

I nodded and jerked my chin towards the door. "Go. We've got a lot of shit to get through today."

My phone rang as he exited the room.

Ivy.

"Don't tell me you're calling for me to fucking take you somewhere today. I'm busy," I said as I answered it.

"I really need you to swing by, King. There's something wrong with the tap in the shower, and I can't get it to turn off. Brian's out taking one of the girls to an appointment, and I'm worried about the amount of water we're wasting."

"Jesus," I muttered. "I'll send one of the boys over. Sit tight."

She turned silent before saying, "Oh, okay. I thought if you came, we could talk over some more of that stuff you helped me with the other day."

She'd made me sit and listen to her plans for getting back on her feet. She hadn't asked my opinion on anything, and I hadn't given it, but it had felt like she'd expected me to make offers to be by her side while she got to work on it all. That had thrown me, but I hadn't brought it up. I figured I was reading too much into shit, because surely she realised we didn't have a shot at ever being a couple again. But here we were again, and I knew I had to deal with this before it got out of hand.

"I'll be there in about half an hour," I said and ended the call.

I didn't have the time for this today, but it was something I had to make the time for. I'd meant it when I told Lily that Ivy was in the past. Now I had to make Ivy understand that, too.

"Thank you," Ivy said when I entered the kitchen after fixing the shower. "Brian would have been super stressed about the cost of all that water if he'd come back to a running shower. He seems worried all the time over money."

I dumped my tools on the table. "It's why I like working with him. He runs a tight ship."

"I wasn't saying it was a bad thing, King. He seems like a good guy."

"That's because he is a good fucking guy."

She frowned, coming towards me. "Why are you so short with me today?"

I raked my fingers through my hair. I'd been in a mood from the minute I'd stepped foot inside the place. Knowing I needed to discuss shit with her had me on edge. I was a bastard for what I was about to do. I'd fucked Ivy up in the past, and now I was about to cut her loose again, and that shit didn't sit right in my gut. But I couldn't figure out another way through this.

"We need to talk about some stuff," I said, holding her gaze, trying to get a feel for her mental state. So far, she'd been happy to see me and had jabbered on the whole time I'd worked on the shower. But fuck knew, Ivy could switch gears as fast as I could, so I needed to tread carefully.

"What stuff?"

"You and I stuff."

Her face lit up and she came to me, moving in closer than necessary. "I'm all for that."

Jesus, she thought I meant something I didn't.

I shook my head and took a step back. "No, that's not what this is about. This won't ever be about that."

Her face clouded over with disappointment. "Really? You expect me to believe you would protect me from my husband and then from Brant, bring me to Sydney, set me up here, come whenever I call you over, fix stuff for me, drive me to job interviews, and yet not want to be with me? I don't buy that bullshit for one minute, King. You want us to be together again."

Fucking hell.

I could see where she was coming from, but what the fuck happened to people just fucking looking out for each other because they cared about their safety and happiness? Why the fuck did there have to be conditions and expectations around stuff like this?

"I don't want us to be together again so you need to get that out of your head now. I did all that shit because even after all these years and after everything we've been together, I care about you. Just not in the way you think."

The disappointment on her face morphed to anger. "That is such utter crap and you know it. Men don't do stuff for women they don't wanna fuck."

"That's some twisted fucking thinking, Ivy. Of course they fucking do. And trust me when I say I don't wanna fuck you."

I hadn't intended to be hurtful, but I saw that reaction in her eyes.

Before I could stop her, she closed the distance between us, grabbed my face, and kissed me.

It was a hard, desperate kiss, and I felt nothing.

Nothing but the realisation we really had reached the end of the line.

I'd already come to that understanding, but this absolutely and undeniably confirmed it. Where her touch had once sparked the kind of passion that would consume me for days, it now left me empty.

I took hold of her arms and forced her away from me. Staring down at her, I bit out, "Don't ever do that again. When I tell you something, I fucking mean it. And I mean it when I say I don't want to be with you."

She stared at me through tears. Hot, angry tears. Not sad ones. And then the rage came, and I knew this was repressed anger by the violence of it. It was also what she needed to get out of her, so I allowed it all to spew out without interruption. That, I would give her. That, she deserved from me. "I fucking hate you! And I fucking love you! And all I wanna do is forget you, but you are un-fucking-forgettable, King. That"—she jabbed her finger at me—"is the worst part of all this. I've tried for years to put you out of my mind, and I fucking failed. I didn't want to come to you about Tony, because I knew seeing you would kill me, but I did. I fucking came, and I helped you, and *this* is what I get for that? I even told Brant not to hurt your friend, and I thought he'd listened to me—"

My body tensed, every inch of me alert as her words triggered my fury. "What the fuck did you just say?"

She flinched at my tone and tried to move away from me, but I grabbed her arm and held her in place. "Tell me what the fuck you mean by that, and so fucking help you God, if you mean what I think you mean, shit isn't gonna be pretty."

Swallowing hard, she said, "You were right about Brant—he was crazy. Insane probably. I didn't know about his past, but I knew he was the kind of man to do anything for the woman he loved. And he loved me, so I let him close and I let him help me escape Tony. But I swear I didn't know he was going to shoot that woman. He'd told me he was tracking the woman you were seeing, and that he wanted to get back at you for all the stuff you did to me years ago. I told him to drop it, because that stuff was in the past, but he was intent on hurting you through her. I honestly thought he meant he was just going to hurt her. I never imagined killing her was on his mind."

I shifted my grip from her arm to her neck. Holding her tightly, I backed her up against the wall, pressing her hard to it. "Tell me the fucking truth. You fucking knew he was going there to kill her, didn't you?"

Fear flashed in her eyes as she clawed at my hand around her throat. "Let me go, King! I didn't know. I promise." She struggled to get the words out, but I didn't give a fuck. I was dancing the line between sane and crazy here with her revelation, and it was a fucking taut line close to snapping and taking us all down with it.

Thrusting my face forward, I stared into her eyes. "Fucking tell me the truth, Ivy! At least fucking give me that!"

Tears streamed down her face, landing on my hand, but I ignored them. I didn't care about her tears anymore. "This is the truth. I might hate you, but I love you more. If I'd known his intentions, I would have made sure I stopped him. I wouldn't allow anyone to hurt you like that. Just like I didn't let Tony hurt you."

Hard, angry breaths forced their way out of me as I

searched her eyes madly for the truth. It was in the blink, and she hadn't blinked. *She hadn't fucking blinked.*

Fuck.

With one last squeeze of her neck, I let her go and jerked away from her.

We stared at each other, a furious and bitter tension sitting between us. After all these years, this is what we had come down to. She said she loved me more than she hated me, but I didn't think she did. Love didn't lead to actions like hers. It was a false love. It was the kind of love rooted in fear and doubt. She might have thought she still loved me, but that was only because she didn't trust herself enough to love herself and let me go. I could blame myself for her broken-ness, but she'd had years to move past what happened between us. She'd had time and resources to help herself, and she'd chosen not to use them. We were all responsible for our own happiness; no one could do a damn thing to make Ivy happy until she decided to make herself happy.

"I'm going to walk out that door and I'm never coming back. You need something, you ask Brian. He sees fit to ask me for help with it, I'll do what I can. Other than that, this is the end of the road for us, Ivy. And as much as you may not believe this, I just want you to be fucking happy."

Her tears still fell, but they didn't register with me.

Not like they once did.

We were well and truly finished.

I got sidetracked with club business that gave me a headache on my way to see Detective Stark, which meant by the time I finally tracked her down and stood in front of her, my skull felt like it had been hit by a sledgehammer a hundred fucking times. Between the bullshit that had gone down with Ivy this morning and the hours I'd spent on club shit, I was in no mood for her to say no to my proposal.

Isabel Stark was grieving the loss of her husband. Well, to the world she was. She'd taken a few days off, so I found her at her home again. She was not grieving the loss of her husband. She was cleaning her oven when I got to her.

She met me at her front door with cleaning gloves on, her hair a mess, and more light in her eyes than I'd seen the last time I called on her. Staring at me through her screen door, she said, "Are you here to finish the job you came for the other day?"

I arched a brow. "If you're asking me if I'm here to put a bullet in your head, the answer is no. However, if you're asking if I'm here to save my club, that would be a yes. Do not send me away without giving me what I want, Isabel. I've had a fucking shit of a day and you won't like the consequences of an incorrect answer."

She unlocked the door. "You better come in then."

I followed her into the kitchen where she pulled her gloves off before looking at me, and asking, "What do you want from me?"

"I want you to drop the fucking case against me and my club. I want you to walk the fuck away from it and never look back. And I'll fucking pay you to do that."

She considered that. "It's tempting, but I don't need your cash. My husband left me a great deal of money. So much that I don't have to work another day in my life if I don't want to."

"Well that leaves you and me with a big fucking problem then."

She took a deep breath. "No, not really. Not if you agree to a deal I have for you."

"What?"

"I've worked my job for too long now that I know how

shit goes down. I put you away, and maybe some of your club, it still doesn't fix the problems on the streets. You guys are a dime-a-fucking-dozen. And you just keep coming at me. I'm tired of working the system legally and never achieving my goals. I do this job so my daughter can be safe from men like you, but I'm jaded and don't buy into the bullshit anymore that what I do makes a difference." She paused for a beat. "But then you showed up here to kill me and didn't go through with it, because of the very reason I do my job—because you want to protect my kid from bad people. That surprised the hell out of me, Zachary. I did not see that coming from you. So here's what I propose—I leave you out there doing your thing, and while doing that, you help me keep the streets clear of as much bullshit as you can."

"You want me to work with you?"

"Not officially. This would be between you and me only. I'll bury the case against Storm, and in return, you'll do everything you can to keep the assholes you work with in line. You appear to have that power, so I figure why not use it for good as well as whatever the hell else you use it for. Keep the streets free of war, and I'll keep you free of jail."

"Fuck, that's a big fucking ask. Streets free of war aren't something you'll ever see."

"I understand that, but I think we can agree you have the power to control a lot of it. You just need to decide to do that."

"I guarantee you our ideas of war are two different things. Some of it is necessary, and that shit I won't ever stop. So if this deal is gonna go down between us, you need to understand that sometimes I'm gonna handle business in ways you won't like. Having said that, I'm all for keeping mother-fuckers in line, so I'm on board with that part of it."

"Good. We have a deal then. And now you can get the hell out of my house and never come back here. In future, you have no reason to come to me. I will come to you if there is a problem."

I moved closer to her and dropped my voice to a dark rumble. "If I have reason to come to you, I fucking will. Do not make the mistake of thinking you have any power here. You don't. If this deal goes south, I will find another way to get what I want."

Without waiting for a response, I turned and strode towards her door.

I'd taken a few steps when she said, "Thank you." The words were delivered with a softer tone, and I knew she wasn't referring to anything we'd just discussed.

Looking back at her, I gave a quick nod, and then I exited her home.

I never imagined the day I would get into fucking bed with the cops, but here it fucking was. I would play this game with Detective Stark and see where it got us. If she tried to switch her rules up at any point, I'd abandon the deal and force my own upon her. But for now, this would do.

26

Lily

"What the fuck is that music?" King asked, entering his kitchen on Wednesday night.

I'd dropped the kids over to Linc after work, stopped at the supermarket to buy the ingredients to cook dinner for us, and had arrived here about an hour ago. He'd given me a key to the place two days ago and told me to use it whenever. I'd told him I really wasn't sure when that would be since he didn't have any furniture in the place, to which he'd called me a smartass and told me he would buy some. That had caused butterflies in my tummy and that in turn had resulted in him receiving a blowjob he'd loved so much that he had then proceeded to fuck me for three hours straight. Needless to say, Tuesday had been a long, exhausting day at work.

I looked up from my laptop and eyed him, noting the tension lining his face. "It's Taylor Swift. Surely you've heard of her."

He put the beer he'd bought in the fridge and came to me. Placing his hand on the back of my neck, he bent and dropped a kiss on my lips before continuing on his way out to the living room. "Never fucking heard that song, and never fucking wanna hear it again," he said as he moved.

I smiled.

All was good in my world.

My man was his usual moody self, my kids were with their father, my sister was with her guy, my mum was out on another date with the library dude, and I had just figured out how to perfect a lemon cheesecake that had given me grief the last time I tried to make it. King would benefit from that on Saturday night, and then *I* would benefit from him being happy. It turned out he had a sweet tooth. And it turned out that I could get him to do all kinds of shit when that sweet tooth was satisfied.

I shuffled the playlist, and a One Direction song came on. Grinning, I called out, "Is this one better?"

He didn't reply, but when he entered the kitchen again a couple of minutes later, he said, "Your taste in music is shit. Anyone ever told you that?"

"Only every guy I've ever dated." His features darkened, reminding me of his demand I never mention another man to him again. I'd momentarily forgotten. *Shit.* In an effort to shift his thoughts from that, I said, "Who's your favourite band?"

My gaze dropped to take in his change of T-shirt into a clean, white tee. I'd never seen King wear white before. It kinda threw me, but in a good way. He'd also taken his boots off and walked barefoot towards me. I loved it when he wore no shoes. I felt like it showed his relaxed state, and that was a state I wanted him in a lot more. I didn't like the idea of my man stressing over shit all the time.

When he reached me, he slid onto the barstool beside me at the breakfast bar. "Is this gonna be twenty questions?"

I smiled as I ran my fingers through his long hair that had fallen across his face. It reached just below his beard now, and I had to admit, it did good things to me. I'd never been into this kind of haircut on a man before, but on King, I loved it. "Will you play with me?"

His eyes searched mine. "Twenty is a fuckload. Hit me with five."

"You play hard to get."

"Metallica."

"Does that mean I only have four left?"

"Yeah, and you're running out of time."

Shit, I had so many questions that my brain scrambled to pick the best. In the end, I decided to keep this light and fun. The deeper stuff could wait. I wasn't convinced he was in the mood for it tonight. "Favourite meal?"

He didn't have to stop to think about it. "Your roast chicken and that gravy you make with it."

Oh God, he was trying to kill me here.

"Favourite number?"

"Who the fuck has a favourite number?"

"I do."

"What is it?"

"Seven."

"And what the fuck makes it your favourite?"

"It's my lucky number."

"How the hell is a number lucky, Lily?"

"I choose it when I put the Lotto in or when I have to take a number at the butcher or—"

"You don't just take the number at the front?"

"No. I search for one that has a seven in it."

"That makes no fucking sense. You'd be waiting there longer than you have to."

I shrug. "So?"

He shook his head and swivelled so he faced me. Spreading his legs, he reached for my stool and pulled me closer. "You do the strangest fucking things, woman."

I lifted my legs so I could wrap them around him. "Pull me closer." Once he had me right next to him, I put my legs around him and rested my feet on the stool behind him. I then placed my hands on his chest. "What things do I do that are strange?"

He rested his hands on my legs. "Lucky fucking numbers for one, but let's list this shit out. You watch Elvis movies like they're going out of fucking fashion, you have bows everywhere on your bags, bracelets, shoes, and underwear, you eat chips with chocolate, you eat fries with ice cream, you read five books at once, you have hard rules around what butter and cheese you will buy, you insist on fucking texting me all the time, you insist on sleeping with the fan on every fucking night, you don't like your food touching other food on your plate, your cookbooks have to be in alphabetical order." He paused, arching his brows. "I could go on."

"Don't knock my bows! You seemed to like them on my panties."

"I fucking like anything to do with your panties. I'd like it a hell of a lot more if you never wore them again, though."

"I bet you would," I murmured, leaning in to kiss him.

The kiss started out slow, but quickly worked its way to being one of King's demanding kisses. By the time he let my lips go, he had a hand inside my bra. Stroking my nipple, he said, "How long do we have before dinner is ready?"

"You're seriously going to stop whatever you have in mind just so we can eat?"

His eyes flashed with heat. "Once I get started with you, we won't be stopping for dinner. I'm also not giving up anything you've cooked, so yeah, how fucking long before dinner is ready?"

I grabbed his face with both hands and kissed him long and hard again. Pulling away breathlessly, I said, "It's ready."

"Fucking hell, woman, why didn't you just say that?"

I grinned. "Because I like to work you up a little."

He smacked the side of my thigh. "Yeah, I've fucking worked that shit out." Attempting to pull my legs from around him, he added, "Get your ass up and serve me my food."

I gripped his hips with my legs, refusing to move. "Oh really, Mr Caveman? You seriously think I'll respond to that shit?"

He curled his hand around my neck and pulled my face to his. Against my ear, he growled, "The longer you fucking sit here arguing, the longer till I get inside you. And I've been thinking of nothing but that today, so stop fucking arguing with me."

I stopped arguing with him. I mean, I didn't care that he went all caveman on me. I just liked to push him to see how demanding he'd get, because that shit turned me on.

As I served up our dinner, he sat on the stool watching me intently. King was always watching, always taking note. He'd proved that when he rattled off his list of strange things he'd observed about me. I loved that he already knew those things, but what I really loved was knowing he paid attention.

I passed our plates to him and said, "We didn't finish your five things. I still have a few questions."

With his gaze firmly locked to mine, he said, "We have dinner. Then we have my time with your pussy. Then we have sleep. Maybe after that, we have five fucking questions, but don't fucking count on it, because the way I'm feeling, I'm gonna need a whole lotta time with your pussy."

I sat next to him and picked up my fork. "I really like your place."

His eyes found mine. "I like it now you're here."

Butterflies. Tummy.

God, this man.

After that, we ate. Then he did all those things he said he would. We never did get to five fucking questions again, but I'd make sure we played that game a lot in the future.

27

King

Lily: How do you feel about cream as a colour?

I stared at the text from Lily. Fuck knew where she was going with this. It was her day off, so I expected this shit to continue throughout the day. But I really didn't have the time to be going back and forth texting about fucking colours right now so I rang her.

"Hey. Did you get my text?" she asked.

"Yeah. What's this about?"

"Well," she started and then stopped for a beat before continuing, "so I was shopping at Target, and I saw this... Wait, first tell me your feelings on girlfriends who take over your life."

"Fuck, Lily, I'm busy. Can this wait until tonight?"

"No," she snapped. "It'll take less than five minutes. Surely you have five minutes."

I forced out a long breath. "Spit it out. What have you done?"

"I may have just bought you a new blanket for your bed. And before you say anything, it's getting colder at night, and I worry about you being cold there. I mean, not that you really sleep there on your own anymore, but you might, and I don't want you to get a cold. But I can return it if this is overstepping the girlfriend line."

Fuck, she hit me fair in the gut with that. "Don't fucking return it."

Silence, and then—"Okay," soft as fuck, causing my gut to tighten again.

"We done?"

"Yeah. I'm going to head over to your place now and drop this blanket off. I'm going to do some washing and stuff, too. I'll try not to text you too much." With that, she ended the call and I leaned back in my chair thinking about her taking over my life. She had no fucking clue that she didn't need to buy me shit to do that; she'd taken it over the minute I'd decided to make her mine. And she could do whatever the fuck she wanted to my place, because I intended for it to be hers at some point, too.

I'd just finished the call with Lily when Axe rang.

"What's up, brother? And where are you?" I asked. After he and Zane had left Sydney, they'd headed back home to Brisbane, but Axe often went away for work if Zane needed him on a job out of town.

"I'm at home. Just checking in on you to see how things have shaped up. The feds still on your back?"

"No, I took care of that shit the other day. We're getting back to business as normal now, thank fuck."

"Good to hear. You speak to Zane yet? Clear shit between you two?"

"Yeah." He'd fucking pissed me off by not giving me all the information I needed, but we'd cleared the air. We'd known each other for too long and had been through too much not to fix shit between us. And I'd decided that perhaps he had a fucking point that I needed to trust him more, because he was right—he hadn't ever let me down.

"So I'm also calling to let you know I'm taking off for a while. Justine walked out on me and has moved in with the motherfucker she cheated on me with. They're talking marriage, and I can't fucking watch this bullshit, so I'm taking some time off work and getting the hell out of town."

"Fuck, Axe. Where are you going?"

"Fuck knows. Where the wind blows for all I care. The baby isn't due for another six months. I'll be back in plenty of time for that. She's made it clear she doesn't want me around, and I'm done fighting."

"Well, you know my thoughts on the matter. It'll do you fucking good to get away. Keep in touch so I know you're not dead in an alley somewhere."

"Will do," he said, ending the call.

I hated that Justine had fucked him over like this, but I was more than happy he was out of that shitfight of a relationship. With any fucking luck, he'd find a better woman fast. Axe had never been good on his own. He preferred to have a woman by his side. I just hoped the next one was the complete fucking opposite of Justine.

I left the office and headed out to the bar. Kree met my gaze as I entered, and hit me with a smile. She'd moved past our previous problems now that her life had gotten back to normal. I appreciated a lot of things about Kree, but the fact she didn't hold grudges had to be one of the best things about the woman. She was low fucking maintenance and handled her business with little fuss, and that shit made life far fucking easier when dealing with her.

I'd come looking for Hyde and found him at a table in the corner. Pulling up a seat, I said, "We need to go over Winter's proposals. You got some time now?"

He nodded. "I've got a couple of hours."

Our disagreement of a week ago was long forgotten. Neither of us held onto that kind of shit. And he'd accepted the deal I'd made with Stark. He'd actually fucking liked the idea which had surprised me.

We ran over the proposals Winter had sent through for the Melbourne operation, and came to some decisions about how we thought it best to proceed. I may have hated that city, but it was shaping up to be a profitable venture for us down there. We'd almost finished working shit out when my phone rang.

Bronze.

I hadn't heard from him in almost a month so I'd figured he'd taken my advice and moved on with his life.

"Bronze," I answered the call. "Why are you still calling me?"

"I've been digging. I told you I would. And I have something you're gonna wanna hear."

"Keep talking."

"I've been tracking Ryland, trying to get to the bottom of whose payroll he was on. He dropped out of sight, which I'm guessing you know, but I followed his trail to South America. Someone paid him a shitload of cash to disappear, and that someone was Dante D'Amato."

I gripped my phone harder. "You sure about that? One hundred fucking percent sure?"

"I'm sure."

Jesus fucking Christ.

"I appreciate the info. And just letting you know, I've

233

sorted my problems with the feds, but I doubt that extends to you, so you need to get as far from Storm as possible."

He turned quiet for a moment. "Watch over Hailee for me, King."

"Yeah."

I ended the call and dialled Lily without wasting a second. "You still at my place?" I demanded, not giving her a chance to get a word in.

"Yes, why—"

"Do not leave there. I am on my way over now."

"King, what's going on?"

"I'll tell you when I get there, but do not leave and do not let anyone in."

"Umm, does that mean I have to kick your neighbour out?"

My blood turned to ice, cooling my veins as it flowed. "What neighbour, Lily?"

She didn't answer. Instead, all I heard were muffled cries before the line went dead.

I pushed up out of my chair. Eyes to Hyde, I bellowed, "It was fucking D'Amato! All this fucking time! And now he has Lily."

Hyde jerked up. "Fucking hell!"

We rounded up everyone we could find and roared out of the clubhouse. My heart beat furiously the whole fucking way there. I couldn't recall the last time I'd been so fucking stressed. If D'Amato hurt Lily, I would hunt down every last member of his family and rip them apart limb by fucking limb. I would make them bleed in ways they never knew they could, and he would wish he'd never laid eyes on my woman.

———

Hyde wanted to be strategic about how we got inside my

place to Lily, but I didn't have the patience for that. D'Amato knew we were coming, so there was no point fucking about getting in there. I gave Hyde half a minute of airtime with his objections to my plan, and then I fucking stormed the place.

"King, you move fast," D'Amato said when we entered my living room.

My eyes went straight to Lily who sat on the couch with her hands bound, her mouth gagged. She met my gaze, and I saw the fear in hers. *Fuck.* I had done this to her when all I'd tried to do was fucking keep her safe.

"Has he touched you?" I demanded of her.

She shook her head. *Thank fuck.*

D'Amato moved to her, pressing his gun to her temple. "You can't imagine how happy I was when it came to my attention you'd found a new plaything. After I killed your previous one, I felt a little empty. I decided that was because you didn't get to see me do it, so this time around I'm fixing that mistake of mine. This time you will have front row seats. All I have to decide now is how long to make you wait for the final performance."

"You're fucking insane," I snarled. "All this for a nephew you hardly knew and didn't like?"

He pushed his gun harder against Lily's head, rage written all over him. "No, all this for my sister whose son I presume you killed. I might not have liked the boy, but after his death, she spiralled into depression and addiction, and killed herself. I lived through those five years of her hell, and I've lived through the rest of these years in my own hell. And that was all on you and your fucking club. I just never knew who to blame until Ryland brought me the information."

I assessed the situation. I had six men at my back, ready to defend me. I could lunge at D'Amato and hope like hell he shot me rather than Lily, at which time my men could save her. My concern was he'd shoot her and take whatever consequences that meant for him. His only goal here was to see me suffer, and killing her was his ticket to that.

I decided to keep him talking while my brain ran through other possible scenarios.

"I didn't kill the baby, but I did deal with your nephew. He was a fool who couldn't keep his dick in his pants. When the club whore turned up with the child and dumped it with him, he panicked about his girlfriend finding out, and killed the whore. It was a clusterfuck for my club, because she had family connections we didn't need to be dealing with if they found out. I only went to your nephew to give him a piece of my fucking mind, but he lost his shit and ended up dead in the process."

"Where's the fucking child now?"

"That was the thing in all of this that threw us—Moses disappeared. Someone took him from his cot. We never worked out who, and we never found him." It was the truth, but I was hoping it rattled him to the point of stepping away from Lily and coming to me.

It didn't.

Instead, he yanked her up off the couch, pushed her in front of him, and put the gun to her head again. Fear flashed in her eyes, but she showed no other emotion. No tears. No muffled cries or screams. My woman stood fucking tall and took what he did to her without anything but that flicker of fear as she watched me.

"Maybe I won't kill her, King. Maybe she'll simply disappear. I'll take her with me and you'll never see her again. Never find her." His voice dropped to a menacing evil tone. "You'll never fucking know what filthy things I've done to her." He shifted the gun from her head to run it slowly over her body. "She looks like a fun plaything, and the more I think about this, the more I like the idea."

I gritted my teeth.

No fucking way was he walking out of here with her.

That would happen over my dead fucking body.

I found her eyes again, silently begging her to stay strong, but she didn't need my encouragement. Lily *was* fucking strong, and she wasn't showing an ounce of fear now. That had disappeared from her eyes. The only thing I saw there now was determination.

D'Amato continued talking, but Lily drew my attention from his voice when her eyes widened and she started shifting her eyes to the side and back, over and over. Like she was trying to give me some kind of signal. Problem was, I had no idea what the fuck she meant. I glanced to the right in the direction she kept moving her eyes, but the only thing there was the couch and above that, the mezzanine level, so that couldn't be what she was trying to get across to me.

"Are you listening to me, King?" D'Amato barked. At the same time, he threw his arms up in the air, showing his frustration.

Lily took her moment. She turned to her right, spinning around to face D'Amato, and pushed him hard as best she could with bound hands. He stumbled back, but he didn't fall. I rushed at them, trying like fuck to get Lily away from him. While I did that, Hyde bellowed, "To the right!" and the sound of gunfire filled my home.

I had no idea what was happening behind me; my only focus was Lily. Unable to get my aim on D'Amato without the likelihood of hitting Lily, I lunged for him rather than shooting him. Lily was in the fucking way, so she went down with us. Our guns went flying, but I didn't need a fucking weapon. I would kill this motherfucker with my bare fucking hands.

Fists flew and legs kicked while D'Amato and I fought like hell to kill each other. Thank fuck Lily got out of harm's way. I couldn't see her, but I knew she wasn't anywhere near him.

I managed to get my hands around his neck, and I reefed him up to a standing position, his back to my chest. However, he then used all his force to ram me backwards against the brick wall, winding the fuck out of me. The loud crack of my head as it hit the wall filled my ears and slowed me down as pain radiated through my skull. It only slowed me for a moment, but it was enough for D'Amato to gain the upper hand.

Turning quickly, he faced me and wrapped both hands around my neck. Squeezing the fucking life out of me, he snarled, "Change of plans, I'll kill *you* first, and then your little plaything."

My gaze focused behind him, taking in what was happening there. D'Amato had brought his own men with him, and they had engaged my men in battle. If I was to save my life and Lily's, I had to fucking do it now before he choked me, because I had no backup to rely on.

And then Lily's voice cut through the battle sounds. "Change of plans, motherfucker. *I'll* kill you, and then my man will kill yours." My eyes landed on her as she put my gun to D'Amato's head and pulled the trigger.

I wasted no time pushing him out of the way, ignoring the blood and shit that splattered over me as she shot him. Ripping the gun from her, I headed into the fucking fray and lost my fucking shit, shooting at every last fucking cunt who'd threatened my woman's and my men's lives.

A fucking hurricane of fury raged out of me as I took down anyone who came at me. That he had put Lily through this drew my demons to the surface. They wanted to dance, and I welcomed that with open fucking arms. So we fucking danced. And when we were done, the place was a mess of dead bodies and blood splatter that fucking sang to me. It was like a goddam orchestra of death and destruction playing in my head, dragging me closer and closer to the edge of no return where the music played twenty-four-fucking-seven.

I'd fought against following that music my whole life.

Had kept my distance.

But it fucking called today.

When my woman almost died because of me, it fucking called.

As the last man standing took my bullet, I looked for her.

I needed to touch her.

Needed to know she was okay.

"King."

I turned to her voice, finding her standing where I'd left her near D'Amato's body. She watched me with that same fierce look of determination she'd had before. So fucking strong.

I closed the distance between us and she moved into my arms. Wrapping hers around me tightly, she said, "I thought you were going to die," right before her first tear fell.

I held her until she stopped crying. Hyde called Nitro who'd been out on a job all day, and asked him to organise a cleaning crew. The place would take fucking hours to clean, but that was the least of my worries. My only concern was Lily and getting her the fuck out of here.

"I'm taking Lily home," I said to Hyde.

He nodded. "Yeah, brother. We'll get this shit sorted. Don't bother coming back."

I cleaned us up and organised for Devil to drive us to her place. I sat in the back with her, not letting her out of my arms. The emotions coursing through me were unlike any I had ever experienced. For the first time in my life, I had felt fear. It was a foreign feeling to me, and not one I ever fucking wanted to feel again.

28

Lily

I'd always wondered if there would be a moment in my life that punched me in the gut and winded me so badly I would struggle to recover. I'd thought I had come close when I discovered Linc cheated on me. I then thought I'd come closer when we divorced. And then when Brynn had been shot, I knew I'd reached that moment. However, when that man had threatened King's life today, I finally knew I'd found the moment that would wind me so badly I wouldn't be able to breathe for a long time.

I'd wanted him to kill me instead.

It had been the most selfish moment of my life, because I never wanted to leave my children without a mother, but in that split second when I thought King would die with that man's hands around his neck, I wanted to offer my life in exchange for King's.

I hadn't been able to breathe.

I hadn't been able to think straight.

All I had wanted was to give my life for my man's.

And then my brain had kicked into gear, and I'd done some straight talking and reminded myself I was a mother with responsibilities. I'd told myself to find a way to save both of us and then I'd done that.

I'd picked up King's gun. I'd been completely focused on my goal. I'd killed a man. Something I never imagined doing.

That moment had winded me, and I was sure it was going to take a long time for me to breathe properly again.

Devil had driven us to my place, and King hadn't let go of me until we were there safely. He'd told me to go inside while he went over some stuff with Devil. Brynn had gone out for the day with Jamie, so the house was quiet as I slowly made my way to my bedroom. My legs felt heavy, my heart, too. And my head was filled with a non-stop replay of that man's gun pressed to my head. I felt the gun still now. Every time I saw it in my head, I felt it like it was still digging into my skin. It continued to make my heart race with fear. And as much as tears threatened, I refused to allow them. I refused to allow his actions today to make me run or hide away from the world. I was stronger than that.

I had just sat down on the edge of my bed when the front door slammed closed. I jumped at the noise in a way I didn't usually jump, but I closed my eyes and breathed through it.

And then King stalked into the room, a rush of wild, angry energy that completely threw me.

Coming at me, his eyes ferocious, he roared, "Don't you *ever* put yourself in harm's way like you did today!"

My heart banged against my chest at his outburst, and I shot up off the bed. "What the hell, King? What's gotten into you?"

"You!" he barked, jabbing his finger in the air at me. "*You've* fucking gotten into me. If you are *ever* in a situation like that again, Lily, you fucking run when you can. You do not fucking hang around and pick my fucking gun up and shoot someone. You get your ass out of there as fast as you can and you save your fucking life. You do *not* think about me."

His anger bled into me. It combined with the adrenaline racing through me, and I slammed me hands against his chest and yelled, "I will never not think about you! And don't you ask me not to. If your life is being threatened, I will do anything and everything I can to save you."

He gripped one of my wrists, squeezing it tightly as he pulled me to him. If I thought his eyes looked ferocious before, I wasn't sure what I'd call them now, because they blazed with more fire than I'd ever seen from him. "This is not something up for negotiation. You have never held a gun before. You have never shot a gun before. That situation could have turned out a whole lot fucking differently than it did today. You could have been killed. Do you fucking understand that?"

I glared at him. "Do you fucking understand that *you* could have died?"

His other hand snapped around my neck and his eyes bored into mine. "I live with that fucking understanding every day of my life. You do not. And I'll be fucked if you're going to start now."

"So teach me how to use a gun. Teach me how to defend myself. Make me as fucking indestructible as you, King, but don't you ever dare take away my ability or right to defend my man's life. I won't stand for it. I'm your woman, and I have your back just as much as you have mine."

His nostrils flared as his fingers dug into my neck. "Fucking hell," he rasped before his mouth crashed down on mine and he kissed me so savagely it hurt. But I wanted that pain. I needed it. And I gave it back to him just as savagely, and when we finally came apart, we were both breathless with desire.

We tore at each other's clothes until we were both naked. His hands then came to my body with the same brutal energy his mouth had, and he wrestled me to the ground. When he had me pinned under him, his hands holding mine down, he thrust his dick inside me harder than he ever had and growled, "I cannot fucking lose you."

He pulled out and slammed back in.

I put my legs around him while trying to struggle out of the hold he had on my hands. He kept pounding into me as I demanded, "Let me go. I need my hands on you."

He didn't let me go.

He bent his face to mine and bit my bottom lip before kissing me.

He then bossed, "Stop fucking arguing with me."

"Stop fucking bossing me."

"Jesus fuck," he said, steam practically billowing from him. He thrust in hard again. "You're gonna spend the rest of your life fucking challenging me, aren't you?"

"Yes, because you're gonna spend the rest of your life not listening to me."

He tightened his hold on my hands even though his hold was already hard as hell. On another thrust, he ordered, "Tell me you won't put yourself in danger."

"Let me go first."

"Fuck, Lily, fucking tell me and then I'll think about it."

"Fine, I'm not gonna put myself in danger, but that's because you're gonna show me how to use your gun."

He stopped all movement and stared down at me. Shaking his head as he let my hands go, he said, "I fucking love you, woman, but you are gonna cause me no fucking end of headaches."

I stilled, all previous thoughts whooshing out of my mind.

Gripping his biceps, I said, "You cannot tell me you fucking love me while shaking your head at me, King. If you really mean it, you need to tell me while not shaking your head."

He continued staring down at me, silently now. And then he angled his face so he could kiss me. This time it wasn't as savage or as urgent. This time it felt like he had all the time in the world to devote to my mouth. I lost myself in this kiss. I never wanted it to end. When King took it upon himself to give a girl a kiss she would never forget, he outdid himself. And when he did finally let my lips go, I felt every ounce of his hesitation to do so. "I fucking love you, and I'll show you how to use my gun, but I will do everything in my fucking power to ensure you never need to use it like you did today."

All my fight disappeared as I smiled up at him. "I love you, too, baby," I said softly.

"Fuck," he muttered as he thrust in again. "You fucking kill me."

He then spent the next two hours fucking me before wrapping me in his arms in bed and holding me close. We didn't speak for a long time until I finally said, "I've listened to everything you've had to say about me not trying to protect you, and you need to know something. Your job is to worry and protect. *My* job is to nurture. And sometimes, part of nurturing is protecting. Just so you know."

His lips twitched ever so slightly and then he kissed me before saying, "Are you good if I get back to the clubhouse and take care of some shit?" He watched me intently for my answer, almost like he wasn't convinced leaving me was a good idea.

I nodded. "I'm made of some tough stuff, dude. Today was hard and it sucked and I'm not keen to ever have another day like it, but I'm okay. My kids and sister are going to be home soon, and I'm gonna spend the afternoon hugging them tightly and loving on them. And then you're gonna come over tonight and love on me. So yeah, I'm good."

He lifted a brow. "Dude?"

I grinned. "Yeah. Dude."

He kissed me one last time before leaving the bed and dressing.

After he'd left, I thought about what I'd said to him. I did feel like I was made of tough stuff, but I was shaken by the events of the day. I wouldn't make a huge song and dance about that, though. King had enough on his plate, and if I believed one thing, it was that while I would share my life with him, I would do what I could not to add to his worries. Life was never easy, but every hardship built a little more strength and a little more character. And I had the grit to weather any storm so long as I had him by my side. He could do the worrying. I would do the nurturing. And together we could protect and look out for each other.

29

King

"You want a beer, King?" Kree asked late Friday afternoon as the boys started rolling in after taking care of business for the day.

I shook my head. "I'm heading over to Lily's soon."

She smiled as she wiped the top of the bar. "She's good for you." At the lift of my brow, she said, "I saw you smile today. She's good for you."

Kick sat on the stool next to me, grinning as he overheard what Kree said. "I saw him smile yesterday, too."

"Fucking hell," I muttered. After Kree had moved on to take someone else's order, I said to Kick, "You sort Brian out?"

"Yeah, I gave him that cash and took care of the repairs that needed doing around the place. And he said to tell you Ivy has found a job."

"Good."

Hyde joined us, a pissed off look on his face. "I just heard the news report on Gambarro. We should have moved sooner on him before they arrested the asshole."

"Yeah, brother," I agreed. "But we've waited this fucking long to get to him, we can be patient for a while longer."

Hyde frowned. "What the fuck, King? Did you take some happy fucking pills or some shit today?"

I moved off my stool and grinned. "Think about it, Hyde. Gambarro fucked a lot of people off who are in prison because of him. Way I see it is that now he gets fucked over in there while they all take their turn with him, and then we can either have him taken care of inside or we can wait our turn and take care of him ourselves when he gets out. Either way, he's gonna get a lot of what's coming to him and we won't have to work as hard to make that shit happen."

The feds had arrested the motherfucker this morning. He'd been my first gift to Isabel Stark. I'd thought long and hard about whether to hand shit over to her so she knew where to look for her evidence, but in the end, I decided my club had been through enough. We were finally beginning to get back to normal business; I didn't wanna put them through another hard battle. I'd let Gambarro go to prison and see where the dust settled. Patience might not have ever been a strength of mine, but a man could fucking change.

A text came through on my phone.

Lily: I think I'm about to take up smoking again.

Me: Why

Lily: Zara.

Me: Fuck

Lily: My thoughts exactly. She has a new boyfriend. God let me down.

I had no fucking idea what she meant about God letting her down, and I wasn't about to get into it with her.

Me: I'm on my way

  Lily: Hurry. And have a smoke on the way so you smell like cigarettes. You may save me from taking them up again.

Jesus, this woman.

———

"Lily," Hannah was saying as I entered Lily's kitchen an hour later, "do you have another dress I can borrow tomorrow?"

Lily had her ass in the air while she bent over searching the cupboard for a container. I settled against the counter, crossed my arms and enjoyed the view.

"Are you seeing the library dude again?" Lily asked while she rummaged. I could tell by the way her actions were becoming jerky that she was growing impatient trying to locate the container. Without waiting for her mother's response, she muttered, "Ma, have you taken my red Tupperware container home? I could have sworn it was in here the other day."

Hannah, who had her back to me, moved to another cupboard and opened it to search in there. "No," she said, and then, catching sight of me, she stopped and hit me with a smile. "Hello, King. I didn't see you standing there. Have you seen that red Tupperware container Lily always insists on using?"

Lily straightened and turned to me. Her eyes went wide and she pulled the face she used when her mother was driving her crazy. She then said to her mother in a snappy tone, "I don't *always* use it, but it's the best one I have."

I jerked my chin at the cupboard next to the one where the glasses lived. "It's in there."

Lily located the container and shot me a smile and a "Thank you" before saying to her mother, "Ma, why don't you go and hang with Brynn? I've got everything under control in here."

Her mother lifted her brows. "I really don't think you do, darling."

As Lily pulled another face, I pushed off from the counter and said, "Hannah, I'll help Lily."

A smile spread across her face. "Oh, you are a good man, King. Thank you." With that, she exited the kitchen, leaving us in peace.

Lily came straight to me, gripping my jacket. She leant in close and inhaled deeply. "Oh, good God, you smell good." She then face-planted against my chest and said, "Between her and Zara, I'm not sure I'll survive this weekend." She lifted her head and met my gaze. "You're free tomorrow, right?"

I curled my hand around her neck. "What for?"

"Ah, smart man. Don't agree to shit until you know what it is. So, Zara has a date with this new boy, and I was thinking you could get eyes on her." She bit her bottom lip waiting for my reply.

My lips twitched and I let her neck go. "Get eyes on her? When the fuck did you start talking like that?"

She smacked my chest lightly. "Since I met you I'm saying all kinds of shit I never used to say, thank you very much. You're a very bad influence." She paused. "So is that a yes?"

"Where are they going?"

"To the movies. I'm dropping her off and picking her up,

and I've told her only one-hour extra time after the movie finishes. It's that hour I'm concerned about."

I didn't tell her she should have been worried about a fuck of a lot more than that hour. I tipped her chin up. "Is this how you want every date she goes on to go down?"

Her eyes widened. "You were the one who told me you wouldn't let a daughter out without eyes on her."

"Yeah, but just because I would do shit a certain way doesn't mean it's how you would do it."

"You don't think I should do this with Zara?"

"You've started talking to her about this shit. You've got open lines with her. Don't fuck that trust up."

She thought about that for a moment. "That was totally not what I was expecting from you. You were supposed to be my go-to guy for this heavy work."

I grinned. "I never said I wouldn't take on the job of sorting out the kid she's dating."

Frowning, she said, "You've lost me."

"I'll drop her off, and while I'm there, I'll find the kid and have a chat to him. I'll lay the fucking law down with him. And if you're not happy with how something goes down, I'll handle it."

She moved close, pressing her body against mine. "Now we're talking. This sounds like a good deal."

I placed my hand on her ass and bent to kiss her. "Fuck," I murmured after I'd had her lips, "I've been thinking about that for hours."

Pushing me away, she said, "Okay, you need to take your ass out of here so I can finish getting dinner ready."

I watched her for a few moments while she located a saucepan and filled it with water. Fuck, I could watch her for hours and never grow bored, but I needed to leave the kitchen so we had half a chance at eating dinner tonight. My need for her body was intense tonight.

I grabbed a beer out of the fridge and headed into the lounge room.

Jamie was on his way out as I entered. He grinned at me. "Hey, man."

I jerked my chin at him as he walked past, and sucked back some beer. I then took a seat on the couch next to Robbie who sat watching his favourite show on his iPad.

He glanced at me. "You wanna watch?"

I smiled and shook my head. "I'm gonna check out the footy."

"It hasn't started yet."

"Who's playing?"

"The Bulldogs and Raiders."

"You gonna watch with me?"

He nodded. "Yeah." He went back to his show for a few moments before looking at me again. "We should get a movie tomorrow night."

"Yeah. Your pick."

He grinned. "Cool." And then he was back to his show, and I flicked through the channels on the TV until I found what I was looking for.

Our peace was shattered when the girls all came in about fifteen minutes later. The couches filled with Lily, her sister, mother, and daughters, and the noise of their conversation drowned out the television. Robbie looked at me with a frustrated expression, and I nodded my agreement while taking a swig of beer.

Lily snuggled up to me on my other side, her hand curling over my thigh dangerously fucking close to my dick. The woman was lethal in her moves when she wanted to be.

"I'm just saying that maybe you should give the library dude another chance, Ma," Brynn said.

It had been just over a month since she'd been shot, and

she was doing well with her recovery. Lily had told me yesterday she was going back to work part-time next week.

"No," Hannah said, "he didn't open doors for me. You know I'm fussy about that."

"God, Mum, I'm concerned you're going to be single for the rest of your life with all the requirements you have," Lily said.

Her mother's lips pursed before she said, "Well, if you can find a man like King who looks after you the way he does, I can certainly keep searching until I do, too."

Lily's hand squeezed my thigh as she chuckled. "King doesn't open doors. In fact, I doubt he would satisfy any of your requirements, so that just shows you that men can still be right for you even if they don't tick boxes."

I stretched my arm across the back of the couch as I ran my eyes over Lily's body. She had on the tightest fucking T-shirt, and I struggled to keep my eyes off her tits.

"What do you think, King?" Brynn asked, drawing my attention to her. "Do you think Mum should hold out for her perfect man or acknowledge that perfection doesn't exist?"

Fuck, how had I been wrangled into this conversation? "Check out how he is with his family. That'll tell you a lot about how he's likely to treat you down the track."

Lily fucking squeezed my thigh again. That was after she slid it even fucking closer to my dick. And before she pressed a kiss to my lips and murmured, "I love you."

I lifted her hand and removed it from my leg. Moving my mouth next to her ear, I muttered, "I'd love you a fuckload more if you stopped fucking with my dick when I can't do anything about it."

She curled her hand around my neck and blasted a smile at me. "Tonight we play five fucking questions and then you get to do whatever you want to me," she said softly enough so only I heard.

I finished my beer. She didn't know that tonight I'd only be playing one fucking question, and if she didn't give me the answer I wanted, I'd fuck it out of her.

———

I stretched my legs out on Lily's bed and rested my back against the headboard while I watched her fuck around getting ready for bed. We'd just taken a shower together where I'd warmed her up for the night. I planned a long night, but first I needed to get her to stop screwing around doing whatever the fuck she was doing.

"Lily," I said, and waited for her eyes.

She didn't give them to me, though. She carried on rifling through drawers.

"Lily," I barked.

Her head snapped up and she turned to me instantly. "What?"

"Bed."

"I'm just looking for the T-shirt I wanna wear tomorrow."

"Leave it."

My tone registered with her, and she hit me with a glare. "No. I don't wanna be running around in the morning, stressing over finding shit. You can wait five minutes for me. And besides, you've already had your way with me tonight."

I moved off the bed and closed the distance between us. Standing behind her, I wrapped my arms around her and gripped both her wrists, halting her movements. Mouth to her ear, I growled, "I haven't had my way with you yet, not even fucking close. I need at least two hours with your cunt before we're even talking close, so stop what you're doing and get your ass on the bed."

She finally fucking did what I said, and I positioned us so she straddled me while I sat how I had been before. Placing her hands on my bare chest, she said, "You're lucky I like your bossy, filthy mouth. I'm not sure there are many women out there who would put up with it."

"I only want one woman, and she's the one who can't get enough of my mouth."

"Let's not get carried away."

I arched a brow. "I stop giving you my mouth in any way for a month and you'd lose your shit."

She wiggled her ass, grinding herself against my dick. Gripping my face, she said, "You stop giving me your mouth for even a day and *you'd* lose your shit."

She wasn't fucking wrong.

"Okay," she said, letting go of my face, "let's do these five fucking questions, so you can get to your favourite part of the night."

I wrapped my hand around her neck and rubbed my thumb over her throat. "It's my turn to ask the questions tonight."

Her eyes lit up. "Ooh, okay."

I kept my hand around her neck. "Beard or no beard?"

"Beard."

"Good fucking answer."

She grinned.

"Morning or night?"

"You are so freaking predictable with your sex questions."

I gripped her neck harder. "Morning or night?"

"Night, but only because there are more hours for you to get your mouth on me at night."

I eased my grip a little. "July or August?"

She frowned. "Huh? What's in July or August?"

I pulled the blue box from my pocket and opened it. "July or August?"

Her eyes widened. "Holy fuck, King." She glanced between the ring and me. She stared at me for the longest time, and then she crashed her lips to mine, her hands grasping my face with the kind of grip that turned me the fuck on. When she'd had her fill, she tore her mouth from mine and said, "Oh my freaking God, yes!" She looked at the ring in the box again, bending her face close, her eyes lighting up, and then looked up at me. "This ring is fucking beautiful."

Jesus, I'd been hard for her all fucking night; I wasn't convinced I'd make it through this proposal without ripping her clothes off and sinking my dick as far inside her as I could.

I pulled the ring out of the box and got it on her finger before she changed her mind. As she held her hand up to her face, checking out the ring, I growled, "Lily." When she gave me her eyes, I demanded, "July or August?"

A smile spread slowly across her face. "You mean you're actually giving me a choice? You're not gonna just boss my ass into one of them?"

Fucking hell, this woman.

"You have exactly three seconds to choose one. After that, I'll boss your ass into a fuck of a lot more than just the month."

She leaned in close and brushed her lips across mine before saying, "July, but only because it comes first. If I had my way, I'd choose September because it would be warmer."

"July it is."

She looped her arms around my neck. "I love you, King. You might be a hard-ass out there in the world, but for me, you're everything I need." She studied the ring for a moment. "And this ring is perfect. Thank you."

I'd taken a photo of her grandmother's necklace that Holly had sent me, and asked a jeweller to design me a ring that matched it. A diamond bow, it matched not only her necklace, but also half her fucking belongings.

I took her face in my hands and kissed her. Deep and slow to begin with, it quickly became the usual demanding kind of kiss we both craved. When we were done, I rasped, "I fucking love you, woman. If I could, I'd marry your ass tomorrow."

Fuck, as long as I lived, I'd never get my fill of this woman.

She'd breathed life into me when I hadn't thought there was any life beyond what I already knew.

She'd given me hope after I'd forgotten what it was.

She'd fucking helped quiet the demons raging deep inside me.

And I was holding on tight.

Wherever Lily went, I would follow.

She may have thought I was running this fucking show, but she was wrong.

She owned the fucking show.

EPILOGUE

King

4 Years Later

I stood on my back deck and watched the kids running around the backyard as I sucked back some beer. Holly pushed Cade on the swing I'd built last weekend while Zara carried Meredith on her hip, laughing at something Lily said. Robbie and the girl he'd invited over for the party sat on the wooden bench I'd built for the back corner of the yard. Lily's meditation bench. The one she spent a good fucking half hour on every afternoon while I played with the kids inside. She called that half hour her Sacred Pause. I didn't give a fuck what she called it so long as she had it. Lily without that pause was wired for my blood. With it, she was wired for my dick.

"Hey, brother," Hyde said, stepping out onto the deck. "We finally made it."

I glanced at him, my gaze going straight to his daughter,

Sage, who held her arms out to me. Letting her climb across to me, I said, "Your dad being an ass today?"

"King," Monroe said as she and Tatum walked past us to head downstairs. Her voice held a warning like it always did when I had her daughter. I cut back my language around the kids, but as far as I was fucking concerned, ass wasn't a word I needed to watch.

"Mama," Sage called out as she spotted Monroe. I put her down, and she ran to her mother who scooped her up and carried on towards Lily.

"Everyone here?" Hyde asked, surveying my backyard where club members and their families hung out laughing and drinking.

"Everyone except Fury."

Hyde met my gaze. "You got him out on a job today?"

"Yeah. I doubt he'll make it." Not with the messy shit he was taking care of for me today. Detective Stark would breathe easier tonight thanks to Fury.

"King!" Kick called out. "We need you to settle something for us." Elizabeth whipped past him, distracting him for a moment. Mostly, though, I figured it was his wife who did that as she chased after their daughter. He'd announced her second pregnancy last week. Fuck, we were having a fucking population explosion in the club these days between Hailee almost ready to pop a kid, Lily two months pregnant, and now Evie, too.

I headed down to where he stood with Devil and Nitro.

"Devil thinks that when you guys built this place, Lily got the final say in everything, because there's no way you would have chosen half the shit here," Kick said.

Lily's hands slid around my waist as she pressed her body to mine from behind. "Wrong," she said. "Well, kind of wrong. I did get the final say in everything, because let's face it, King wants his dick sucked at night, but he chose more than half the shit in this place. My man has immaculate taste."

"No shit," Devil said, smiling at Lily. Fuck, every fucker in the club had a soft spot for my old lady. A hell of a lot of respect too, which was deserved. The past four years had shown Lily's grit in ways I fucking wished we hadn't had to live through.

"No shit, asshole," I said. "Now give me a minute with my wife."

As they walked away from us, I turned to face her, my gaze landing on the bruises on her neck. Tracing my finger over them, I said, "Fuck, I need to go easier on you." Especially now that she had our child in her belly.

"Don't you dare."

I found her eyes. The heat in them caused my gut to tighten. I'd had her cunt twice already today, but it wasn't enough. I'd arranged for her mother to take the kids tonight so I could dedicate a long stretch of time to her. We'd need it before I headed away for up to a week tomorrow. I had shit to take care of in Melbourne. Shit that was giving me nothing but fucking headaches.

"I spoke with Jackson yesterday," I said, broaching the subject guaranteed to piss her off.

She frowned. "Why?"

I kept my gaze pinned to hers. "Because he needs to hurry shit the fuck along and make you part-time already. He's been promising you that for months."

"Fuck, King, I told you to stay out of that. I can fight my own battles with Jackson."

"You've been fighting this one for too fucking long. I've sat back and let you handle shit, but I'm done waiting. I told him I wanted a call within the week to confirm your part-time status."

"King," she started, but I shook my head and cut her off.

"Lily, you're exhausted. Hell, if I had my fucking way, you wouldn't work at all. But I know better than to push you for that, so I'm pushing you and Jackson for what I know I can get."

She stared at me silently for a few moments, before muttering, "You drive me fucking crazy half the time."

"You return the fucking favour."

Moving closer, she jabbed me in the chest. "I'm going to push you on something then, too."

Jesus. "What?"

"You need to quit smoking."

"Fuck, woman, we've already discussed this. Don't give me hell over it again."

"Your doctor said—"

"I don't give a flying fuck what my doctor said."

Her face softened. "Yeah well, maybe you should, because I don't want you to die sooner than you have to." Tears welled in her eyes, and as she wiped at them, she grumbled, "God, I hate pregnancy hormones."

That fucking made two of us.

"Daddy!" Cade ran at me, arms outstretched, and I bent to lift him up as he said, "Auntie Skye got me a twuck for my birfday!"

I jerked my chin at Skylar who'd just arrived with her latest boyfriend. I gave him a month at the most before she kicked him to the kerb. Skylar couldn't seem to find a man who would stand up to her and her bullshit, and this dick-head didn't fit that category either. I'd told her to get some advice off Annika who had finally married the guy she'd met two years ago. He had some fucking balls on him that I could respect.

I eyed my son. It was his third birthday today. I'd managed to knock Lily up fast after I'd married her. If I had my way, she'd have a baby in her belly more often than not, because my kids made my fucking life. But Lily had told me six was a good number to stop at, so after this current pregnancy, I'd be heading into a new kind of battle. The day we were married, I'd told her I wanted four more kids, and I hadn't been fucking about. I intended to win that battle, but fuck, I wouldn't complain if it was a long, drawn-out one. Going to battle with my wife got me hard as fuck and led to some crazy shit going down between us. It was the kind of shit a man could die happy having experienced.

I smiled at Cade. "Why don't you and Meredith play with it in the sandpit?" Eyeing Lily's mother, sister, Jamie, and Adelaide coming down the stairs, I added, "Grandma's here."

He squealed with delight, wiggled out of my hold, and took off in Hannah's direction.

Building this place had been one of the best damn decisions Lily and I had made. We'd sold the place in the city after the shit that went down there and bought this land. And neither of us had looked back. Lily had surprised the hell out of me by how she'd handled the D'Amato shit, but it had just been the first in a line of incidences she'd had to stand tall against as my old lady.

"Oh God," she muttered, her hand landing on my chest, scrunching a handful of my shirt.

"What?" I asked, following her gaze.

"Zara. Shit, shit, shit. Now is not the time for her to get distracted from her studies."

I found what she was looking at, and I didn't fucking like it either.

"I'll have a word with him," I said firmly as my shoulders tensed.

Lily looked at me. "King, don't be hard on him. It's not his fault Zara's watching him."

I clenched my jaw as I watched Fury making his way through the party toward me, oblivious to the fact my daughter had her gaze trained on him. "That may be the case, Lily, but if I'm not hard on him, he won't have a reason to keep his distance from her." And no fucking way was a man like Fury getting anywhere near my daughter. She may have been eighteen now, but I still saw her as the fourteen-year-old I'd handled little shits for.

Fury stopped when he reached us. Glancing between Lily and me, he said, "Hate to interrupt, but I need a word with King."

Lily smiled and nodded at him. "Sure." Then she turned and gave me her wide eyes that meant I should pay attention to what she'd just said about not going hard on him. I had no fucking intention of doing that so I ignored those eyes.

Fury watched her leave and then said, "I've taken care of what you wanted. There was some collateral damage, though."

"How bad?"

"Nothing I couldn't handle. It's all been cleaned up."

"Good."

"You got anything else for me today?"

"No, but it's come to my attention that my eighteen-year-old daughter has eyes for you." My voice dropped to a hard command. "Under no fucking circumstances are you to look at her, speak to her, or fucking touch her. If I find out you've done any one of those things, I will make it so you wished you fucking hadn't." I paused for a beat. "We clear?"

His brows lifted. "I'm not into eighteen-year-olds, King, and I'm sure as fuck not into anyone related to you, so yeah, we're clear."

"Good. Keep it that fucking way and we won't have a problem."

"If you don't have anything more for me, I'm gonna go off-grid for the day."

"Do that. We've got a fuckload of shit on when we hit Melbourne, so make sure you're ready for that."

"I'll see you tomorrow."

He passed Zara on the way out and didn't so much as look at her.

I found my wife again. "I've sorted the problem."

"King, I hate to break it to you, but the problem is Zara. Not your guys. And that's the kind of problem I have no clue how to sort."

Zara had given Lily hell for years when it came to boys. And since Zara had turned her attention to Storm members, it had become my hell, too.

"Well, as far as I'm concerned I've handled it. Now, are we gonna do the cake, because the sooner we get this party done, the sooner I can clear people out, and the sooner I can get inside you."

"They only just arrived like an hour ago. You can't start kicking them out soon."

I lifted a brow. "You wanna fucking watch me?"

She shook her head at me, but her eyes had that heat in them again. Moving into my embrace, she said, "I'm so glad I decided to grow old with you and your filthy ways."

My hands landed on her ass. "You had no fucking choice in the matter. I decided for you."

She smiled up at me. "Yeah, baby, you did, because you're bossy like that." She kissed me long and hard before adding, "Right, I'll go get the cake. You round everyone up. And then we start working on getting them to leave."

My gut tightened as I watched her walk across the lawn, up the stairs, and into the house. I hadn't ever imagined finding a woman like Lily. She was my opposite in almost all ways, and yet we worked. Fuck how we worked. And now I couldn't imagine a life without her.

I'd laid myself bare for her.

I'd bled for her and wouldn't fucking hesitate to do it again.

I fucking breathed for her.

And while my family and my club were everything to me, I existed for Lily.

ACKNOWLEDGMENTS

There are two people who this book would not be possible without - Jodie O'Brien (she's a lot of things to me, but for the purposes of these acknowledgements, she was my one beta reader for this book) and Becky Johnson (my editor). These ladies worked around the clock for me to help me get King ready for you. From the bottom of my heart, THANK YOU <3

I also need to give thanks to Letitia Hasser my cover designer for creating my fave cover ever for this book, and Wander Aguiar for taking the sexy photo. You guys are both so very talented and I am so grateful to work with you <3

Now! I really need to give HUGE thanks to some of my Levine's Ladies for helping me build the King's Reign playlist. I have one for every book, but this has been the best playlist I have ever built. I didn't use all the suggestions, but without them, I wouldn't have been led through the Spotify jungle to discover songs I had never heard of before now. Thanks must go to - Bethany, Lee Anna, Sara, Tiffany, Rhiannon, Cindy, Melissa, Laurie, Fern, Alana, Diane, Lisa, Monica, Jennifer, Suzan, Paula, Larissa, April, Wendy, Silvia, Jessica, Angela, Ronda, Missy, Nadia, Melissa, Beth, Shannen, Jolena, Jo, Lisa, Sallie, Megan, Melanie & Tracy. I hope I got everyone! You ladies rock!

To my mofos, you know who you are. Love you girls for having my back xx

To my bloggers & reviewers & street team! I FREAKING LOVE YOU GIRLS!!! From the very bottom of my heart, thank you <3 Also, I suck at ARCS but I'ma try really hard on the next book to get them out early! *dies of laughter*

To my beautiful readers, this one was for you. I wrote a book I truly love, but I did it for you. I worked the longest hours I have ever worked in my life to get this book done in a month, and while I am sitting here today feeling like I am from The Walking Dead, absolutely exhausted, and happier with a book than I have ever been, I am blessed to get to spend my days making up stories about alphas I adore, and I only get to do that because you continue to buy my books and love my alphas as much as I do. Thank you for waiting so long for King. I hope you loved his story. And if you didn't, I am sorry for that, but I wrote him exactly how he has been coming to me for years, flaws and all. I, at least, can tell you I poured my heart and soul into his story. <3

ALSO BY NINA LEVINE

USA Today Bestselling Author

Storm MC Series

Storm (Storm MC #1)

Fierce (Storm MC #2)

Blaze (Storm MC #3)

Revive (Storm MC #4)

Slay (Storm MC #5)

Sassy Christmas (Storm MC #5.5)

Illusive (Storm MC #6)

Command (Storm MC #7)

Havoc (Storm MC #8)

Sydney Storm MC Series

Relent (#1)

Nitro's Torment (#2)

Devil's Vengeance (#3)

Hyde's Absolution (#4)

King's Wrath (#5)

King's Reign (#6)

Coming Soon

Storm MC Reloaded Series

War of Hearts (October 2018)

The Hardy Family Series

Steal My Breath (single dad romance)

Crave Series

Be The One (rockstar romance)

The Vault Books

Risk (billionaire romance)

Keep up to date with my books at my website -

www.ninalevinebooks.com

ABOUT THE AUTHOR

Dreamer.

Coffee Lover.

Gypsy at heart.

USA Today Bestselling author who writes about alpha men & the women they love.

When I'm not creating with words you will find me planning my next getaway, visiting somewhere new in the world, having a long conversation over coffee and cake with a friend, creating with paper or curled up with a good book and chocolate.

I've been writing since I was twelve. Weaving words together has always been a form of therapy for me especially during my harder times. These days I'm proud that my words help others just as much as they help me.

www.ninalevinebooks.com